Facing the Queen ...

Without warning, the queen alien jumped.

It sailed through the air, and landed just short of Dr. Begalli. Stunned and disbelieving, Begalli tried to turn.

A long set of secondary jaws streaked out from the alien's mouth, slicing and hammering into the back of the scientist's head, boring through and pushing his eyes out of their sockets like red Jell-O being squeezed through cookie cutters.

Kozlowski was stunned. The thing wasn't supposed to be able to do that. Wasn't its ovipositor fastened to the pod? But then wasn't that just something else they didn't know about these aliens?

Only a flicker of a second of thought, though. Already her rifle was going up, aiming, squeezing off a round.

Henrikson fired at the exact same moment.

Their fire converged upon the exact same spot on the queen. It hissed and wailed, a hole blown in its thorax. Its blood rained down upon Begalli's head and boiled his face away. The alien started toward them, forelimbs clutching and seeking.

Kozlowski lifted her rifle and aimed at its head. It still came forward.

If you enjoyed this book, look for these other exciting titles
from Bantam Spectra:

By Iain Banks
CONSIDER PHLEBAS
USE OF WEAPONS
AGAINST A DARK BACKGROUND

By James Blish
STAR TREK: THE CLASSIC EPISODES 1
    (written with J. A. Lawrence)
STAR TREK: THE CLASSIC EPISODES 2
STAR TREK: THE CLASSIC EPISODES 3
    (written with J. A. Lawrence)

By Stephen R. Donaldson
THE GAP CYCLE
THE REAL STORY
FORBIDDEN KNOWLEDGE
A DARK AND HUNGRY GOD ARISES

By David Gerrold
VOYAGE OF THE STAR WOLF
THE WAR AGAINST THE CHTORR
VOLUME 1: A MATTER FOR MEN
VOLUME 2: A DAY FOR DAMNATION
VOLUME 3: A RAGE FOR REVENGE

By Kathy Tyers
STAR WARS: THE TRUCE AT BAKURA

By Timothy Zahn
STAR WARS, BOOK ONE: HEIR TO THE EMPIRE
STAR WARS, BOOK TWO: DARK FORCE RISING
STAR WARS, BOOK THREE: THE LAST COMMAND

ALIENS™

GENOCIDE

David Bischoff

(Based on the Twentieth Century Fox motion pictures,
the designs of H. R. Giger,
and the Dark Horse graphic novel by Mike Richardson, John Arcudi,
Damon Willis, and Karl C. Story.)

BANTAM BOOKS
NEW YORK • TORONTO • LONDON • SYDNEY • AUCKLAND

ALIENS: GENOCIDE

A Bantam Book / January 1994

All rights reserved.

ISBN 0-553-56371-8

Published simultaneously in the United States and Canada

Bantam Books are published by Bantam Books, a division of
Bantam Doubleday Dell Publishing Group, Inc. Its trademark,
consisting of the words "Bantam Books" and the portrayal of a
rooster, is Registered in U.S. Patent and Trademark Office and in
other countries. Marca Registrada. Bantam Books, 1540 Broad-
way, New York, New York 10036.

PRINTED IN THE UNITED STATES OF AMERICA

OPM   16   15   14   13   12   11   10   9   8

For the Haldemans—
Jay and Vol
Joe and Gay
Thanks for everything, folks!

Prologue

The planet was not hell.

It just looked and smelled and tasted like it, according to the marines who had come there and raped it.

Its denizens were not demons.

They were far worse.

The marines simply called it Hiveworld, although the navigators of hyperspace had an obscure numbered tag for it. They had come here, to this blighted planet, and they had plundered it, stealing its queen mother.

Without the psychic bonds of the ruler to guide the lives of her minions, genetic drift occurred. Different queens, pretenders to the throne, developed and flourished.

All were killed by the most dominant of the bunch, a traditional creature who could have been an identical twin to the queen mother who had perished in a nuclear blast in the Pacific Northwest of Earth.

Call them "black."

Call her the "black queen mother."

And the new group, the changelings.

Call them "red," though they were not red. To a casual observer, they looked identical. But to the "blacks," through touch and smell and morphic fields, they were anathema. Strangers, aliens. Freaks that had to be destroyed.

Leader of this new brood, living against all calculable probability, was the "red" queen mother.

Bearer of recessive genes, any sign of whose chromosomal changes had brought instant death in the hive before.

The red queen mother and her minions fled. In the confusion of reorganization, they escaped and they established a new hive far enough away to thrive.

The red queen mother spawned, using the herds of animals that roved this bleak planet.

A new rival kingdom was created and for years the kingdoms lived in peace.

But each knew instinctively that the other hive was the enemy, that this peace would not last long. And when war came, the principle weapons would be in the numbers of warriors.

And so the creatures bred . . . and bred . . . and bred.

While others of their ilk were hunted under different suns . . .

1

The alien hive was exactly at Hollywood and Vine.

The god of the bugs alone knew if the sliming, sucking, skulking bastards knew the cultural significance of the intersection they'd chosen. In truth, that section of La-La land wasn't exactly what it had once been, but then nothing in Los Angeles was these days. And the fact that they chose to infest the old creaking bank building, in what after all was comparatively open territory, testified to the fact that this batch's IQ seemed rather low.

Still, thought Captain Alexandra Kozlowski as she stood a block away from the sun-faded concrete dialing the polarizing filter down on her faceplate against the grim and gritty southern California sun. You could count on each and every one of the merciless mother-killers being just as

mean and nasty and ornery as the worst of the last
hive she'd exterminated for Uncle Sam.

Who ya goin' to call?

Bug Busters!

Oddly enough, it felt good to be back in an
E-suit, clunky helmet and all.

She turned to the hunky lieutenant to her left,
already sweating in his armor.

"Got your jock strap on tight, Lieutenant Michaels?"

"You want to check?" The square jaws grinned
defiantly and the blue eyes crinkled.

"Maybe later." She winked and chinned her radio. "Approaching hive zero zero nine, LA sector B
forty-seven." She chinned her radio off and gave a
significant look to the platoon under her command: 69th platoon. AOE. Alien Occupation Eradication. The toughest soldiers in the biz. They all
looked back at her, smiles covering what she knew
was fear.

A fear she felt in her own heart.

A fear every time she got near the things.

"Roger, it's a go, Captain," crackled the command voice over her radio. "Commence explor-
atory and extermination. Backup targeted."

In Captain Alexandra Kozlowski's humble opinion, the "backup" should have been all that was necessary. A couple of borer missiles with multi-K
payloads, primed to go off when the sensors were
buried in alien hive musk. Just burn the bastards,
erase them, destroy. However, with the numbers of
aliens so significantly reduced on this, the eigh-
teenth year following the Alien-Earth War, scientists
and private interests wanted carcasses, pickled eggs,

photographs, and any royal jelly that could be scarfed up.

This meant Personal Delivery. Service with a Death Grin. Rock and roll and kill.

Well, it kept a lot of kids out of gangs, anyway.

The other twenty members of this assault squad had the same radios in their suits and heard the same message, but Kozlowski gave the hand signal anyway, just to reinforce her command—and to assure herself of it as much as to remind her "bug guys."

They rolled out. They were just foot soldiers marching alongside the anchor vehicle, a Mark 23 Access Tank. In this kind of operation, if you needed extra ammo or just a quick ham sandwich, not to mention a little close-up heavy artillery, it was nice to have a Big Metal Brother along. The metal treads chewed up old concrete and worn metal stars on the Walk of Fame as the troop approached their objective. Almost immediately they broke through the ribboned "perimeter" that had been staked out when the authorities for what was left of Los Angeles had determined the existence of the hive in the old Bank of America Building. Basically, this informed the natives that this was a danger zone, that if they trespassed—no sweat off legal backs—you were likely to become egg-fodder.

Even here, fifty meters from the objective, Kozlowski could see the hardened ooze of the hive stuff filling up the building's windows and frozen down the side.

"Hey, Koz!" said Lieutenant Michaels. "Why did the bug cross the road?"

"To get to the other side, wreak havoc, kill and

spread its kind, and generally give 'life' a bad name, you asshole," she barked back.

"You heard it before!"

"You know I hate jokes while I'm working."

"Just smart-ass remarks."

"As long as they're *mine*, subordinate officer Michaels."

He glared at her and she started defiantly as they marched along. It was a way they'd found they could get up for a heavy mission like this. Afterward, when the acid got sluiced from their suits and any wounds were mended, she and Michaels also had another tradition.

Strip and hump each other's sweaty bodies like bloody bunnies.

Ain't love grand? thought Kozlowski as she let her keening hormones blend with adrenaline and regulation Army boosters for what brewed up to be a regular Kamikaze Cocktail. She and Michaels had been an item for a year now, which in this Idiot's Army was just about a lifetime. The favorite gag around the barracks was that if the captain and the lieutenant ever got hitched and pregnant, the spawn would come charging out its birth parent (it was still up in the air in the minds of the privates as to who that would be) with a flamethrower in one hand, a missile launcher in the other—and a grenade in its mouth.

As for Kozlowski, she was always just glad that they could spend any time together at all.

They'd met in the service and he fit her like a hand in a glove. He was a couple years younger than her twenty-eight, an army brat who'd spent his younger years first in a safe area on Earth, then offworld after the evacuation . He was smooth and fit, a devotee of exercises and sports, a big blond package of sexuality that she never grew tired of unwrapping. Captain Alex's muscles—and scars— had been earned in the field. Even before she'd joined the army she'd been battling the aliens. Her parents—landowners in Montana—had stayed and battled the things. She'd lost her brothers to the monsters, her mother had died of a broken heart— and her pop . . . Well, her pop was a tangle of mean gristle and bone and determination, eternally guarding his ranch under the big blue sky against the critters from beyond.

And Alex? Well, Alex was just a chip off the old tendon, a small-breasted, big-hipped storm cloud of a gal, feisty as an undefeated bantam-weight fighter. She had a brunette haircut from the Bowl-on-the-Head Salon, dark eyebrows like accents over burning hazel eyes, and a pair of scars like parentheses over a classically cut face. She could fight or make love with equal abandon. She just wasn't sure which she liked better.

A burnt stench was hanging over the area, moving down from the Cahuenga Pass like a curse. Smog hung over the rest of the city like a stubborn spirit condemned to hell but staying put. The squad rolled along with practiced ease to the hole that was the principle entrance to the nest.

Ten meters from the entrance, she chinned her radio and commanded a halt. "Okay. Main thrust force. Double line. Let's move it."

However, before they could even assemble, the defenders struck.

Five large bugs, the sun gleaming sickly on their

carapaces, their prehensile skeletal tails snapping
behind them, scuttled from the frontmost tunnel,
just below the crooked sign that read BANK OF AMER-
ICA.

"Jesus! Guns!" she cried, unstrapping her own
.45mm blaster. "Rodriguez . . . Swivel and fire.
Take cover!"

Like the crack team they were, the soldiers broke
ranks and took positions as though this were all in
the plan. Even as Kozlowski lowered her rifle, the
turreted guns of the tank angled and aimed. A
nanosecond later, they spoke, hurling a frenzied
hail of fire at the enemy.

Kozlowski found her crosshairs, aligned them on
the closest alien—a twisted thing with a burned or
deformed forelimb—and squeezed off a charge.

The stream of fiery energy tore off its feet at
what served as its kneecaps. The thing acted as
though losing its limbs was an everyday affair. Slavering as though in anticipation of burying its secondary jaws in Kozlowski's throat, the xeno raced
onward.

The others let loose with their own weapons,
only staggered beats behind Kozlowski and the
tank.

The resulting fire tore the X's apart. Arms and
heads and deadly acid blood flew and splattered.
Entrails blew across the street. One of the banana-
shaped heads rolled toward them like a lobbed
bomb.

Instinctively Kozlowski aimed and fired, crushing
and rendering the thing a charred, fragmented
skull.

She gave them a moment to play a little more

fire at the things, just in case, and then ordered a cease.

The smoke slowly cleared, revealing the scattered, steaming remains of the bugs.

"What the hell was *that*?" said Michaels, taking in a hoarse breath, sweat now pouring down his temples.

Ultimately, as always, it was their trained reflexes that saved them. This kind of offensive action in midday hardly ever happened with the aliens.

Kozlowski shook her head. "Don't know. These bugs . . . they're getting weird."

"Big sons of bitches," muttered Sergeant Garcia, lifting his helmet to spit onto the street.

"Yes," said Michaels. "Maybe we'd better send a robo in there."

"Right? You think the Army's going to waste good robots when they've got cheap soldiers?" Kozlowski snorted disgust, lifted her faceplate, hawked and spit out a gob of phlegm on one of the smoking bodies. "C'mon. These xenos have got something in there they don't want us to have. Which makes me want it!"

Michaels nodded, but Alex detected a glint of fear in his eyes, of vulnerability and foreboding. A pang of empathy sprang inside her: the poor guy. Spiking the X's wasn't second nature to Peter Michaels. He hadn't jammed his instinctive horror and terror of the things back into a rock-hard ball to use against them. For a moment she wanted to hold him. Hold him and tell him that it would be okay, that this was just a destructive game and when it was over, she'd soothe his hurts and make everything all right.

But she couldn't. She was in charge here. She was the dominant, and she had to pretend she'd left her femininity back in the makeup case in the locker.

"All right, groaners. Pop 'em if you got 'em, and let's get in there while their carapaces are around their ankles!"

A halfhearted cheer sounded in her earphones as she dialed out a pill for herself. One second, two seconds. Hold the nose, open the gums—look out, stomach, here it comes. She opened her mouth just in time to accept the dosage of Wail. Getting it intravenously was faster, but the designers of these suits hadn't figured out how to safeguard soldiers from accidentally getting jammed with drug-filled needles.

Pills were just fine with Koz. She had an oral fixation anyway. She took lots of pills. Oodles. The higher-ups not only didn't mind, they helped supply them. Yep, things were sure different in This Gal's Army.

"All right, assholes. Let's roll!"

Holding her gun at the ready, she waved them on and the mechanical pack kicked into motion again, heading for that door into X-land.

By the time they made it to the otherworldly entrance, the drugs had kicked in. Kozlowski felt a power, an elation—a sense of belonging and an Army urge to fuse her forces into a brilliant battering ram and crush out this threat to Earth. Primal territorial urges were tapped. She was the leader of a Neanderthal pack, guarding her tribe from sabertooths. She was the head of a village on the English coast, guarding her kin from marauding Vikings, broadsword gleaming in the lightning. She was Gaia, guarding her precious brood from cosmic crawly interlopers.

The suited soldiers entered the hole into the bank building without incident. They continued down the tunnel. It was like a tube through a cancer. Noxious drippings oozed along the sides. X-holes always had an acrid, unnerving stench. Alex had already kicked in her filters.

"Looks like a normal hive to me," said Michaels. "I hope this is a by-the-book."

"Only these xenos want to be stars. I bet they're all wearing sunglasses and sporting tans!" said Garcia.

"Well, this is the only take we're going to have on this production," said Alex, bringing up her rifle. "Lights, camera, action, guys."

They came up to a narrower passage that dived downward.

"The tank won't fit," barked the machine's operator into her ear.

"Yeah," said Alex. "I figured as much. Okay, you stay here. Sentinel duty. The rest of us—we go down. *Looks* routine to me, but expect the unexpected anyway. Got it?"

"Yes, sir!" chimed the voices of the units cacophonously in her ear.

"Good. I want the short rangers out on the horn tip."

Two men with Mark Five Crankers—the equivalent of high-tech sawed-off shotguns—trundled up to take the lead, and they were off to see the lizards.

Within twenty-five yards, the tunnel opened up

into a large underground chamber—the remains of a huge vault basement, daubed with alien gunk.

"Gimme some light!" said Alex, and the guys obliged her by turning up their suit lanterns. The chamber blazed with incandescence, but as usual in these kinds of places, Alex Kozlowski wasn't crazy about what she saw.

Against one of the tenebrous walls hung people.

Alien egg sacks.

Live people, impregnated with alien young. Chest-bursters that looked like they were about to blow at any minute. The victims—ten men, five women—hung at the edge of death, dangling like corpses that had forgotten to rot.

"Agents," said Garcia.

"What?" said Kozlowski.

"Hollywood agents. That building got overrun by bugs last week down the road." The dark-skinned man nodded toward the ropy remains. "The Creative Talent Agency, one of the diehards of the entertainment industry that stuck it out here in LA." He walked forward to have a closer look, remaining cautious.

"Yeah. Yeah, I remember," said Michaels. "Whole building blew up. The assumption was that everyone was killed."

"Looks like they're still making deals," said Kozlowski.

One of the agents, a woman in a shredded dark black jumpsuit, her hair a mat of grease, slimy green threads clamped into her skull, seemed in some netherworld of delirium. She had on an ear-tab that sprouted artfully into a thin microphone, and she was mumbling dramatically into it.

Garcia stepped back into ranks, clucking his tongue. "Too far gone. All of them."

Kozlowski nodded. She'd suspected as much. If you caught on egger early, you had a pretty good chance of squeezing out the spark of new life in it. But this far along, a baby xeno was so linked up in its parasitic position amid vital tissue that even if you were able to yank the X out without it boring a hole in you, there was no way you could save the donor.

Kozlowski knew what had to be done. There were precedents. She'd done it before, and would probably do it again. She was just following orders. Orders that made sense.

That didn't mean that she liked it.

"Needles," she whispered.

There of the men were certified executioners in this kind of circumstance. They brought out their air pistols, tapped in cartridges of darts filled with a fast-acting poison that shut down the nervous system first, then destroyed the body. Two of the men had grim frowns as they aimed. The other man, Dickens, was an LA native. Dickens had been a writer and producer and actor in LA.

Dickens was grinning.

"Put the poor bastards out of their misery," commanded Kozlowski.

Thwip! Thwip! Thwip!

Three of the hanging bodies shuddered, and then were still.

Quickly, the executioners finished their task, then stepped back. "Okay, quick—before the bursters hit their ejection buttons!" Kozlowski screamed.

Two men had readied themselves. They stepped

forward. One sprayed a thick fluid on the bodies, stepped back. The other, with a high-density flamethrower, stepped forward and with fire condensed to incredibly high temperatures immolated the dangling egg sacks.

When the smoke cleared, all that was left was blackened, incinerated ashes.

"Good. Now let's go slag the Xes that did this!" barked Kozlowski.

"Amen," said Lieutenant Michaels, pale, with sweat shining on his brow.

Of course, they weren't just here to slag xenos.

Nope, that would be too easy.

In this day and age, in a disintegrating place like the City of Angels, theoretically you could just slip a limited nuke down a nest and skedaddle. Easy, quick, and a minimum of lost soldiers. However, although that nuclear holocaust up in the Pacific Northwest years back had certainly turned the tide in the Alien-Earth War, giving humanity a hope of getting its planet back, such extreme measures weren't used these days, for more reasons than just the glowing glands they tended to produce in neighboring villages.

No, these xenos had their uses these days.

And damn them for it.

"Okay. Fall out. The chamber's probably down that tunnel there," called Kozlowski. "Garcia?"

"You got it, sir," said the grizzled vet. "These bugs haven't changed that much, and this tunnel looks like the anteroom to where we're headed. What I ain't seen though is enough bugs. These hellhounds know we're here. I don't get why they didn't try and protect their progeny. Something stinks."

"Could be they're out somewhere," said Michaels. "Could be lots of things."

Garcia grunted. "Yeah. Lots."

"We're here, we'll do what we came to do, and second-guess later. We've got artillery guarding our asses, and we've got firepower. Now move it!" Kozlowski growled in a low, no-bullshit voice. She'd perfected it when she realized she had to order men around. Lowered voices worked well with dogs and human males.

The troop descended quickly but cautiously, illumination lamps picking out their direction for them down the foul, mucousy passageway.

Kozlowski would have liked these missions much better if she could just obliterate all the xenos. However, there were two things that the Army wanted her to haul out these days.

A couple of bug bodies, dead of course.

Random DNA samples.

And whatever royal jelly from the queen's chambers they could tap. Gold from outer space, some of the top brass were calling it these days. Bug juice. The lab coats were going absolutely nuts with it, and there was talk about all kinds of new possible uses for the stuff. With the U. S. government pretty much busted, private industry had suddenly become the main financial backer for the armed forces. Drug companies, mostly, along with other medical and scientific researchers. The government wanted their share, of course, but when push came to shove, the interest groups holding the biggest bucks in their outstretched hands got the biggest shovelsful of goop.

Alien royal jelly.

The stuff that made the right kind of drones into queens. Food of the xeno gods. Kozlowski wasn't entirely sure what they needed it for. Hell, it could just be gab, and they were collecting the stuff for nothing. But it was what the upper brass told them to do, and so they did it, without questioning.

The scuttlebutt that she heard was this:

Each hive was based around a queen. Queens bred drones. However, only a certain kind of bug could breed queens—the so-called queen mother. None of which existed on Earth now. Rumor had it that it was the queen mother royal jelly that was the primo stuff. Regular jelly had its uses, but it was nothing compared to the Q-M gunk. In truth, though, Kozlowski had other more important things to think about. Like staying alive.

There were all kinds of differences between alien hives and insect hives on Earth. Scientists didn't really understand the full activities of the beasties. Was their communication telepathic, or some weirder somatic buzz? It had already been established that the wavelengths of a queen's call could be picked up by human dreamers. One of the best ways of scoping out obscure hive locations was listening to these sensitive dreamers who acted as receivers, and in the best circumstances as locaters.

Just what did the monsters want? Where had they come from? What were they doing? Where were they going? What was their cosmic destiny? Were they so grouchy because the race had gotten up on the wrong side of their galactic beds in some prehistoric starday?

Kozlowski had a theory.

They'd accidentally eaten all their males, and were on one hell of a PMS jag. The theory wasn't exactly scientific, but it did explain a lot. Here were all these hysterical bugs, with no men to scream at.

Anyway, the core truth of what they were doing down here was the tanks in the cart that Private Henderson drove. Of course, to get to the jelly, you had to off the royalty first, and this was probably the most onerous task anybody could want in this kind of situation.

Corporal Michelin's head snapped up from a radar set.

"Incoming!" he said. "Twenty-five yards ahead. Sensor range. Picking up five bogies, coming in at five klicks per hour. Same direction."

Kozlowski was almost relieved. This dead silence was getting to her. "Okay, dig in, and I want a man with his weapon trained on the ceiling. Adams— you can shoot skeet. I've seen them break through and jump down from above. If they do that, I want 'em dead before they hit the ground."

"Yes, sir!"

She didn't have to notify the front or rear guards. They were already down and dug in, ready for the attack. Kozlowski threw a beam of light down on the floor. Solid-looking enough, but she was ready if any of the bastards popped up from that direction. With bugs, you just didn't know *where* they could pop from. They couldn't teleport, that much was known. But for all of that, sometimes it seemed like they *could*. And the commanding officer who underestimated them usually ended up just as dead as her men . . .

Or worse.

In this case, though, what the sensors showed was all the hive was throwing at them.

Five bugs.

Plenty, though.

As soon as they scrabbled into view, the frontmost boys let loose a barrage of fire. Down here in the claustrophobic darkness, Kozlowski felt the familiar tug of total irrational fear. Trapped-in-a-coffin fear. Preternatural mammal-hiding-from-the-dinosaur fear. That was one of the unnerving intellectual aspects of the bugs. They seemed to have been designed specifically to grip those hard claws deep into the softest parts of your soul. And squeeze.

The bugs dodged the first bolts. Awareness of human weapons was either bred or trained into them by their maturity these days. These were Earth bugs and they were ready to scrap with Earth people.

However, the soldiers had also been trained, and better. Countless simulations gave them a sense of exactly where the things would hop in their erratic jumps.

A bolt hit one. The explosion shattered it, splattering its viscous blood over the whole corridor.

"Duck, dammit!" cried Kozlowski, hitting the dirt as the acid blood sprayed every which way. The stuff could bore through the best armor if you got enough on you. She peered up through the smoke. The boys were still firing away, but crouched low and off to the side. "Knees and head!" she cried. "Knees and head."

You hit the head, the things died with a minimum of acid splatter. You hit the knees, you had the bug on the ground and a good chance for the head.

Alex Kozlowski immediately saw that she was going to have a chance to show them. A bug minus a right arm had broken loose and was scampering along the side wall. Alex lifted her weapon and squeezed off two quick but carefully aimed shots. The first missed, exploding far away. But the second caught the left knee dead on, shattering the joint and causing the alien to go down.

Garcia's next shot caught it right in its banana brain with a satisfying thud and soft *ker-plow*, like an M-80 in a gourd.

With this guidance, the boys calmed down and picked off the rest of the things. The fire boys cleaned up the wiggling jaws and claws with a dose of concentrated high temp, and then applied a splash of acid-neutralizing spray to get through.

Kozlowski allowed herself a smile. They'd killed lots of aliens already, without so much as a stubbed toe. "Good work, chums, but don't get cocky. The toughest part is straight down there, in the general direction of hell."

"Hey, don't we know it!" said Michaels.

"Pretty dumb bunch of bugs, though," said Garcia.

"They're not exactly known for their high IQs," said Kozlowski. "But then neither are grunts, so I don't want any slackers. Move it! We're not exactly in unfamiliar territory now."

Chances were the xenos were about as ready as they could be for the attack, but that didn't mean it was good for the men to rest on their laurels. Best to use the adrenaline and the other performance-augmenting drugs while they were peaking.

They traipsed over the dead, crackling things in the tunnel, trundling into the darkness.

The corridor widened, and their lamps illuminated a chamber.

In the center, like a giant flower bulb of chitinous flesh, grew the "throne"—the storage place for the royal jelly and home of the spawning queen.

Kozlowski had been in these places before. That didn't mean she was used to them. The hole was like Death's uterus, with hubs and cordings and odds and ends of effluvia that while biological seemed antilife. Every cell in her body rebelled at the sight presented here. Training and experience and resolve fought with a deep instinct in her to turn and run.

A bent, insane frieze of alien sculpture, a mockery of life.

Otherwise the chamber was empty.

"What the hell?" said Michaels. "Where are they?"

Garcia looked like if he hadn't had a helmet, he would have very much liked to have scratched his head. "I don't understand. Where's the freakin' queen?"

"Off at the Hollywood high spots?" quipped a jokester.

"I don't like it," said Kozlowski. "Get back. The queen doesn't leave her chamber unless there's a damned good reason."

Michaels shook his head. "Look. We've got a pot full of royal jelly waiting to be tapped. Half the time, the stuff gets blown up or burnt." He grabbed a tapper and started walking toward the bulb. "I say let's get this stuff tanked right now and we're assured a good supply, no matter if we take out these bugs or not!"

"Michaels! Halt!" screeched Kozlowski. "I'm not certain that junk is all that valuable. It's certainly not worth the extra risk. You're not going anywhere—and that's an order."

Michaels stopped in his tracks. He turned around, his eyes flaming. Kozlowski could see the drugs in those eyes, and the male pride. Don't do this to me, Koz, said those eyes. Don't be so damned protective.

"Yeah! Lover boy might get himself a boo-boo!" said a veiled voice in baby talk.

"What have you got on the sensors?" Kozlowski demanded.

The private looked up from the telltale board. "Activity, but nothing close."

"Come on, Captain. I could have started tapping by now!"

"Yeah. We get our quota, we get extra leave!"

She didn't like it. Not one bit. But there wasn't any good reason to say no. And if she didn't let Michaels do this, the other jerks here would call favoritism, and she couldn't deny that.

"Okay, but I want the rest of you to back him up. And, Daniels . . . you go along."

"No problem," said the tough Army man.

Damn it, Peter. Why are you doing this to me?

"The rest of you. Fan out and check for other exits."

The men, grateful for action, spread out.

"What do you think, Garcia?" she asked the sergeant as Lt. Michaels strode for the huge bulb.

"I don't know, sir. It's not like the bugs to leave their jelly unguarded."

The soldier walking off to one side looked up from his instruments. "Sir! I'm reading lower rooms. They're chambers, sir, and just as big as—"

The lieutenant was just driving in the tap, connected to a couple of storage tanks. Daniels had slung his rifle in order to help with the tricky manipulation.

It came to her like thunder.

This wasn't the main chamber! And if it wasn't what they were really after, then it was a—

"Michaels! Daniels!" screamed Kozlowski. "Get away from—"

Trap!

The bulb split open like a pregnant belly. And the baby was deadly as death itself.

"Jesus!" cried Daniels, leaping back, pulling his rifle down.

The emerging bug struck with the speed that still was astonishing to see, even though Kozlowski had seen it many times before. It grabbed Lieutenant Michaels by the arms and pulled him up.

It had been hiding inside. The alien was just waiting for them to tap.

Michaels screamed as he was hoisted upward in the claws. The secondary jaws, slathering drool, rammed against the reinforced helmet, cracking it.

Michaels screamed again.

Automatically Daniels fired his rifle.

Only yards away, the shell hit its mark. The mark, though, was the torso of the beast. A gory hunk of creature was torn away, and like a burst vessel, alien blood pumped.

The secondary jaw whacked into Michaels's helmet again, cutting a hole before the thing began to crumple. Michaels fell under it, and Kozlowski, helpless, watched as the alien blood spouted into the interior of her lover's helmet.

Directly into his face.

The scream ratcheted through the radio, until the radio was killed. It seemed to grow louder and more horrible carried only by the fetid air.

The acid worked with amazing quickness upon the face. It was as though she were watching time-lapse photography. The skin sizzled off, snapping with gooey bubbles. The eyes boiled and melted.

The screaming stopped.

The skull began showing and then the acid began to eat through that, frying Lieutenant Peter Michaels's brain.

"Nooooooo!" cried Kozlowski. She grabbed up her rifle and was about to riddle the beast with slugs.

A hand on her suit's shoulder stopped her. Garcia. "Don't. You're in charge here, Captain. *Stay* in charge."

The alien slumped, twitching.

The burnt remains of her lover mixed into a liquid, unholy embrace.

"Check on him," she said tersely.

If only I hadn't let him go. I knew there was something wrong!

"He's gone."

"I said *check* on him!" she bellowed. "If he's not, I don't want him to suffer!"

Garcia nodded. He stepped over to the bodies, gingerly nudged the lieutenant with the butt of his rifle.

Acid mixed with smoking gore riveted out into a horrible puddle.

It burned straight through the floor, leaving a ragged, smoking hole.

"Dead."

"Right," said Kozlowski. She could feel the iron grip of control exert itself and she was in command again. "There's another chamber, and that's where we're going. No more heroics, you assholes." She took a breath. "No more carelessness. Or I swear to God, if the bugs don't kill you, *I* will."

The silent squad followed the telltale to their destination.

Lieutenant Alexandra Kozlowski tongued for another pill. She swallowed it and her tears.

2

Victory.

The smell of it was in the air, alongside the fading stench of the ruins of war.

Victory.

Domination.

Excellence.

He could feel the demand for it throbbing in his sinews, pulsing in his veins. He could feel the need in the stadium crowd outside, the impatient stamping of their feet, their calls and their applause. Its power and its glory electrified the air.

Now it was time to electrify some nerves. Goose some synapses. Nudge some neurons.

Jack Oriander stood in the shadows of the tunnel. Outside, his fellow contestants milled around, waiting for the officials to call for the beginning of the hundred-yard dash. He felt more secure here, away from the open space. He was slightly agoraphobic; anyway, that was what his dad had said. He wasn't so sure about that himself, since he didn't really have a *fear* of being outside. He just preferred walls around him.

Pop was dead now. He'd been a captain in the Alien-Earth War, and he was dead now. The Army had not supplied the details, nor did the Oriander family want details. Not when it came to the aliens.

Jack Oriander took a sip of cold water from a paper cup, swished it in his mouth, and spat it out. The Middle Eastern sun was hot out there. Jack wanted his mouth wet, but he didn't want his stomach bloated. He had his sunblocker lotion on, and he'd taken care to drink lots of fluids yesterday and today as well as "carbing up" for the contest. At twenty years old, he was in absolutely peak condition. His muscles, trained and corn-fed in Iowa, sang with health and speed and proportion. He'd run track and field in junior high and high school and now college at Iowa U, now that these kinds of things were getting back on track. The Earth had lost some time—and so had Jack, because of the war and reconstruction. But time didn't mean that much when you were young. There seemed lots of it behind you and lots of it ahead of you. Even though you saw people older than you with bald heads and paunches and lines around their eyes, the idea that *you'd* be like that one day seemed absurd.

"Win today, grow old tomorrow," Coach Donnell had said, his eyes glaring down like lasers into Jack. "We're counting on you, Jack, to put us on the map." That's what the graying, grizzled man said every day of the training.

He got his message across in more ways than one.

The tension in the air was thick. Jack's nerves seemed stretched as tight as violin strings. He knew that if he was going to get some help, he'd have to get it now. Around his waist was a light flesh-colored belt of synthetic material. Jack de-Velcroed a pouch, pulled out a small bottle. A fresh one. Best if fresh, his mom had always said, and though Jack wasn't sure if that applied to this stuff, his obsessive-compulsive nature made him use a fresh bottle even though there was a half-full one in his luggage.

Jack cracked open the safety seal and knocked out a pill.

Hell, why not?

He rattled out another one into his palm, then quickly screwed the top back on and stuffed it back into the pouch, readjusted his oversize shirt, tucking it into the elasticized top of his shorts.

He looked down at the capsules. They were a deep green, seemingly embedded with silver sparkles.

For a moment he heard the old man's voice at the back of his head. "Take it from me, Jack. You've got all the drugs you really need in you already. Learn to tap those first before you go for other ones." But he discounted it as he'd always done, listening to the voice of the coach instead. "Tell you what, Jack. You do what you got to do to *win*."

Jack slipped both capsules between his lips. He took the paper cup and used the small amount of water left to wash them down. Not too much. Didn't want to get too much moisture inside of him. Balance. That was the ticket. The old man was always keen on balance. Yin and yang. Now the old man was dead. So if what Jack swallowed tipped the scales a little to his favor, what did it matter?

Xeno-Zip.

Street name: Fire.

From Neo-Pharm.

Great stuff.

He'd been taking Fire ever since it first came out. He'd asked the coach about it and the guy had taken a few seconds to read the label. ALL NATURAL INGREDIENTS. That was okay with the coach. Just as long as there weren't any steroids in the mix. Not that the man had anything against steroids himself. Anything that could give you that extra edge was really okay by him. Judging committees were a lot more laissez-faire these days.

Besides, it wasn't any worse than a couple of extra cups of coffee in the morning. That's what the ads implied, anyway.

He hadn't looked into it very closely. Jack immediately noticed that not only was he more alert and self-confident after swallowing one, his athletic abilities improved. Concentration, agility, coordination: all jumped into higher levels. Not only that, he *felt* better. Fire gave a little more zing, a little more oomph.

The official line was that they made the stuff from alien queen mother royal jelly.

Rumor had it that they used ground-up alien bodies from the war.

Jack didn't care. He liked the stuff. The glow that it put on life's horizons was just the icing. What Jack liked was the edge it gave him in sports.

Jack waited for the glow to start, listening to the sounds outside, peeking into the light, shading his eyes.

The stadium was a spectacular tribute to the reconstruction of Earth, a wonder spawn of new technology and architecture. Lots of companies had tossed in contributions to build the thing, and not just demicreds. Big coin. A tubular confluence of lines and efficiency, of new and mighty alloys, centered around a traditional field. Wedding of the new and the old. Blimps and zeppelinlike hovercars hung in the sky, bristling with tracking devices and media sensor arrays. Field Humanitas was the name, and these competitions in which Jack Oriander participated had been dubbed the Goodwill Games.

Now that the Olympics had been destroyed, along with much of old Earth, you had to start with something, after all. Something to unite people, something to celebrate the New Humanity, something to take civilized minds off the savage past.

A sweeter conflict among nations.

A good-natured competition among athletes.

Jack Oriander leaned out into the sun a bit. He could smell the familiar humanity out there. He smelled the popcorn and the hot dogs, the spilled beer and the excitement in the air. He intended to be the center of that excitement now, yes, sirree bob.

He felt a lick of the drug playing around his nerves, and blinked.

Ah!

"Yo! Oreo! You want to get your ass out here!" called Fred Staton. Staton was the other guy from the States. He was clean-cut and slender like Oriander, only he had neatly clipped blond hair instead of black, with no widow's peak. A strapping young man. As Oriander's senses sharpened, squeezed into a fine focus by the tongues of fire, he smelled his friend's lemony deodorant and the talc on his hands. Caught a wisp of grape jam from today's breakfast, along with the astringent touch of Gatorade. "We're just about set to line up!"

"Uh . . . yeah, right."

"Hey, man. You okay?"

"Sure. Why?"

"I dunno. Your eyes . . . they're a little odd."

"This sun . . . it's kind of getting to me. That's why I'm staying in the shade as long as possible."

"And your hands. They're trembling some."

Oriander lifted his hands. He fancied he could feel special blood pouring into them now. Fiery blood.

But they'd never shaken before on Fire.

"Man, I just guess I'm a little nervous!"

"Aren't we all."

"I'll be fine. Just give me a sec."

"Sure. But seconds aren't mine to give. And those officials are oiling up their guns." He slapped his friend on the shoulder. "You'll be fine. Take a deep breath. You're only a few feet away from a hundred yards." He snapped his fingers. "It'll be all over like that and we'll go out and celebrate, huh?"

"Yeah. Right." Jack grinned.

Fred was right. He should move on out. He could see the milling racers not just lining up, but slotting themselves in their starting posts.

Yet the sun was not only hot, it looked terribly bright now, much too bright. Fire had never sharpened his vision up *this* much before. He felt like he had just been blessed with telescopic sight. Such incredible detail!

Maybe he shouldn't have taken two pills after all.

Squaring his shoulders, pushing back the razory feeling along his spine, Jack Oriander trotted out to assume his position.

As he slotted himself in line, he got the A-OK signal from Fred. "C'mon, Oreo. Let's show them that American sneakers can still kick butt."

Jack smiled and waved. He fitted his feet into the metal stirrups, leaned down onto his knuckles. A buzzing began to keen in his ear, like an amp feeding back. He cocked his ear, waiting for the starting pistol. The finish line loomed ahead like a magnificent promise.

Glory. Achievement.

Winning.

The crowd noise died down to a hush.

But the keening in his ear grew to a roar.

What was—

The chemical rush hit Jack Oriander like the hammer of Thor. Molten energy poured into his muscles and lightning exploded from his brain.

The signal pistol went off, and his legs answered as though they'd been waiting for this moment their entire life. They pushed him forward, shooting him off like a bullet down a rifle chamber. Suddenly he wasn't just Jack anymore. He could feel the atoms exploding in his sinews, he could feel a cosmic power gushing through his entire being.

He was a god!

The crowd went crazy.

The PA system rumbled with the announcer's astonishment. "Unbelievable! Jack Oriander of the USA is literally burning up the track!"

His face had grown a rictus of determination and sweat burst from his brow in rivuleting globules. His feet seemed to have grown wings. The air rushed past him like a wild river and the determination to win inside his breast burst into white-hot brilliance.

The yards streamed by in a flash.

Jack Oriander crossed over the finish line, well ahead of the others, his feet a blur and his mind hot as an incandescent filament in a megawatt bulb.

And Jack Oriander kept on going.

The crowd in the stadium and the millions watching the race would never forget the close-ups.

Jack Oriander's arms pumping.

His legs slamming onto the turf outside the track like John Henry's sledgehammers.

His eyes gazing into madness.

The young athlete from Iowa did not seem satisfied in shaving off a solid four seconds from the world record for the one-hundred-yard dash. As though eager to get on to yet another race, unseen by any but him, he loped over the finish line, covering the distance between the edge of the track and the wall in a couple of blinks of the eye, reason and sanity burned out in chemical conflagration in his cortex.

He smashed through the corrugated plastic of the wall.

Only the steel girder just beyond stopped his demented run.

And the blood . . .

The blood was *everywhere*.

You can buy black market videos from media vultures. You can see shreds of skin and veins and hair torn from the speeding body and hanging from the edges of the shattered plastic wall in clumps of gore. You can see the twisted remains of the rest of the body, lying akimbo under the harsh glare like road kill in a cleated tank run.

And, if you look closely in these tapes, you can see the medic take something from Oriander's blood-spattered pouch belt, and tuck it into his own pocket.

Xeno-Zip.

3

The sun shone down gently and pleasantly on Quantico Marine Base, Virginia. It wasn't often these days you got sun, not with some of the clouds that still hung in the atmosphere, not with the strange weather since the invasion. Colonel Leon Marshall had his drapes flung wide to let the warmth into his office.

He sat at his desk now, the report printout neatly encased in clear mylar before him. He glanced over the neatly listed facts and figures and smiled to himself, feeling a pleasant rush of anticipation.

Amazing.

Absolutely astonishing.

Puissance to the formerly powerless, power to the formerly impotent, is heady stuff indeed, and the close-cropped, burly colonel was feeling positively giddy with the prospects that lay before him.

The digital clock on his desk turned silently to 11:00 A.M. The general was a prompt man. He'd be here any moment. Colonel Leon Marshall had been preparing his demonstration since seven hundred hours this morning, and all was ready to go. Now he could afford to take a quick breather, relax and enjoy the prospects that lay before him, his career and, of course, the future of this battered country in its efforts to build a strong defense even as it rebuilt its cities and its economy.

The digital clock was just threatening to transmute to another number when his intercom chimed softly and the adenoidal voice of his secretary swept through.

"Colonel. General Burroughs is here."

"Excellent." Colonel Marshall slapped his desk and its thin burden lightly and stood up. "Send him in."

The door cycled open with a whir and the burly figure of General Delmore Burroughs marched in, his eyes turreting like offensive guns on a land carrier. They lighted on Marshall and a flicker of camaraderie shone in them below the grim and businesslike exterior. "Leon." Pudgy fingers were extended. The general's grip was certain and firm.

"General Burroughs. Thank you so much for coming."

"I believe the words 'urgent' and 'maximum importance' were used in your communication, Colonel. I tend to respond to those words. But I am a busy man." The eyes turned stony. "I hope that my time here is not misspent."

General Delmore Burroughs was a beefy black man with a bald pate rising up from grayed temples. He had a broad nose and a voice deep and full. He smelled strongly of bay rum and the Instistarch of his uniform. He was a general who had gotten where he'd gotten by taking no shit, and Marshall respected that. If he was a person who trifled with such things as mottos, then this general's motto would have been "The ends justify the means." That was why Colonel Marshall needed to get him in on the project.

"I'm not a man to waste time, you know that," said Marshall. "Tell you what—you think it's a waste of time, you get to use my ski chalet in Vermont for a weekend . . . complete with my little black book."

The general's eyes glimmered a bit. A hint of a smile played on his lips. Then his teeth clamped down, his face assumed its normal grim posture. "Fair enough."

"Good. Then lean back, drink some Kona, and have a cigar. This will take a couple of minutes and I might as well kiss your butt awhile as well."

The general couldn't help but chuckle. "Cigars? Where you getting cigars, Colonel?" He sat down.

Marshall stuck a cup of steaming java beside the general's elbow. Then he pulled out a humidor from one of the drawers. Smith y Ortegas. "They're just swinging into production again, and my sources dug up the best of the first batch."

The general rolled it, sniffing. "You know, soldier. It's been so long since I've had one of these, this might just kill me with pleasure." He chuckled and took up the clipper Marshall offered, dealt with the cigar end in an almost reverent fashion. "Now exactly what have you got on that scheming mind of yours?" He stuck the cigar in his mouth and allowed Marshall to play a flame over the end. He puffed, blew out bluish smoke. His eyes seemed to roll back with pleasure.

"General, do you recall that unfortunate incident last week with the Iowa boy at the Goodwill Games?"

"Sure. Put the world record in the American camp firmly. Probably for years to come." Puff. Spume. "Too bad about the accident."

"Colonel, did you know that drugs were involved?"

"Nonsense. Good American talent and muscle pulled that boy over the line."

"You didn't read the results of the autopsy? Oriander had Xeno-Zip in his blood."

"Xeno-Zip? Fire? What, that silly pick-me-up they're putting in the stores now? Marshall, he probably had caffeine and lots of good old-fashioned testosterone, too. Ain't nothing that great about those pills. Hell, I tried a couple. Goosed me a bit is all, but with no crash and burn. Nothing that would make me win a race!"

"That's exactly what everyone says. But I did a quick search of news cuts for the last couple of months. And then I had the boys at biochem do some quick testing. Came up with some remarkable findings."

He gave the general a moment to exhale his last puff of smoke, and then he tendered the plastic-enclosed paper to the man. General Burroughs grunted. He murmured a whiff of annoyance, and then dug into a side pocket for a pair of half-frame spectacles, which he put on. His eyes strafed the paper for several moments, then he shrugged and handed it back to Marshall.

"I've got a team of science boys to read this stuff for me and digest it. I don't get much out of it on my own, I'm afraid."

"That's all right, General. I had to have most of it explained to me. Just a few items of jargon, some facts and figures to illustrate the fact that I've done some serious work on this."

"Right, Colonel. I believe you, but I still don't see where you're coming from." The general tapped off some ash from the cigar, then left the smoking thing sitting in the tray. He folded his arms. A sure sign of impatience. Time to cut to the chase.

"You're aware of the active ingredient of Fire, aren't you, General?"

"Sure. The PR is that it's alien royal jelly. Actually, there's more to it than that. It's alien royal jelly, with a drop or two of queen mother extra royal jelly. All that comes from one source, the queen mother who got nuked. Can't get it anywhere else. A minuscule amount of this mixture acts in a positive boosting fashion on the human nervous system." The cigar remained in the tray. It went out. The general ignored it.

"Correct. However, even with a minuscule amount, Neo-Pharm, the manufacturer, found itself running out of the regular jelly. They started manufacturing synthesized stuff, with mixed results. It still needs a few molecules of queen mother royal jelly to work, though."

The general grinned. "Right. I'm not surprised they're running out of jelly. We blew most of the bug bastards straight to hive hell!"

"Absolutely and we did a fine job of it, too—and a *better job* of reconstructing. But that leaves us, as the military, in a bit of a quandary, doesn't it? And I don't have to give you a sheet of facts and figures to prove it. The enemy is mostly defeated, all the governmental money is pouring into rebuilding or into outer space. Now that the military's done its job, it's the same old story. No respect. We get squat in the way of money to develop what we have to develop to stay modern."

The gray eyes sparked with anger. It was a sore subject with all career military sorts. The general had taken the bait. Now all Marshall had to do was to reel him in.

"Public sentiment is also very antiwar machine. I think it's a historical distrust of power. The media tends to think that if the military has too much resources in a time of peace, they get antsy and take over the government. So the other extreme occurs. The military gets weak. And so when the country needs us, we get thrown into the fray, unprepared . . . and get clobbered. *That's* provable history, General."

The general nodded, anger etched into his face. He picked up the cigar, stuck it into his mouth. Marshall happily relit it for him.

"What can we do about it? We're not getting the funds to build new and improved equipment. So . . . why not build a new and improved soldier?"

General Burroughs squinted suspiciously. "What? Synthetics? Cybernetic? DNA jobs? That costs a pretty cred, too, Marshall."

The old boy wasn't following the line of reasoning. That was one thing about Burroughs, he was a little thick sometimes, a little bullish. But like a bull, if you pointed him in the right direction, all you had to do was grab the tail and he'd take you where you wanted to go. That was why Marshall had cooked up his little exhibition. In show-and-tell, the "show" carried the greatest weight.

Marshall smiled. "How about if you could do it for just a few bucks a head, General?"

General Burroughs barked a growly laugh. "Pull the other one, Colonel." He pushed out a stream of smoke and palpable disbelief.

Marshall checked his wrist chronometer. The players in the game would be just about ready. "General, if you'd care to step out on my balcony, there's a little demonstration I'd very much like to show you, courtesy of some of the men in my company."

Burroughs shrugged. "I'm here. I've smoked your cigar. I've listened to your curious nonsense. And I must say, you must have used some of the government money I'm responsible for to throw together this bit of research. So I guess you've put me into a position where I don't have much of a choice in the matter." He took out the smoking cigar and pointed it gruffly toward the colonel's nose. "But let me tell you, Colonel. I'd better see some serious justification for the use of this taxpayer's money."

"Naturally, sir." Marshall got up and marched over to a side wall, hung tastefully with mementos, weapons, and equipment. He pulled out two pairs of electronically enhanced binoculars from rechargers and handed one to the general. Then he pointed toward the sliding glass doors and the open spaces beyond.

"Come on, General. Wait till you get a gander at *this*."

The "balcony" was actually an extension of a cat-walk and stairs system that connected a number of buildings in the newly built assembly of offices, barracks, and warehouses that comprised this portion of Quantico.

Beyond, a bank of obsidian-bottomed clouds hung on the horizon. A storm was brewing. Nothing unusual on Earth now, storms. Marshall shivered a bit at the prospect. They moved fast, those storms. Dark battalions of weather, phantom marchers left behind after the war. But there would be time for the exhibition.

Marshall picked up a walkie-talkie from the desk.

The two officers walked to the edge of the balcony. Marshall leaned against the railing and pointed down at the open yard below. Some yards away, a group of enlisted men seemed to be milling about, up to nothing much more than loitering.

The general glowered. "Looks like a bunch of men goofing off!"

"If you'll just direct your binocs toward that lone private over there in the corner, sir . . ."

General Burroughs harrumphed. But he angled the cigar off to one side of his mouth and put the binoculars up, finger expertly adjusting the focusing vernier. "Looks like just a normal grunt. And a mighty doofy one, come to think of it."

Marshall brought up his glasses and took a look. Yes, there he was, the poor guy, looking a little lost and oblivious as usual. Gawky. Geeky. Big Adam's apple, tiny brain. Colonel Marshall was a collector of mid-twentieth-century cultural remnants and he remembered one of Edgar Bergen's puppets. That was who the guy reminded him of.

Mortimer Snerd.

"That's Private Willie Pinnock. And if I may say so, your assessment is right on the money. Private Pinnock barely made it through boot camp. His reflexes are slow, his IQ is low. He can barely handle latrine and KP duties . . . but he can, which is why he isn't booted."

"So what's so special about this particular private?"

"Just a moment. You'll see." Marshall opened up the walkie-talkie he'd taken with him. "Corporal Glen. Can you read me?"

The walkie-talkie sputtered and spat back. "Roger. I read you, Colonel."

Marshall pointed to where the corporal was standing on a crate, snapped to attention, waving at them. "Our referee, if you will, General." He clicked the channel back on. "Corporal, you may proceed with the exhibition."

"Yes, sir," spat the walkie-talkie.

Up went the binoculars.

Corporal Glen, a well-built specimen who looked good even in fatigues, semaphored to the private off to one side of the courtyard. However, Pinnock did not respond.

Glen signaled again.

Nothing.

General Burroughs arched an eyebrow.

Cripes, thought Marshall. This had better come off or my butt is cooked.

"What's wrong with that soldier?" he barked into the walkie-talkie.

"Off in his own little world, sir."

"Well, drag him out of it and let's get the show on the road. The general hasn't got all day."

Glen "yessirred," then trotted quickly off to where Private Pinnock stood, spinning rainbows. He tapped the nerd on the shoulder, flapped his gums in traditional mad army Drill Instructor fashion, and Marshall didn't need binoculars to see Pinnock jump, flinch, and generally cringe at the chewing out. A bob of head from the private, and then Glen trotted back to his monitoring duty.

Pinnock's shoulders were slumped. He looked quite hesitant and more than a little frightened at the prospect before him. Nonetheless, he slipped his hand into the pocket of his fatigues and drew something out.

"Get a close-up on what he has in his hands, sir," suggested Marshall.

"A bottle of that drug . . . Xeno-Zip."

"Yes, sir, that's right."

Pinnock visibly drew a deep breath. He turned toward a wall, as though he were doing something shameful, and then dragged a shaky hand through his blond short-cropped hair. He opened the bottle of Fire, poured out three tablets, then choked them down, without the benefit of water.

He stiffened, and visibly shuddered.

"Doesn't look like he's having much fun, Colonel."

"No, sir. May I give you a brief personality profile? Pinnock is a meek fellow with a minimal aggression quotient. His adrenaline levels are low;

he doesn't get mad when the other soldiers tease him. They generally just put up with him, since he tends to do the distasteful chores for them."

"With no resentment."

"None that is reported." Marshall looked at his chronometer. The increased dosage in the subject was his order, to increase the speed of release of the chemicals in the bloodstream. The last thing he needed was an impatient general. The results were going to have to be fairly immediate, or Burroughs would just about-face and leave. A minute since ingestion. That would be about right.

"Glen. Next step."

"Yes, sir," snapped the walkie-talkie.

The colonel signaled the milling group of men. They loosely ordered themselves and began marching toward the lone private like a gaggle of surly Teamsters headed for a manager. They were bulky lads, with rock muscles earned by constant drilling and exercises. Marshall could hear a couple of them, joking with one another. They had no weapons, only their fists. Marshall had planned it that way. He didn't want to see Pinnock or anyone get hurt, exactly. Scuffed up a bit, that was all. A little red on the turf was always a dramatic underline.

Besides, these barracks bullies might be in for a little something they hadn't bargained for.

The frontmost of the group, a beefy tower of a man, stepped up to Pinnock, grabbed him by the shoulder, and spun him around. A few obscene motions and words were made. Pinnock did nothing. Another man stepped forward and shoved the private. Pinnock shuffled backward, still not reacting. Not even cringing, which was a good sign.

Then another grunt snuck up behind him and got down on all fours. Big Pecs stepped forward, executed a sharp, swift push. Pinnock tumbled onto the ground. The smallest of the men, a little guy with a rat face, stepped in and gave a sneaky kick to the private's backside.

"What the hell is going on?" said the general. "This is absurd!"

Marshall tensed. There should be some reaction here by now. Was all this going to be a ridiculous fiasco?

The ratty-faced man sneered and went in for another free kick. However, this time, he did not step back after the blow was delivered. And the sneer melted into a look of alarm.

Something snapped. There was a scream, and Rat Face was flung ass over elbows backward. He was slammed into the corrugated metal of a barracks wall and left a smear of blood as he poured onto the ground, out for the count.

The burly bully boys took a step back.

Private Pinnock jumped to his feet.

"Holy shit," said General Burroughs.

The officers' binoculars leapt to their eyes.

Pinnock's eyes seemed to glow.

"Three tablets of the synthesized version of Fire," said Marshall. He brought up his walkie-talkie. "Okay, Glen. Have the boys subdue the private."

The corporal barked out orders. The men stepped forward again, looking quite a bit more tentative now, and probably a damned sight startled. Still, they were good military men and they followed orders.

They advanced, closing in on Pinnock on all sides. There would be a wonderful tussle, but there were a good eight tough boys there and they'd pin the guy down and then they'd get in the restraining leg cuffs and force jacket and let Pinnock burn off his sudden energy.

"We did a genetic workup on the men, and Pinnock proved to be the most susceptible to the effects of the drug," Marshall explained. "Of course no one understands what the hell happens, really, or what's likely to. Sometimes it appears to have no effect at all. Pinnock is a most suitable specimen, don't you think, sir?"

"He's outnumbered . . . but what's happening to him?" said the general. "This is remarkable!"

Up with the binocs. Down with the jaw. It wasn't just the man's attitude and spirit that had changed. His whole physique seemed—altered. Latent muscles seemed pumped up, and the whole face seemed chiseled purpose and resolve. And those burning eyes . . .

Pinnock grabbed the first of the men and with lightning speed lifted him off his feet and hurled him back, knocking over five more Army men.

. . . those burning eyes. His face seemed twisted into a mask of hatred and anger.

From Mortimer Snerd into Superman . . .

"Amazing," said General Burroughs, echoing Marshall's thoughts. He had no idea . . .

Pinnock didn't give the others a moment to rally. He charged in, punching and throttling. Gobbets of blood flew into the air, along with shrill shrieks and gurgles.

Maybe he shouldn't have used *three* pills . . .

Glen's voice erupted over the walkie-talkie, but the device was hardly necessary. Marshall could hear him yelling desperately down in the courtyard.

"Colonel! Pinnock's getting out of hand!"

Pinnock leapt onto the back of Big Pecs, and grabbed ahold of the man's neck. Big Pecs tried to throw him off, but Pinnock was as firmly planted on him as the Old Man of the Sea. The crazed private gripped the head, and wrenched, his tendons standing out from his neck. A loud *snap!*, a pulse of arterial blood, and the big man wilted to the ground, his neck broken, his head almost torn from its mooring.

The other soldiers had watched this, stunned and stuck in indecision. The bloody demise of their fellow soldier sent them racing away.

Pinnock, grinning like a death's-head, caught two and slammed their skulls together. He raced and tackled another, pummeling him into a pulp with fists.

Perhaps, thought Colonel Marshall, I should not have chosen a soldier with such understandable resentment buried in him.

The walkie-talkie spoke again. "Colonel! He's out of control. We need armed soldiers out here. We—"

"Oh, my God!" cried the general. "Behind him!"

The crazed berserker that had been a meek private leapt upon the corporal, grabbed the walkie-talkie, and slammed the hard metal-plastic over and over again into the man's face, until *it* was a bloody mess.

Colonel Marshall did not pause long to watch.

He was screaming into another radio channel for backup. *Armed* backup. There'd been absolutely *no* indication that this exhibition would get this far out of control.

Two soldiers, one with a machine gun, one with a blaster, raced into the courtyard.

Somehow, in the sudden blur and explosion of fire and bullets, and despite a bullet wound and the loss of part of an arm, Pinnock managed to wrest the machine gun away and use it on the backup soldiers killing them instantly.

Amid the decimation, Colonel Marshall watched with horror as the bleeding and burnt chemically charged maniac slowly swiveled around like a gladiator surveying his kill—and seeking out the emperor . . .

"Christ!" said General Burroughs. "He's looking at us!"

. . . and *not* for approval.

"General. Quickly. Back to the office!"

Even at their first step, a hail of bullets splattered over their heads; Marshall was stung with flying cement chips. Ducking, they lunged through the office doors, and the glass windows exploded. Burroughs took cover behind a desk, and Marshall leapt for his wall of weapons. He tore two loaded semiautomatic Hyper machine guns from their racks and threw one to the general.

"I haven't used one of these in *years*!" moaned Burroughs.

"Watch!" Marshall clicked off the safety. He ran to the billowing curtains, took cover, and squeezed off a salvo at the approaching maniac. No hits, but he got the feel of the thing. He dodged as another hail of bullets crashed through the door, tearing up a wall of certificates and pictures. Marshall retreated, letting off two more burps of fire.

There was a moment of silence, and then Pinnock marched in like he was Superman. He gripped the gun and the grin on his face was like an ax wound. One eye was a bloody gouge, but the other gleamed like diamond. Blood rivuleted down his face. One whole side of his body was burned.

He lifted up the machine gun, like a crazed zombie with firepower.

Burroughs had figured out how to use the Hyper and he ripped off a clip. However, only a couple of bullets hit their mark, the others splattering along a wall. Pinnock was knocked off his feet, falling back onto the balcony. But with iron determination and a brain burning with chemicals, he began to get up.

Marshall lifted his gun to fire again, but it jammed. He did not waste time on the weapon, flinging it down and leaping to a rack. The nearest weapon was a bazooka. He tore it off the wall, grabbed a shell, loaded up, and ducked back behind a chair just as a new hail of bullets chunked and screamed into the weapons wall.

A pause. Pinnock was out of ammunition. He *had* to be.

Marshall thumbed off the safety, checked the golight of his weapon, thanking the Powers That Were he'd kept up on his weapons training. He brought the short barrel of the mini-bazooka up and gave himself only a fraction of a second to aim.

Private Pinnock, smoking and smelling of burnt

flesh, still grinning, walked toward him, death glaring from his one good eye.

Marshall squeezed the trigger.

The shell whooshed out of its pipe and whacked directly into the maniac private's chest, pushing him back through the door into the balcony before it detonated. The explosion of the shell blasted the private and his gun to pieces, not even leaving smoking boots behind.

Marshall gasped and collapsed, dragging ragged breaths into his weary lungs. What a fiasco! A catastrophe of the first order! Support from the general? He'd be lucky now if he didn't get his chops busted, didn't get demoted or sent to deal with some alien infestation in northern Alaska.

General Burroughs cautiously poked his head from behind the desk. His uniform was torn and he had a stunned look to his eyes. He regarded the tattered gore, the remnants of Private Pinnock spread over the balcony like an explosion in a butcher shop.

He smiled slowly. "I believe, Colonel, this drug bears some further investigation. But please—not while I'm around."

4

War is good business.

War is even *better* business after the war is over, especially if there was massive destruction on the order of the kind administered by the alien infestation. When humanity fought off its enemy it found many of its cities ravaged. But like London after the Nazi air blitz of World War II, this was not necessarily a bad thing. Sure, some good buildings were destroyed by bombs in that case—but also destroyed were massive numbers of creaky docks and ancient buildings that should have met the wrecking ball years before.

The result of the devastation: reconstruction and a better city.

Such was the case with the alien infestation.

Take New York City. Manhattan in particular. It had been rotting for years, its roads and subways tottering on the brink of disaster.

The extermination of the aliens had left behind many ruins and much potential. Nothing on the order of Los Angeles, which was still pretty much a smoking ruin with odd nests of the creatures still needing to be wiped out. But the Big Apple needed a big overhaul.

The U.S. government, weak but still there, brought in two traditional weapons in this particular struggle: free enterprise and deregulation. Any entrepreneur, any company that had the stomach for it, were awarded the privilege of going in and wrestling with the wreckage and the building.

A man named Daniel Grant not only had the company and the willpower for such a job, he has a cast-iron stomach and platinum business nerves as well.

Now, Manhattan's towers were shiny again, and majestic bridges spanned the East River and the Hudson. Its subways were streamlined and the aliens were all dead here, though not necessarily all the vermin.

Rats, like Daniel Grant, were survivors.

Although his chic East Side penthouse was only ten blocks away from the infamous Grant Tower, Daniel Grant always had himself driven to work in one of his sleek fleet of robo-chauffeured turbostretch limos.

You had to put on a show.

You needed leverage for business deals. Flash and illusion and glitz helped gain leverage. Sometimes, when the numbers in your bank account were either preceded by negatives or promises, flash and illusion and glitz were all you had.

This was why Daniel Grant always made sure that

he entered his building through the front door, so that the spectacle was available to the local media.

Today was a brisk spring day in Manhattan and Grant had his window open so that he could see his tower as he approached. God, it was gorgeous! A hunk of gleaming obsidian thrusting up toward the sky from the famously firm island bedrock, Grant Tower dwarfed its surrounding midtown neighbors. Of course a lot of these were still in twisted ruins, which gave Daniel Grant's skyscraper the edge. In fact, it looked like a streamlined monument in an urban cemetery. Still, Grant only had to look at it to feel like the Top Dog, the King of the Hill, the Duke of New York.

"Nice day for a skyscraper, eh?" he said to his female companion, tucked away in the plush, dim corner.

Candy (or was it Bambi?) barely looked up from her compact mirror. "*Very* impressive, Mr. Grant." She glanced at the erect structure, nodded, and winked coyly. "Reminds me of last night!" She extended a long, sleek leg and teased his ankle lightly. Grant smiled, glorying as much in his own manly scent as in the mists of perfume and femininity that wafted his way from this choice little bundle of boobs and buttocks and blond hair he'd bedded down with last night, after the *de rigueur* champagne, caviar, and camera clicks. Hopefully, his nightclub antics would make *Spy Sheet* again this month. Let his competitors think he had money to burn—which, of course, he didn't. These days, though, the newshounds checked your clothes and your chicks—not, fortunately, your checkbooks.

"You're the best, honey," he said as the limo

smoothly cruised up to the new permacrete fronting of the G.T.

"You won't forget my number, will you, Danny?"

Grant tapped his sternum. "Your digits are stamped in my heart, babe." He pulled out a microC-card, tapped in a five-hundred-cred-buck limit for the day, and tucked it into her sweet palm. "Go buy yourself something nice, sugar cheeks."

"Oh, Danny, thank you." He got a face full of lips and bosom for his effort.

"Gotta be at Lipshitz and Garfunkel's in Brooklyn Heights, though, sweet cakes. The car will take you there and back to your digs." He puffed up importantly. "But I'm going to need it at twelve-thirty for an important date."

Actually, he had the thing leased out through his car service then, but an important man had to look like he had full use of his limo, right?

"No problem."

"And remember what I told you if you see any signs of aliens?"

She nodded her head importantly. "Call *you!*" Her voice was slightly and unpleasantly squeaky, and as he began to open the door and some sunlight got at her, he realized it didn't flatter her as much as candlelight did.

Unlikely she'd see any aliens. But you never knew. "That's right, darling. Last night was wonderful. I wish our time had never ended. But even billionaires have to work . . . probably harder than most people!" He swept off the seat carefully so he wouldn't crease his trousers. "Ciao, baby!"

She blew him a kiss just as the clatter and flashes of cameras began. Nimbly, he jumped so that a few photographic images would record décolletage and blond tresses (for his ex-wife as much as envious male competitors) and then shut the door.

The robo-limo smoothed off toward Brooklyn Heights and the perma-thrift department store he owned. Fortunately, Candy (Bambi?) was far too dumb to know the difference between new merchandise and restructured merchandise.

Daniel Grant swiveled around to greet the chroniclers of his arrival, trying to looked annoyed.

"Can't a busy man have *any* privacy?" he groused, straightening his power neck jewelry so that it would look right in the pictures. Daniel Grant was sheathed in his usual sartorial splendor. His tailored camel-hair coat hung over his tailored suit perfectly, every angle and nook and color complementing the jut of his square jaw, the tilt of his brain-filled brow, the steely slate of his penetrating eyes. Even the tousle of his hair was follicle-calculated to be photogenic.

Today, even Grant was surprised.

There were usually one or two people here to record his arrival and ask a few questions.

Today, there was a *mob*.

From the corner of his eye he caught a reporter with a new face and an old question. "Mr. Grant. How do you account for your meteoric rise to success? What's your secret?"

Grant paused, lifted his hand like a heckled but patient monarch requesting heed for his proclamation. He went into automatic speechifying mode. Mental tables appeared before his eyes. He chose from column A and column B.

"No secret! I just make a point of proving an old saying: 'You can learn something new every day.' "

Whew. What did *that* mean? Sounded damned good, though.

"Mr. Grant, what led to the recent split between you and your last wife?"

"No comment."

"Can you confirm rumors that you are planning to enter politics?"

"Of course not."

Loved those kinds of questions. You give a definite answer that didn't mean a goddamned thing.

"Who was that young lady you drove up with?"

A slight smirk tugged at the corner of his mouth. "A friend."

"Is it true that your financial empire is in trouble?"

He feigned total astonishment. "Where did you hear *that* one?"

"Mr. Grant, could you comment on the alleged lethal side effects of your new wonder drug?"

Oops. Time to check Column C.

As there was nothing appropriate there, he just had to wing it. "I'm unaware of such reports." A lie. But he honestly didn't think the "wonder drug" actually was lethal. But these impromptu news conferences were no place for complex ethical and biochemical delineations. "I have full confidence in all my employees. Especially those hardworking people at Neo-Pharm."

Yes, that good old tried-and-true method. Head 'em off the track with a statement. In a legitimate question and answer session, Grant could keep up the palaver for so long, a reporter was lucky to remember his *name*, much less his original question.

Still it *was* an alarming question, one that he really hadn't been ready to deal with, despite the news reports.

Time to beat the retreat.

He spun around on the sole of his spit-polished wing tips, again a busy businessman, immersed in the burdens of accruing riches, and stamped away, letting the hail of further questions slip off him. He dodged between two uniformed, sunglassed guards into the building, waggling the finger of command. The thick-necked men stepped between the press and the door, preventing them from further pursuit.

Grant stepped into the marbled halls of the first floor and made a hasty hop and skip for his special turbo-elevator.

He put his face up against a window for a retinal read, even as he placed his thumb into a hole for a quick DNA check.

In this kind of political and economic atmosphere, you just couldn't be too careful.

The car closed behind him and he punched a button. Thus, he was zoomed down to the basement offices and labs of his principal company, the foundation from which Daniel Grant had boosted into the wheeler-dealer stratospheres.

Neo-Pharm.

When he'd sent the message via sub-space to his folks on Beta Centauri colony that he'd used the money they'd given him to purchase a little-known drug company, his old man had thought he'd said "bought the farm"—and thought he was dead. From a friend back on the colony, he'd heard the old fart had just shrugged and poured himself another boost of booze. Fortunately, his mother had replayed the message and gotten the true gist of the message before she poured *her*self another drink. Then, in celebration, they'd bought everyone at the bar a drink and promptly gotten stinking drunk.

Of course, with the Grants, that was nothing new.

They drank so much at the New Town bar, the old man went ahead and *bought* it to minimize expenditures. Daniel Grant had to convince his father that the loan was a good business investment by sharing several bottles of cognac with the man. Over multiple ounces of the gut-searing stuff, Grant had pointed out that the alien-torn Earth, now in reconstruction, was ripe for business opportunities. A man who had vision there could have *immense* power. Old Man Grant wasn't so sure of the financial soundness of his son's plan, but he did have money. Money that he wasn't sure what to do with. Lend me some of that money, Pop, said Daniel Grant, and let me show you what I can do.

Daniel Grant had the money transferred to an Earth bank before his father sobered up, and then followed immediately thereafter, by a slower route.

The New Earth was violent and exciting and dynamic, a phoenix rising from ashes. World governments bent over backward to encourage growth. Restrictions were cut. Regulations either forgotten, ignored, or repealed. It was the freest market imaginable, and Grant studied it. He decided that what Earth people really needed—and would always need—were pharmaceuticals. Aspirin for headaches. Harder drugs for those harder-to-deal-with biochemical problems. Euphorics. Other moodalterers. And with a crack team of scientists at his bidding, he could map out new directions of bio-chemical technology.

So he bought the Pharm.

Since Neo-Pharm was one of the few drug companies still operating, under the helm of Grant's cunning and ruthlessness, unbounded by law or ethics, it burgeoned. Cash and credit flow were astounding. Grant expanded, buying out other companies, building himself an empire. Real estate, retail, hotels, space shuttles—even gambling casinos. Daniel Grant wanted to make a strong, swift impression.

Unfortunately, his first buy remained his best. None of the other companies did anywhere *near* as well as Neo-Pharm—and often he found himself dipping into N-P's black ink to try to neutralize the other companies' red ink.

If something happened to Neo-Pharm, some financial disaster like a successful class-action suit or (shudder) having to shut down production of Fire, their most popular product, then the whole card castle would crumple.

And he wouldn't be able to make certain personal payments.

Failure would not mean just bankruptcy.

His *ass* was on the line.

Dammit, he thought as the doors shut behind him. He'd paid back the old man. He'd pay his other debts. And he'd still have his cake and eat it, too . . . even if it *choked* him!

The door whispered open before him, and the familiar subdued colors throbbed over him. The acidic smells of the lab assaulted his nostrils.

As always, he could almost *taste* the freaking

bugs down here. At first, he thought the taste was sweet, because it tasted like money. Now, Daniel Grant wasn't so sure.

He stalked across the catwalk that spanned a pit where biochem workers in silvery suits worked over tables and tanks. Along the walls were aquariums filled with pickled bugs—whole bugs, half bugs, bits and pieces of bugs.

And the hellish bug juice—their acid blood—was carefully controlled, the vicious stuff. That was why the technicians worked in the specially lined pit. Anything that got loose, you could sluice it away, and it couldn't get into where it would damage things—or kill people.

"Mr. Grant!" called an alarmed technician from the floor below. "You're not wearing your suit!"

"Well just don't squirt me, guys," said Grant sarcastically. "Is Wyckoff in?"

"Yes, sir. He's in his office!"

"Great. What about the doctor's blood? Does that stuff burn through human flesh?"

"Not that we know of, sir."

"Good. I won't need a suit with him, then."

Helmeted heads swiveled and hooded looks exchanged.

Grant grinned to himself. Let 'em talk. Kept them on their toes!

He finished crossing the pit and entered the bank of offices belonging to the scientists of the firm. Here the air was tinged with a sweetener to clear out the bug stench—but still the stuff hovered.

A door labeled DR. PATRICK WYCKOFF loomed. Grant opened it, not bothering to knock.

The little gnome of a man was huddled among a stack of paper. Paper, paper, everywhere—even covering his computer. Wyckoff liked to figure and doodle on paper. He was a whiz with computers, but for some reason the man far preferred a number two pencil and cheap bond to scratch and fiddle with than one of these overpriced wangdoodles he nevertheless *insisted* was vital to his operation. Wyckoff was so immersed in what he was doing, the shiny-headed, cobalt-nosed little munchkin didn't notice his chief coming in the door.

"Wyckoff! Hey! Look alive. I could be a bug!" he growled in his big, booming I'm-pissed-off voice. *Worse, I'm your rampaging boss!*

The little man did a double take. His round, Coke-bottle glasses flashed in the indirect lighting. Jaw dropped, he stared at Grant for a moment, then recovered his aplomb.

"Good morning, Mr. Grant. I hadn't expected you so early," said the man in a nasal twang.

Grant loped over and slapped a plastic news sheet from his home News Service machine on the desk, featuring a highlighted article about the latest Fire boo-boo. "But you *did* expect me, didn't you, Wyckoff?"

"Ye . . . ye . . . Yes, sir. I knew you'd at least call. The truth is, I thought I'd hear from you yesterday or the day before—"

"Maybe I just trusted my employees to do their job . . . To deal with this ridiculous matter. I didn't realize that I'd have a microphone shoved up my nose as soon as I'd stepped out of my car, and be hounded by news of the lethalness of Xeno-Zip."

Wyckoff shook his head sorrowfully. "No, sir, Xeno-Zip's perfectly fine."

It was Grant's turn for a double take. He blinked, twisted his head around, and examined his scientist from another angle, as though to make sure he wasn't seeing some one-dimensional projection. "People seem to be reacting rather *poorly* to it for it to be perfectly *fine*, Wyckoff!"

"That's just it, sir. As soon as I heard the reports, I did a complete check of our supply. You may not have noticed, but your PR people have been doing their jobs . . ." Wyckoff seemed to be back in control now, though he still was clearly intimidated by his ranting and raving employer. "They've put out the notification that these are counterfeit bottles of Xeno-Zip that are affecting people poorly. Meanwhile, we're exploring the possibilities, and I believe we know now what the problem is."

"Well, why don't you *tell* me, instead of mincing words and hemming and hawing."

"Sir, it's the active ingredient."

"Regal jam, you mean?"

"Um . . . Royal jelly. Anyway, that's what we call it—there are so many equivalencies to the aliens and their nest/hives and the Earthly insect kingdom. Our supply is obtained by free-lance mercenaries who destroy the many hives still around the world. We pay them to take the royal jelly first before they destroy the hive and pass it along to us."

"Yes, yes, I know that—"

"As I said, our main supply of Xeno-Zip is perfectly all right. The effect of a tiny amount of regular royal jelly combined with precipitant molecules of queen mother royal jelly ingested by a human being within the proper biochemical suspension is a safe serotonin booster and nonabrasive stimulant, improving perception and performance in nerve relay. Part of our work here is to either synthesize both or genetically create creatures that will manufacture both types of royal jelly without the less . . . benevolent aspects of the aliens. We have introduced synthesized regular royal jelly already into the market. Even with the precipitant Q-M molecules it, alas, effects a percentage of users negatively. Why, we're not sure yet."

"Because you're a bunch of *morons*, that's why!"

Wyckoff looked chagrined. A pained expression was etched on his face, and he sighed. "There is a possibility that these effects can be controlled by a higher Q-M jelly content. However, doing that would rapidly deplete our supply. Perhaps someone else can explain this to you better." He leaned over and thumbed a toggle. "Dr. Begalli—would you mind coming into my office, and bring some of those charts you showed me earlier. Mr. Grant desires the full scoop."

"Begalli?" said Grant.

"Yes, sir. The researcher you bribed to jump ship from MedTech."

Grant grinned, remembering his coup. "Oh, yes— that bug expert. Cost me a pretty penny . . . but it was worth it, knowing I stomped on Foxnall's nose!"

"You did indeed, and believe me, sir—he's worth it. He not only has the best handle on the genetic makeup of the things, he's got unparalleled field experience and a grasp on the behavior of the things like I've never encountered before. As soon as he heard about this—ah—little problem, he started an amazing amount of work in conjunction with our computers and the other scientists."

Grant, who had felt a tantrum coming on, was intrigued.

He found himself flopping into a formafit chair and allowing himself to be served some soothing medicinal tea concocted by Neo-Pharm—thankfully not derived from anything alien. The scientist who Wyckoff had summoned showed up with surprising speed, not even allowing Grant an edge of impatience.

Dr. Amos Begalli slouched in, as though burdened by the computer-generated charts and diagrams he carried under one arm.

"Morning," he whispered in a hoarse voice to Grant, almost seeming to bow in obeisance. If he didn't have the charts in his hands, Grant suspected that the man might rub his hands together in the manner of Uriah Heep.

Grant grunted and leaned back, the expression on his face clearing communicating "Show me."

Begalli's eyes flicked over to the pot of tea that Wyckoff had just brewed. "Might I trouble you for a cup of that tea?" he said. He coughed, in an annoying phlegmy fashion.

But then, just about everything was annoying about Dr. Amos Begalli. Grant had always found him an unctious, queasy worm, and would never have hired him at all but for his expertise—and the extreme harm it did to MedTech. He was a darkcomplected man with limp black hair that looked greasy even when clean. It dropped down over a sloping forehead in ridiculous bangs, emphasizing an almost Neanderthal brow. Dark rings underlined dark, bloodshot eyes. Only in the center of those eyes could intelligence be discerned—intelligence of a searing, sneering variety that even thick-skinned Grant found a little unnerving.

A weak mouth below a long, hooked nose twitched, showing a flash of eellike teeth as he spoke.

"Thank you," he said, accepting the steaming brew. He pulled out a small bottle of Xeno-Zip and took out a tablet, which he washed down with a gulp of tea. "Marvelous stuff, Mr. Grant. I would not be able to perform at peak mental ability for such long hours without it."

"Good to see you putting some of the money I give you back into the firm," said Grant. "But I'm a busy man, Begalli. You want to get on with this show-and-tell?"

Begalli put the tea down and began to prop his charts up on an easel. He spoke in a hoarse, low but audible voice as he did so.

"Mr. Grant, I believe you are aware of my background and many other important things. But I do not believe you are aware of the amazing number of secrets comprised in the genetic makeup of these marvelous xenotropic creatures, so interwound with human experience."

"I'm a businessman. You're a scientist. I have the money, you have your work."

"Indeed, indeed, but you have to understand something of what's going on here in order to have a grasp on not only the essence, but the cutting edge of this business." Slender, snaky fingers were tapping on a chart, which looked like some modern art collage of the alphabet connected by lines and squiggles and the incomprehensible. Grant recognized it as an incredible tangle of genetic code, with some new symbols that had been invented just for the silicon-based segments of the alien creature's makeup. Begalli gazed at it for a moment, absorbed and fascinated.

He snapped out of it just before Grant was about to get mad. "This is the closest we can get to an actual chart of typical alien DNA. There's so much we do not understand—so much to learn." Eagerness and awe crept into his voice. "So much opportunity . . . But look what I have discovered, Mr. Grant!"

His eyes widened and he tapped the edge, where the code performed a curious curlicue.

"A goddamned crossword puzzle?"

Begalli laughed an oily laugh. "The whole DNA is a puzzle, sir—but what this is, is nothing less than a recessive gene!"

Grant did not pretend to understand. "Look, talk in English, will you?"

"Mr. Grant, when we first started getting reports of the hyperactive results of some doses of Xeno-Zip, I was among the batch of scientists who immediately investigated the biochemical reasons. The reason that some people have been reacting in this fashion to the drug is that their biochemistries are sensitive to the unique properties of the synthesized regular alien jelly."

"Yes, dammit, but what else are we going to use? We're running out of the natural stuff, right. We've got to synthesize the jam or jelly or whatever."

"Yes, sir, but if you'll allow me, there's more. Apparently the berserker antics were the result of a batch of Xeno-Zip in which too much of the precipitant was introduced."

"What a waste!"

"Indeed. Nonetheless, normal amounts still affect a portion of the populace negatively."

"So. What are we going to do?"

Begalli shrugged. "I for one would like to study the possibilities in this recessive gene."

"What does that have to do with our problem?"

"Mr. Grant, you're going to have to face up to facts. We need more royal jelly, and we need more queen mother royal jelly. At the moment, our understanding of the genetic makeup of the aliens is not sufficiently advanced to clone either. We need to go to the source. I have reason to believe that the DNA avenues I have been exploring could result in drug breakthroughs far beyond mere Xeno-Zip. At the very least, we could obtain a source of the active ingredient in the cornerstone of your drug empire that would allow you to manufacture safe batches for a long, long time. And I have the feeling that the answer to my questions could lie at the source of what we need."

The man nodded significantly as though Grant was supposed to catch the significance from these words alone.

Grant shook his head, jumped to his feet, and let the frustration out, full volume.

"Look, goddammit! I'm staring at the possibility of lawsuits buggering me from now till kingdom come . . . I'm going to hear from sales as soon as those spineless assholes get up the courage . . . and you know what I'm going to hear? A drop-off of sales for Fire. That will kill the cash flow, which

will kill Neo-Pharm . . . And I'm in hock for everything else!" He stalked nearer to the cowed scientists. "And you're telling me I ought to give a rat's
ass about a blip in a weird ladder? You're telling me
that I've got to spend more money than God owns
for a trip to an alien planet?"

Begalli blinked and smiled uneasily. "In every
seeming disaster, there is incredible opportunity.
And this particular discovery . . . well, sir, it simply
reeks of it!"

"What, because it makes people as crazy as aliens?
I just don't get you guys! I'm running a business
here, not a nonprofit research group. I'm in desper-
ate straits! I need help, not homilies! I need—"

The vid-phone chimed. Wyckoff jumped for it, as
though for a lifeline to pull himself from the storm.

Curiosity and deep respect for that demigod of
the business world, the telephone, caused Grant to
stop mid-spew. Begalli watched the proceedings,
engaged but more than a bit bemused.

"Yes?" said Wyckoff. His eyes swung toward his
employer, still wary and more than a bit relieved by
the interruption. "Yes, he's here, but this is a—" He
blinked. "Oh. Oh, I see. Well, very well, I suppose . . .
Yes. Right away." Wyckoff turned to Grant and
handed him the receiver. "It's General Burroughs of
the United States Army, sir. Vital communication."

As Daniel Grant reached for the vid-phone volume button, he saw Begalli's lips tilt up into a half
smile, as though he'd expected something like this
all the while.

5

There was only one thing worse than the nightmares.

The nightmares, plus a hangover.

When the phone kicked Colonel Alexandra Kozlowski out of sleep at 0600 hours in the morning, she was experiencing both.

"Yeah?" she said, fumbling with the vid-phone control. She was covered in a snarl of sheets. She was still dressed in the civvies from last night. From what, for where? Her pounding brain came up empty.

First things first.

"Who is this?" she demanded.

"Colonel?" Unfamiliar face.

"That's right." Inventory. All her limbs seemed intact and still attached. No empty bottle of whiskey on the counter. Even better, no naked body be-

side her. That limited the possible damage of last
night. Shreds of memory and the dinner tray in
front of the vid told the story.

Too much video, too much vino.

She hadn't raised hell outside, she'd just raised it
inside. Much more discreet. Far more destructive.

"Colonel, this is Burroughs. General Delmore
Burroughs." She sat up, ran a hand through her
hair. "I'm sorry to bother you this early in the
morning, but we've got an important meeting today
in Washington. I'm going to have to ask that you
get on a jump-skip."

"Yes, sir." Civility and duty won over surliness.
Why the hell had she stayed in this stinking profes-
sion anyway? Why was she taking this bullshit?

"Good. There will be a plane ready for you at
eight hundred hours. The meeting is scheduled for
eleven hundred hours, sharp."

"Yes, sir." She struggled for the proper words.
"Begging your pardon, sir . . . but could I inquire
about the nature of this meeting?"

"I'm afraid not, Colonel. Top secret. Priority one.
You'll know soon enough."

"Thank you, sir."

"And, Colonel. Wear your dress uniform. Wear
your medals . . . and some kick-ass boots."

"Yes, sir."

She disconnected. Well, it wasn't any problem
getting to the transport. She was living on base at
the moment. All she had to do was call up her adjutant and get him to wheel her all of two miles to
the airfield.

The trouble was going to be getting out of bed.

Dammit! she thought, groaning. I wait around

for months for something important to happen, and it happens on my day off, hours after I've had a snootful. The karmic balances of the universe were just getting far too hair-trigger for Alex Kozlowski's taste. The stupid Eastern theories were immediately banished for the colder, more mechanistic, and less vengeful rules of Western science. You drink too much, you get sick. Moreover, if you're a career officer, you took it all like a good soldier.

Groaning, she heaved her compact, muscular body out of bed, wishing she'd been working out more lately. Cripes, she felt like a pair of hips with a torso and limbs tacked on as afterthought. She peeled off her clothes, then walked (no, Koz, she admonished, more like *waddled*) to the shower stall, avoiding the mirror. She turned on the water, hard and hot, held her breath, and jumped in. The pounding heat against her neck and shoulders immediately improved things. Suddenly she had an afterthought head, too.

It wasn't like she was an alchy or anything. She'd go for weeks with just a glass of wine or a shot of bourbon and beer with the gang now and then. Every once in a while, though, when she started thinking about Peter too much, she found herself motoring for a jug of wine, gallon size, and just going apeshit.

Peter. Peter Michaels. Lieutenant Peter Michaels.

There had been men since him, just as there had been men before him. Hell, soldiers in foxholes and all that stuff. Nothing like sex to ease the tension. But there had never been anyone like Peter ever again. No one she cared about. No one she could love.

Had it been love with Michaels? Hard to say. She just knew that she didn't have much in the way of tender emotions anymore. They had got eaten up with that alien acid. All that was left was guilt and nightmare—and a large sturdy pile of grit that was the essential stuff of Alexandra Kozlowski.

The grit. The iron. The hard stuff. That was why she was a colonel now.

After that nasty business with the Hollywood nest, she transferred to the Marines. They took her in a shot. She found herself immersed in space and the vessels that traversed it. It was a way to get her brain out of the acid. She was a top student and her rank just increased and increased. She was on Camp Kennedy base now, doing some prelims on a possible space cruise, but it looked as though her superiors had something different in mind for her, which was just hunky-dory.

Busy. That was what she needed. To be busy, to immerse herself in work. When she worked hard, she slept hard. When she slept hard, she didn't have nightmares.

When she didn't have nightmares, she didn't see Peter's dissolving face again.

Dammit! Just shut up! she told herself, pounding the tile of the shower stall, letting the hot water sluice down her face. Just shut *up*! It *wasn't* your fault, why are you *torturing* yourself? It was Peter who'd been getting weird, who had to show his independence. If he hadn't demanded to go up to that bulb, if he had *listened* to her, he might still be alive.

After his death, they'd cleaned the nest out. It was as though all her men had become an extension of her need for revenge. There wasn't much alien jelly. They'd taken the piddling amount out. Not worth the bother, certainly. But no alien bodies, no DNA samples. They slagged all that. It was like a dementia. It was like nothing that Alex had ever experienced before. If the bugs had had half a brain between them, they would have run, because there'd seldom been a killing machine like her and her men, taking revenge for that sneaky little alien trap. Somehow they'd all made it through alive, too, which was a wonder. They'd used part of their extra leave for a wake for Peter Michaels. It should have been enough for her, it really should have.

But it didn't bring back Peter.

The thing about it was that they'd both known that something like that could happen. They'd promised each other that if it did, they'd get on with their lives, not cling to memories and hope. But it *had* happened and now Alex had to live with that and somehow there were always other kinds of pain she'd rather have.

She dried herself off. She put herself together. She made herself some coffee. Then she called her adjutant to pick her up. She found her good uniform, she put on her pants—one leg at a time, as usual. She combed her hair and she had another cup of coffee.

The pounding in her head had subsided, but she still felt weak and weary.

She looked at the clock. Five more minutes to pickup time.

She looked at her hands. They were trembling.

Damn and double damn! What was happening to her? She wasn't nervous, yet she couldn't function. She'd never been like this after drinking.

She took a deep breath, but it didn't calm her. She sighed. Then, wearily, she went to her medicine cabinet. She took out one of the bottles there, opened it, and tapped a pill into her hand.

She took it with a gulp of coffee, and almost immediately began to feel better.

Damn this stuff, she thought. Damn it to hell.

She tucked the bottle of Fire into her carry-bag, and put her face into her hands.

Daniel Grant smiled.

He felt the room lighting up around him from the effects of that wonderful smile, and he reveled in its power.

"Gentlemen, all I ask for are three things." He turned the smile wattage up just a tad higher. "Guns. Grunts. And a gondola. Send my team of specialists and scientists on a little voyage, and I promise to bring back happiness and satisfaction for us all."

The meeting place was a high-level war room, streamlined angles, all polished wood and chrome and underlit attitude. It smelled of after-shave and leather, and was about five degrees cooler than it had to be. Architecture and technology contrived to create a crib of spare power, with acoustics that made the most of monosyllabic speeches.

There was enough brass in the room to supply knuckles for an army of hoodlums. They sat around a black oval table, bracketed by uniform high-backed black chairs, still and forbidding as monuments in a nighttime cemetery.

"To the alien *homeworld* for God's sake?" said Admiral Niles. The old man moved forward in his chair. He was a good-looking man, with a shock of gray hair and a slash of a mustache below an aquiline nose. His face was lined with weariness, but his eyes were sharp as a hawk's.

"Not homeworld, sir," a supernumery corrected. *"Hiveworld."*

"The source of all the aliens that have been encountered in this quadrant of the galaxy, from all signs. The source of the queen mother that was brought to Earth—not of the race," tendered another expert.

The extent of the spread of the xenos had not yet fully been determined. So far they had been found only on isolated planets; all the clues pointed back to this so-called Hiveworld. The Hiveworld had been the source of the Alien-Earth War.

However, naturally, there was great concern. Any newly discovered planet had the potential of being infected. And no one knew if any eggs had been illegally exported from Earth.

Admiral Niles grunted. "Whatever. This place must be hell. I know that the xenos are comparatively well contained here on Earth." He looked at Grant, and it felt like those coal-black eyes were boring into him. "In some ways, perhaps, even *farmed*. But on their own turf, surely—"

Grant snapped his fingers.

The AV portion of this morning's DC festivities.

A holotank eased down into its moorings and lights flickered. Three-D film flashed of brave soldiers and mercenaries in the latest getup, carrying the most modern weapons, slamming through the ranks of an alien nest. He would have enjoyed splicing in some martial John Philip Sousa, but his PR people had talked him out of it.

"Not bad, huh? And lots of these folks are yours. Just crack teams! Crack! And I even understand you've got a real handle on the alien-blood-in-battle problem. Wonderful!" Grant was all enthusiasm.

"I know those films!" said the admiral. "They're from the North Carolina campaign earlier this year. A piece of cake, true—but we're talking about a place where aliens have total sway."

"Not necessarily, sir," an expert's nasal voice twanged. "The Hiveworld may also be inhabited by the alien homeworld original predators—or corollary predators. There's got to be a similar ecology to some extent for them to have developed there the way they have."

"Hmm. So you're saying an expedition there is feasible, and not overly risky," said the admiral, settling back in his seat.

"Any environment containing these critters is going to have an element of risk, sir," said Grant. "But then . . . I know your people can handle it! And the rewards would be spectacular!" He leaned forward confidently. "I mean, it was General Burroughs here who approached me on the subject. And I found it to be not only a fascinating concept—but a mutually rewarding alliance. An expedition into the adventure of free enterprise and the onward evolution of the American soldier! General Burroughs? Would you care to elaborate?"

The black general glared at Grant through slitted

eyes. "The admiral has been thoroughly briefed on the benefits of the royal jelly you can supply." The man was playing poker here, and that was okay, because Daniel Grant appreciated a good negotiator.

It brought out the best in him.

"Yes, but before me I see intelligent eyes, *questioning* eyes!" Grant stood and gestured outward at the assemblage of frowning brass. "And as I am the pitchman here, and you've granted me time—please allow me to properly present my pitch!"

Again, a snap of fingers.

The moving pictures flickered into a different round.

The Baghdad Goodwill Games. Oriander's world record, and his unfortunate demise.

Ratty videos of the horrible slaughter at Quantico.

He heard the sharp intake of breath.

"I'm sure you're aware of these tragedies and others like them that have caused a huge number of lawsuits to be leveled at my company," Grant said gravely, deep into presentation mode.

Then: soldiers, looking noticeably calmer, performing tasks and exercises with sharp precision and sharp eyes.

"Here we have a group of men who have just taken small doses of regular Xeno-Zip . . . which I shall call Fire from now on. This, as I hope you know, is derived from normal alien royal jelly. My company Neo-Pharm has patented the proper methodology of transforming normal alien royal jelly utilizing molecules of queen mother royal jelly so that tiny doses will perk up a normal human's day—and enhance any soldier's performance. A little costly, perhaps—but worth it.

"However, as you no doubt are aware, the supply of normal royal jelly has been dwindling. We have synthesized the jelly . . . with mixed results . . . however we need not go into that right now. What is significant is that a batch of the synthesized jelly Xeno-Zip was accidentally spiked with extra queen mother royal jelly. In a marked percentage of those who ingested it, the result was quite incredible. Properly modulated, the results of this new drug will create nothing less than a supersoldier."

Another picture appeared on the screen. A gladiator soldier, hammering away at robots with sword and machine gun—but under control. A berserker without a doubt, but with orders and a plan.

"The good general here is already at work experimenting with this new kind of jelly. However, our supplies of queen mother jelly are reaching depletion. And may I also add, we're still not exactly well stocked in regular royal jelly, either, which is our own bread and butter, far preferable to us than our synthesized sort."

He waved away the audiovisuals, and motioned for normal light. He leaned forward emphatically on the table.

"It's very simple. My company needs more regular royal jelly as well as Q-M royal jelly—and a way to get a regular supply of both. Your company—I mean, your armed forces—already staggering under heavy opposition and funding cuts—need to make maximum use of every soldier in conflict. I have the scientists and the talent—you've got intergalactic vessels, pilots, and soldiers. My scientists predict the certain existence of what we both need on the Hiveworld." He smiled. He held his hands up in an eloquent shrugging gesture. "So some of my kiddies go, some of your kiddies go. We get what we want. We make a little pact. You help me, I help you. You scratch my back—I save your butt."

"Pardon me, Mr. Grant . . ." chided the admiral, shaking his head a moment as though to clear it. "Just a moment. I thought it was *your* company that was inundated with civil suits."

"We've got a few legal problems, sure. So sue us!" Grant chuckled. "Besides, I'm sure a few military words in the attorney general's ear will go a long way toward helping the company you'll be climbing into bed with."

"Mr. Grant! This is a lawful assembly," said the general, but with a hint of irony to his deep tones.

"Absolutely. Without a doubt. Unquestionably. But my association with a powerful legal force isn't going to do my legal standing any harm. And by the time people understand why we're doing what we're doing—by the time they see the benefits of our research . . . They will surely not be so vehement in our pursuit." Again, a shrug. "But only time will tell. In the meantime, no skin off your noses, eh?"

He could tell his spiel was getting to them. Everyone loved a rascal, especially when what he was coming up with could do big time good. He might as well get out the victory cigar in his vest pocket and start smoking it.

A new voice sounded from the assemblage. "Pardon me, Mr. Grant, but are you planning on accompanying this proposed mission?"

Grant blinked. "Hell no!" He looked over at the originator of the suggestion. A woman. Short hair, nice chin, scars. She would have been pretty if she wore makeup. Now she was merely . . . handsome. "I've got an important business to run here!"

The woman leaned forward, clasping her hands together. "Mr. Grant, with all due respect, have you ever put on a suit and gone into a hive?"

"Well, no . . . but what difference does that make?" He looked over at the general as though for help. The black man's eyes twinkled with amusement. Let's see how you wriggle off *this* hook, those eyes said.

"We're apparently talking about a whole *world* filled with bugs, Mr. Grant. Glib as your words may be, this assignment would *not* be simple. In fact, I'm willing to bet that stochastic prophecy would predict losses," said the woman.

"Not the ones projected by our figures!" Grant said. Who the hell *was* this woman? What was she trying to do—scuttle his boat?

The woman swiveled her head back and forth, catching each of the assembly eye to eye for just an instant of seriousness.

"Let me tell you all. I *have* been in alien hives. Miracle weapons or no miracle weapons . . . there will be losses. Are you willing to be responsible for that?" said the woman intensely, teeth gritted as though she were in some kind of pain.

Some of the upper brass began to hem and haw. This was entering touchy territory.

"Aw, goddammit," said Grant. "Give us a break. Is there not a war on? Is this not directly and indirectly a mission against the enemy? Casualties are *always* a possibility. But who's to say they're a certainty?"

He stared at the woman defiantly.

Her eyes were ice. She wasn't giving an inch. "I just wanted to ask a question, Mr. Grant. And state a fact that you seem to be trying to avoid. That's all." The lips curled into a private smile. "As for me, the idea of going to this Hiveworld and killing bugs and stealing their life's stuff is . . . rather appealing."

Christ Almighty! Who was this bitch?

The general and the admiral leaned over and privately conferred. The admiral looked over to his other officers and met merely nods and encouraging eyes.

"Well, Mr. Grant," said the admiral. "It seems as though your intriguing proposal has made the first hurtle. I believe we can work something out."

Grant could not suppress an ear-to-ear grin. His muscles unknotted. "Glad to hear it, Admiral. Glad to hear it!" He put out an impulsive hand, pumped away at the plump paw he'd grabbed. He nodded at the others. "My companies have had a long and prosperous liaison with you fine folks in uniform. I'm glad it's taking off for other worlds!"

There were a few embarrassed coughs, and a couple of members of the meeting made excuses and scurried off into labyrinthine Washington hallways. Grant just mentally shrugged it off. He was used to stepping on boot toes in this business, almost reveled in it. He'd never much liked military people, and secretly resented having to work so much with them, particularly in harvesting the precious royal jelly, far preferring to encourage the mercenaries in the business. Money was something that Daniel Grant could understand when it was the bottom line. When you got into the halls of politics, sex, personality, and power, things got a whole lot murkier.

"Now then," said the admiral, "I believe we have the necessary deep-space tactical vessel at our disposal. It will take some time to prepare it for this special journey. And of course we'll want a staff other than the people that Mr. Grant is supplying."

Grant sat back down. "Of course, you'll get me the best men for the job."

"Naturally, Mr. Grant. Naturally. We have some fine veterans and pilots who would be perfect," the admiral said. "What the expedition needs most is a commanding officer with the right feel both for leading troops and dealing with the quite unpredictable alien bugs!"

"That's your call," said Grant. "I'll leave that one totally up to you."

The general and admiral conferred for a moment in whispers and then the general spoke. "We anticipated the need for such a commander, Mr. Grant. So we invited a certain colonel along to this meeting. The youngest holder of the Congressional Medal of Honor, specifically for a pivotal role in the final cleaning up of the aliens in North America . . . and with special training for further work in space, dealing with infestations on other planets and colonies . . ."

"Sounds good to me. When do I get to meet the man?" said Grant.

The general turned to the small, coal-eyed

woman. "You've already met. The question is, will the colonel agree to such an assignment?"

The intense, scarred young woman leaned over, showing small pearly white teeth in a smile.

"I'd relish such an assignment, sir. Thank you."

It was the general's turn to smile. "Excellent. I cannot commend your expedition into better hands, Mr. Grant. May I formally introduce you to Colonel Alexandra Kozlowski, your commanding officer."

Grant's jaw dropped. He was glad he hadn't lit up a cigar. It would have fallen right onto his expensive Italian suit, spilled embarrassing ashes all over the place. He recovered quickly, converted his surprise into a laugh. "Well, well, well! How marvelous. And I thought you were the one who hated the bugs."

"I do," said Colonel Kozlowski. "I want to see every last one of them either cindered . . . or perhaps even harmless, if that's possible. That's why I'm in this business, Mr. Grant. That's why I'm here today." She leaned forward and tapped the table. "Make no mistake, though. I don't believe in the Devil, Mr. Grant—but if there *was* a Devil, I doubt if even he would be evil enough to invent these bugs. This is not going to be a field trip to an ant farm. Tell your people that."

Those smoldering eyes again.

There was something else in those eyes . . . something that looked at him in a peculiar way that bothered Grant. Bothered him intensely. He shrugged it off, turned to the men in charge.

"Well, seems like a fine choice to me. I like a woman with intestinal fortitude." He pulled out a handful of cigars from his breast pocket. "A celebration seems to be called for. Anybody care to join me?" He flashed a handful.

The general took one.

The admiral accepted one.

"Me," said Colonel Kozlowski, holding out a hand.

Grant had one passed down.

He watched as the petite but hard-looking woman accepted the cigar, examined it, sniffed it, then pocketed it.

"You're not going to smoke it with us?" Daniel Grant said, slightly miffed but playful nonetheless.

"Mr. Grant," said Colonel Alex Kozlowski. "Celebration is hardly in order yet. I'll smoke it when the mission is over and my rear is seated safe and sound back in this chair for a debriefing."

The woman asked for and obtained permission to leave from her superiors.

"Well, what do you think of our choice for your commander?" said the general, an eyebrow raised.

Grant let out a gust of smoke.

"I'd say, I feel damned sorry for those Hiveworld bugs!"

6

"**N**ice-looking boat, huh?"

Daniel Grant flashed the cube-shot to his date sitting in the restaurant booth next to him. She was a hot, big-busted brunette with her spangled dress spray-painted on. Long hair, delicious perfume, and foreign territory for the old Skyscraper Man to plumb. He was impressing her with this nightclub, black and white and dazzle all around— and now, for what reason he knew not, he was impressing her with his power that extended Yea! even to the ends of the Universe!

Her name was Mabel.

"Weird! What kinda thing is that?" Mabel spoke with a New Jersey accent, which gave her flamboyant body a certain earthy charm.

"That's a spaceship, babes. That's *my* spaceship. Pretty, huh?"

"Pretty strange. What you want a spaceship for, Mr. Grant?"

"I told you, you can call me Daniel, sweetheart, just as long as your pretty fingers aren't anywhere near a keyboard."

"You're so kind to take me out tonight, Mr. Grant!" Mabel batted long thick mascara at him. "And me, hardly having worked for two days at your offices. And I don't *care* what the other temps have said—you're *such* a gentleman! Such a scrumptious meal, such delicious champagne—and you haven't laid a hand on me!"

Grant mimed a kiss at her. "I know, and it's damned hard, too, make no mistake about it. But Mrs. Grant brought her little boy up right, I guess."

Truth was, you get enough bubbly percolating in those pea brains, display enough dazzle, and blow enough pheromones in their faces, and women touched *you*. A little trick Daniel Grant had learned early on which kept him out of trouble. Oh, well. He had his share of trouble all right, what with *letting* all those women touch him that wanted to, while he was still married to old Iron Drawers and building his companies. But you tread a fine line, and trouble that came your way tended to be the fun kind of trouble, the thrilling trouble, the trouble that made you feel like you were dashing down a ski slope on a power sled, not a garbage-can lid.

"Anyway, really—what do you think of it?"

The picture was of the U.S.S. *Razzia*, hovering in parking orbit above Earth. Right now, it was getting loaded up with supplies, weapons, men, and whatnot for the expedition to the alien Hiveworld.

A trip that would bring back royal jelly, preserved DNA, and other treasures that would spell not only full financial recovery and put paid to any lost lawsuits—but place him, Daniel Marcus Grant, squarely back into the pure honey of wealth.

"I don't know. It's . . . well, it's kind of ugly."

They'd had more than a few glasses of champagne, so things were kind of blurry. Grant examined the picture again.

There it was, a whale of a ship, bubbles and glassine protuberances making it look like some kind of colorful exotic beetle that had been pumped up with gas to the point of bursting. Aesthetically, it *did* look rather odd. Kind of like a strange cross between the jewelry kind of carbuncles and the flesh-bump kind. Of course, that wasn't the way Grant saw it. He saw it as his beautiful, thrilling hope for riches beyond avarice.

"What is it?" said Mabel.

"Never mind," said Grant, tucking the photo back into his jacket pocket. "Just a little business venture of mine. Let's talk about *you*!"

"Oh, but, Mr. Grant! Daniel! I'm fascinated by business ventures!"

"Stick with Grant Industries, kiddo! We've got our share of businesses. Maybe we'll set you up as a special secretary for one of our branches."

The eyes went wide. A slender hand touched his knee. "Oh, but, Mr. Grant! That would be wonderful. I'd *have* to prove my skills to you first—"

Grant plucked up the bottle of Dom Fauxgnon from the ice bucket and poured some more champagne into her glass. "I'm sure you will, my dear."

He winked at her. "And I for one am looking forward to the fruits of your official labors!"

They clinked glasses.

Feeling positively ebullient, Grant tippled.

This fake stuff sure wasn't classic—but it tingled and did the trick.

He was just finishing off the glass when a booming voice almost made him choke.

"Careful! Careful there, my dear, dear chum!" A dim form moved out of the swirling, milling shadows of the hip night spot and clapped him on the back. Grant sputtered, struggled, and recovered, watery eyes blinking.

"Foxnall!" he said, working hard to keep his voice neutral. "What portal of Hades did you pop from?"

"Ah, believe it or not, dear boy," said the cultured voice from the thin and wiry man with affected square spectacles and billowing silk clothing, "I have not come here to torment you. In fact, if you ask any bartender or regular here tonight, they'll assure you that I am not a stranger to Flickers. But this *is* a treat, especially with you in the company of such a charming young lady. Are you going to be a selfish cad and refuse to introduce us?"

Grant felt a distinct leveling of spirits.

However, everything was still well within control.

"Mabel, this is Lardner Foxnall. Principal stockholder and CEO of MedTech. Lardner, this is Mabel Planer, an employee and . . . ah, new friend."

"My pleasure." Foxnall kissed the woman's hand to her obvious delight.

"MedTech! Why, they make Wonder Diet! I use

that all—" Suddenly aware of her diplomatic error, Mabel cringed. "Oh, dear. I mean . . ."

"No problem, Mabel," said Grant. "MedTech makes a quite reputable line of pharmaceuticals. This is a free enterprise system in which we work—and yes, Neo-Pharm has quite worthy competitors and we value them. After all, if there were no other companies, who could we constantly outperform?"

A muscle in Lardner Foxnall's jaw flinched. However, his eyes remained amused. "Yes—quite. And this new enterprise of yours . . . this journey . . ."

Grant felt a thrill of alarm. "Ah, you must mean—" He began groping for some fake enterprise, to put Foxnall off course.

"Oh, you mean the spaceship! Yes, isn't it exciting?" Mabel fairly jounced with elation. She looked over for approval from her boss, her gentleman date—and found cold eyes instead.

She shut up immediately, to her credit.

"Indeed, Neo-Pharm is looking toward colonial expansion . . . but then what Earth drug company worth its salt isn't?" said Grant aggressively.

An artificial tic of a smile from Foxnall. "Absolutely. And may we all prosper!" He winked. "But some, more than others!" A tip of an imaginary hat. "By the way, Ms. Planer. We're always in need of good help at MedTech. Whenever you care for a free supply of Wonder Diet, please remember us!"

"Quite unlikely!" called Grant after him, barely hanging on to his temper.

He waved for a waiter, and a photosensitive robot

promptly smoothed up. "What's riffraff like that doing in a reputable club like Flickers?"

"Pardon, honored guest—but Mr. Foxnall is the new owner." Lights blinked obsequiously.

Grant started, did a double take, then smiled. "Then that must be why the fellow ordered a bottle of Dom Perignon for the young lady here!" He scratched his nose. "And the caviar and crackers for me, come to think of it!"

"I will see to it immediately."

"He did?" said Mabel as the robo-waiter trundled off.

"Oh, yes. A tradition between pharmaceutical rivals, my dear."

"Oh, Mr. Grant. I'm so sorry if I said anything wrong. Is there anything I can do to make it up to you?"

"Well, let's drink this next bottle of champagne and eat our caviar and have a serious discussion on the matter."

The caviar was cold and quite good, and the Dom Perignon turned out to be far superior to the Dom Fauxgnon. However the conversation in the next half hour grew sour in Grant's mouth and ears, unspiked by sensual desire and the urge for sexual conquest.

Dammit!

Could Lardner Foxnall have gotten wind of what he was up to? Could he possibly know the destination of the U.S.S. *Razzia* and the reason for the trip?

If so, that could mean many things, none of them particularly good, several of them very bad.

His mood seemed to grow fouler as he helped

the increasingly drunk secretary finish their late night treats among the wistful smells and pulsing sounds of Flickers nightclub.

"Mr. Grant!" she said, giggling at some stupid sarcastic statement he'd made about some politico. "You are so *funny*!"

"I think we've had a little too much champagne, Mabel."

"But not too much caviar. I never could have believed that I ever would like fish eggs, but this stuff is just delish! I really am enjoying myself."

"I hope you've saved some for friends," said a cold voice from the darkness. A swath of mist swirled away, and there stood a husky man with a scar riding along his bald pate like a bolt of lightning. He wore good clothes and he smelled of good cologne.

"Gee! Another competitor, Mr. Grant?"

Grant froze. "Not exactly."

Fisk. Morton Fisk.

What was this, old home night for demons from hell?

"Good evening, Grant." The man did not even look at Mabel. His piercing eyes just hooked on to Grant and hung on. "I don't usually visit people personally. However I do have a tradition. I like to make sure that my face is branded on the retinas of dying men."

"Fisk. What are you talking about?"

Grant had a suspicion, but he didn't even want to think about the possibility.

"Who is this guy, Mr. Grant? What's going on?" said Mabel.

"I told you, Grant, when you got me to bail you

out, that I was a patient man . . . until I wasn't patient." The scar on the head seemed to glow a livid
pink. Pulsing with contained rage. "And I haven't
been. You're months overdue, and you haven't even
had the dignity to send partial payments. I am truly
offended."

"Fisk! I'm not sure what you're talking about.
You've been getting regular installments!"

A big fist grabbed a handful of his shirt, lifted
him up so that Grant began to gasp for air. "Lie! He
lies to my face! You well know that I haven't gotten
a penny for months."

Indeed, Grant did know.

All too well.

In the scrabble for solidity and power after the
Alien-Earth War, not all of the fortresses of fiducia-
ry control were entirely legal. And often as not, to
get the leverage you needed for truly inspired buy-
outs, you had to go to these underground people
for liquid assets.

Unfortunately, they were criminals.

Violent criminals.

Self-confidence was always the antigrav stuff for
Daniel Grant, the by-your-bootstraps talent that
hoisted him above the rest. Unfortunately, self-
confidence could also be a blindfold. He well knew
that he personally owed millions to Fisk and company, but since for Daniel Grant mañana was always golden—well, he'd pay them mañana, when
he had the money.

Alas, he saw no mañana in Morton Fisk's eyes.

"Look, Morty. Sit down, pull up a glass of the
warm south, get to know this delightful creature . . .

and for heaven's sake, let's jaw awhile, huh?" Grant patted a comfortable cushion.

"Sorry."

The big man spun on his heel, and was swallowed up by the stylish mists and the nightclub gloom.

"Mr. Grant ... Daniel ..." said Mabel. "What kind of gorilla was that?"

"*Not* the gorilla of my dreams!" said Grant, scooting over to the end of the booth. "Look, I'll be right back, Mabel. Got to visit the little boys' room!"

What had happened here? Had Foxnall tipped Fisk off to his presence here? That bastard! That must have been what had happened.

Geez! There were such sharks in business these days!

He was at the edge of the booth, when he heard a *click*. Instinctively he dived for the floor.

An explosion of bullets whacked over the top of him like lateral hail. He could feel their heat. He hit the floor and rolled, the sound of the machine gun echoing in his ear, the scream of his secretary joining in.

He got a glimpse of the poor brunette, jerking amid the passion of the bullets, blood yanked from that sweet body, making a mess of her dress. Glass and champagne and caviar spattered every which way, in a fantasmagoric slow-mo fountain.

The will to live turned Grant away from this death dance, and he scrambled away, like a rat from a pack of cats.

7

A month of her life, just getting this show on the road.

Colonel Alex Kozlowski took a swig of her coffee, and watched as the last batch of supplies got loaded into the shuttle. She managed to get down to a quarter capsule a day of Fire, but she'd already taken that now, and damned herself for wanting more. The stuff wasn't like booze, you didn't see creepy crawlies if you went dry. It was like cigarettes. And just as hard to kick. She wanted to kick it, to show her own superiority to herself. Which was why she felt bad now, wanting another hit.

In just a few hours they'd be boosted up to the *Razzia*, stored away with the rest of the stuff Daniel Grant and his scientists wanted on this mission—along of course with the rest of the marines, her own hard ass included.

Alex Kozlowski was sitting on the apron of the ramp, the lip of which sided a wing of the shuttle that would soon trundle out of the hangar and wing up through the atmosphere. To the other side of her was a warehouse-sized security checkpoint and storage room. Dawn had just shouldered through a cloudy horizon.

She slouched in the chair, watching the crates being loaded.

Hell of a lot of stuff going up there.

She'd been in charge of everything her crew was going to need. She'd wanted to be in charge of the whole shebang. Unfortunately, that was not in the cards.

A bored-looking deliveryman walked over and handed her a piece of paper on a clipboard. "Sign please, Colonel."

Alex took the clipboard.

SUPPLIES, said the checklist. That was all.

"How can I check 'em in, if I don't know what they are?"

"Look, Colonel," said the man, "I'm just doing my job. I'd like it a lot if you could just take a crowbar and prize open a couple and have yourself a gander. I'm afraid, though, that it's all pretty insulated and locked up and you'd be pretty hard-pressed to lock the stuffing back in."

The guy was a civvy, probably worked for the government. Kozlowski could tell by his attitude. She didn't like any man she couldn't give orders to, or take orders from, and the man annoyed her. What could she do, though? Make him clean the latrines? He was the equivalent of a third-rate, truck-driving, trolley-pushing bureaucrat.

It hit her then: what was important to bureau-
crats?

"Ooops!" she said, and tore the papers she had
to sign into shreds.

The man looked at her, stunned. "Colonel. I'm
going to have to go and get another form now!
Why . . .?"

"File a complaint, toad-breath," she said. "But
have some respect next time you give a lady a form
to sign . . ."

The man went off, cursing under his breath, to
get another form. Kozlowski went off to sniff
around the crates.

TOP SECRET, they read.

THIS SIDE UP.

HIGHLY FRAGILE.

One was even fitted with elaborate refrigeration
equipment.

"Oh, well," she said, drumming her fingers
against a crate. "You can bet I'm going to find out
what's going on when we're light-years away."

She was almost sorry she'd signed up for this gig.

Not that she minded going long distance in in-
terstellar space. That would be fun. And the idea of
blowing away xenos en masse still tickled her pink.
However, all the mystery and bullshit attendant to
her duties had not exactly thrilled her, to say the
least. She thought that *she* was in charge of this
mission—but over the weeks, the fact had gradu-
ally seeped through her thick skull that she was
only in charge of the military aspects. Neo-Pharm's
other operations on the *Razzia*—and there was
plenty of extra room for that, which was doubtless

why the ugly scow had been chosen—was strictly out of her control.

Which was one of the reasons they'd probably chosen her.

She could hear the old uniformed farts now, gassing. "Kozlowski! Yeah—she's tough, good, but she's a woman. She's got some give to her."

Alex Kozlowski smiled to herself. The preparations were only part of the whole story. She'd taken the shit dished to her, fried it up nice, and put some ketchup on it. When the Neo-Pharm boys were out there among the stars and planets and xenos, they had better just hope they'd brought some condiments along to stomach what they were going to get from her.

Yep. This was going to be an R and R trip for her, if it killed them *and* her, along with those bugs.

It would be nice to get away from the planet where Peter had died. Maybe, just maybe, she'd find the kind of peace—or war—she was looking for.

She was just sauntering back for another pour of coffee when a man whirled through the door. At first she thought it was Mr. Mover, pissed off and running back with that form to sign.

However, it was not the bottom-level bureaucrat at all.

It was Daniel Grant.

He didn't see her. He ran toward the gangplank of the loading car for the shuttle, looking as though he wanted to climb on along with the baggage. He looked really bad, too, fancy duds all tattered and torn, shoes scuffed, and fancy haircut all frazzled.

"Yo!" she called out.

He swirled around, and the first thing that Kozlowski noticed was how bloodshot his eyes were, how baggy. He looked like a man who hadn't slept much last night . . . only worse.

"Look, soldier. Tell me where I get on the shuttle?"

"Grant?" She went closer, eyeing him suspiciously. What, was the Drug King flying high or something?

"That's right, soldier. You want to help me out? I'm in charge of this mission."

"Colonel Kozlowski here, Grant—and the last I heard you were going to keep your oxfords firmly hugging ground." Unfortunately, she was a bit too astonished to be properly sarcastic.

"Oh, yes . . . Colonel . . . of course. I'm sorry. It's been a rough evening." He sighed, looking back at the access room as though half expecting something to be following him. For a moment he looked lost and vulnerable, and quite a different human being entirely than how she'd seen him before. Something troubled her deeply about him . . . There was an aspect here that reminded her . . .

"Rough evening?" But the sun was rising . . .

"Er—yes."

He seemed uncharacteristically at a loss for words. He kept on looking behind him.

"Don't worry, Mr. Grant. Whoever's chasing you can't get through the base's security unless they nuke the perimeter."

"Chasing?" He seemed to shake something off. "Nothing of the sort . . . I just couldn't sleep last night . . . That's all . . . Got a little groggy, fell down a couple times—"

"Shouldn't you see a doctor then?"

"No. No, Colonel, I'll be just fine."

Before her eyes, he seemed to be putting himself back together again. An amazing act of will. Somatic repair: straightening of poise, sucking in of stomach, stiffening of upper lip. Psychological repair: the psychic armor erected. The eyes recovered, and the willpower returned, the arrogance.

"I made a monumental decision last night, Colonel."

"Did you."

"Yes. This mission is far too important to my companies—to *me*—to allow . . . I mean, not to contribute my presence. I called both the admiral and the general last night and made arrangements. I'll be going along with you, Colonel Kozlowski, to help oversee and participate in the effort." He took in another breath, looking stronger by the moment.

"Are you." Oh, this was just peachy keen.

"Yes. Specific orders are even now being sent over. Now, if you'd kindly drive me to the passenger portion of the shuttle?"

"No bags, Mr. Grant?"

"Er—uh—no. The decision was so abrupt, I did not have time to pack. I'll use whatever's on board. However, the admiral assured me that there are communications facilities available aboard the shuttle that I can use to let my people know what's happening—and dub someone to take my place while I'm gone."

"That's going to be a long time, Mr. Grant. Four months at least. A lot can happen to your company while you're gone."

"I trust my officers here . . . just as I trust you

and your people on the *Razzia*. I'm not dealing with amateurs in either case."

"No, of course not. But don't be mistaken. It's going to be plenty dangerous out there."

Whatever danger was "out there" did not seem to phase Daniel Grant. He seemed far too preoccupied with whatever he was running away from here.

However, there would be plenty of time to find out exactly what that was later.

"Fine. We'll put you on the shuttle with your boxes and the last group of marines going up."

"Excellent, Colonel. I'm looking forward to working with you." He could not seem to help himself, looking furtively around. "Ah—perhaps you could bring me some of that coffee and one of your military style donuts . . . oh, and an Alka-Seltzer. That would help a lot."

Kozlowski stepped forward and poked him on the shoulder.

"Look, Grant. You're in my territory now. I'm not your slave." She pointed, cringing a bit. God, he smelled of alcohol. "There's stuff over there in the office. Get it yourself."

Then she stomped off to get on with her work . . . and check on the promised electro-dispatches. Only way she was going to allow Grant on the *Razzia* was if she was ordered to do so.

This little wrinkle in the future did not bode well.

8

When Grant closed his eyes, he could see Fisk's face, grinning at him.

But he was tired. So tired.

He sat in a corner grav-couch of the shuttle, dimmest part, telling himself he was safe, telling himself it was okay, that he was in charge again.

Rest. He needed some rest.

He was alive, that was the important thing, he told himself. Miserable, but alive. Why had he ever gone out last night? He knew that he hadn't made the payments to Fisk. He knew that Fisk's temper got out of control sometimes.

A mistake. A goof. A snafu. It wouldn't happen again, that was for sure. Of course, he had a few months to get the opportunity to high-life it again. By then, hopefully, the money due to Neo-Pharm and thus Grant Industries and thus Grant himself—the financial entity in direst need—would have arrived. He'd just called his CEOs and ordered them to pay Fisk what they could of his blood money . . .

Deal with the whole disaster, weep with poor Mabel Planer's family, and make sure the insurance company paid off as though it had been on company time the girl had been shot . . .

And, above all, do what Grant was doing.

Survive.

He'd come damned close to falling off the edge of *that* state last night.

Even now he wasn't quite sure how he'd done it. When those blasts had ripped through the booth and Mabel, some auxiliary mode in his musculature must have kicked in, because he'd never scrambled and dodged and ducked so well in his life. Some survival node in his brain must have clicked on as well. He'd done exactly the right thing, headed right on down to the dance floor. The wrigglers and flailers there, doubtless thinking that the explosions above were part of the show, were still going at it to the heavy localized pounding. He hadn't dared to stop for the slightest moment. He'd dived to the exit, skipped his limo, sprinted blocks and blocks, falling down a few times, until he felt safe enough hailing a cab.

And still the chase had not been over. He'd spent most of the night hiding behind cans of garbage in an alley, waiting for one of his aides to come and pick him up. Then he'd directed him on a Toad's Wild Ride to the launchport—and thus, he'd made it to the base, after a sleepless night, grateful to be alive.

In the comparative safety of the shuttle, strapped

in above the equivalent of thousands of tonnes of GeligNuke®, Daniel Grant shuddered at the thought. No, he didn't want to think about it . . . not for a while, anyway.

Sleep. Some blessed sleep . . . that was what he needed. Fisk's ugly mug or no . . .

"Hey there. That seat by you taken?"

Grant's eyes snapped open.

There, looming over him, was a Nordic god.

Thor with a haircut.

Well, not exactly. He was big and strapping, with blond hair and blue eyes and a smile above his square-cut chin. He looked not only damned competent, but perfectly content in that state, and perfectly comfortable in the fatigues that snugly fit his muscular limbs and torso.

Now this guy, thought Grant, looked like a leader.

"Ah—no. No . . . please, be my guest."

The blond god secured a carryall bag in a storage bin, and then slid into the couch, not yet buckling himself in. "Name's Henrikson. Corporal Lars Henrikson." They shook hands. "You must be one of the Neo-Pharm fellows."

"Yes. I'm Daniel Grant. I *own* Neo-Pharm."

Henrikson did not react immediately. He took the information in thoughtfully. "Ah. I had been told that you would not actually be on our expedition, Mr. Grant."

"A last-minute decision."

Henrikson assimilated this information and nodded, as though this were the most natural thing in the world.

"I see. Well, good, I say . . . with all respect. It's good to see bosses take a personal interest in important tasks." A slight bend of the mouth. "Get their hands a little dirty, you know."

Grant smiled, the first time for what seemed like millennia. "Maybe I'm just trying to turn over a new leaf, Corporal Henrikson."

He closed his eyes, hoping to give the man a clue that he'd like a little privacy inside his own head, maybe rest his bloodshot eyes.

Henrikson wasn't the clue-taking kind.

"This is a special mission," he said. "I can feel it in my bones. Nine times out of ten a group of marines head out into space, all they come back with are handfuls of boredom. I've had some of that out there, let me tell you. Soon as I got wind of this mission though, special duty entailing a beachhead on the alien Hiveworld . . . Well, I just jumped at the chance. *Jumped.*"

"Couldn't get your fill of bug duty on Earth?"

Henrikson shrugged. "I've killed some bugs. Europe, mostly. Special services. That's probably why I got this gig—the experience. No, that's not it though, sir—you see, I've got this feeling that the human race is destined for great things in this universe. *Destined.* And I'd like to do my bit to make that possible. And I guess I'm vain enough to think I'm a talented enough guy to deal with the kind of situation we've got lined up for us."

Granted expected an inner groan of cynicism to echo in his head. Instead, he found the words oddly striking a sympathetic chord within him.

"That's a compellingly homocentric view of the universe, soldier."

Henrikson nodded. "Yes, sir. I'm sorry . . . I've had people tell me that men are just accidents in the scheme of things. I don't think so . . . Why . . . Because we're *men*. We *stand* for something, goddammit. We've got values and order and . . . hell . . . *purpose* to bring to what amounts to a lot of godless space."

"Indeed. Indeed! That kind of feeling would be a wonderful rabble-rouser . . . I mean, that would go a long way to heal the wounded spirit of humanity!"

"I know, sir. I know." Henrikson nodded gravely. "And that's why I'm here."

"Excellent. Well, you know, Corporal, I think we're going to have lots of time to discuss pertinent applications of that philosophy while we're on our mission. In the meantime, I think I'd like to take a little time to compose myself before the blast-off of this shuttle. You know . . . for meditation . . . a little cat nap, perhaps . . ."

Henrikson looked over at Grant. "Ah. Yes, you do look a little tired. How thoughtless of me. Please, close your eyes. Relax. Snooze. I have my own inner warrior's form of meditation. We shall meditate together."

With that, the corporal's eyes trained onto the front of his couch, and focused.

Well, so much for that. Rest and meditation was even valuable to big boy here. He should have tried that tactic before.

Oh, well. He knew he'd have someone of interest to talk to on the mission. He just wished now he'd brought along one of his PR men to jot all these golden thoughts down.

Grant let his heavy eyelids close.

He found peace for perhaps thirty seconds, before he heard the clamor of feet boarding the boat,

closets opening, packs being stored, voices jab-
bering among one another.

". . . look, chum. I'm telling you, that was the
way it was . . . the *music* was the soul of the beats!
The hot, cool black music of the streets, man.
That's where the streaming ice lava of the poetry
came from to begin with!" The voice was annoy-
ingly adenoidal and high-pitched.

"Look, Jastrow! I make one single comment the
other day that I enjoyed reading the old free verse of
the twentieth century . . . and you think I'm talking
about the beat poets! I'm talking about a number of
writers, including William Carlos Williams . . ."

Grant cracked his weary eyelids.

Couple of privates in fatigues and caps. White
boy, black boy. White boy was the one carping on
the literary and music themes. Unfortunate, but he
could tune them out.

"Williams! But Williams *was* John the Baptist to
Allen Ginsberg!"

"Sorry. Never heard of him."

" 'Howl'? You read twentieth-century free verse,
and you've never read 'Howl'?"

"Well, come to think of it . . . Perhaps I have . . .
but I still don't see the connection between free
verse poetry and jazz."

"Sheesh. Not just jazz, budz. *Be-bop!* Here, let
me show you."

The conversation had become detached, as
though Grant were listening to it through a tin-can
telephone as he drifted into exhausted sleep.

Blaaaaat . . . !

High-pitched, running hell-for-leather up some
spidery octave.

Bleeet . . . BLEEEEET . . . !

The sounds were fingernails and Grant's brain had turned to chalkboard.

He jumped up, awake and disoriented. He hit his head on a low overhang and flopped back onto the couch.

Honk . . . honk HONNKKKKK!

He looked over. Sitting on the edge of a grav-couch was a black man wearing glasses and a grimace. His hands were over his ears. Opposite him was another bespectacled guy with a pocket-protector face. His thin lips were clamped on the mouthpiece of a big baritone saxophone.

Both had boot-camp bodies, but faces innocent of the heart of war.

Blat . . . blat . . . Blat!

"Can't you hear it, Ellis?" he said, unclamping. "I have seen the finest minds of my generation—"

The natural force that was Corporal Henrikson reared up like a vengeful statue. "You guys want to give the rest of us in here some peace?"

His muscular hovering said it all. The salt-and-pepper twins blinked, flinching back.

"Gee—sorry, Corporal."

"Just playing a little Bird, man."

Henrikson stood rock-hard. "Well, I'm clipping your wings! This is not a place for *that* thing. Now over your head . . . maybe."

Ellis looked as though he agreed, but Jastrow got a hurt-little-boy expression on his face as he put his musical instrument away in its case.

"I could use a few Z's anyway, Jazz," said Ellis.

"Yeah. Maybe you're right. We'll continue this conversation later, though, huh?"

"Whatever." The man sounded resigned.

Henrikson bent over Grant. "You okay, sir?"

"Sure. My ears are still ringing and I'm wide awake. But I'm okay."

"We got a good fifteen before formal boarding, so maybe you should use them."

"I'll try, Corporal. Believe me, I'll try."

Henrikson shot one more warning look at the newly arrived duo and then resumed his grav-couch. Grant found Ellis and Jastrow peering at him curiously, obviously wondering who he was.

Grant could feel it even through his closed eyelids.

"Name's Grant. The reason you're on this mission," he said. "Mind if we meet formally later? I'm trying to get a little rest."

"Oh!"

"Oh, sure, sir. Sorry."

"Yeah. Right. We'll be real quiet." Whisper. "Sheesh. That's Daniel Grant, man! And you had to squeal that sax in his ear."

"How could I know? I didn't even see him!"

The whispers died into uneasy silence and once again Grant found himself slipping into an uneasy coma.

Which ended all too soon.

He'd been having a dream about his parents, and he hated to dream about his parents, so it was just as well. Still, it was all a little annoying.

The *clump-clump* of steps didn't wake him. He barely heard it: background noise.

The shifting of bags, the snap of storage cases. No problem.

However, when a body fell directly onto him— *that* woke him up.

"Ooophhh!" he said.

"Gahhh. Oh, dear . . . damned floor! All these knobs and braces. Sorry!"

That the person was prominently female mitigated the hurt and shock somewhat, and not just because of the softer bits. She looked good and she smelled good, even in fatigues. She was a busty brunette with hair about as long as the Marines would let you wear it if you weren't male, and rich dark eyes that now looked thoroughly repentant.

"That's all right," said Grant, flashing on the immediate lady smile. "I was hoping to get some rest before takeoff, but these things happen."

She pushed herself off of him with ease and a great deal more grace than she'd shown in tripping onto him. "I do better in faux grav, for some reason. And null grav? I'm a swan." She shrugged. "I'm just a space babe, that's all there is to it, and I'll be glad to lift off this—" She batted those splendid doe eyes. "Say. Haven't I seen you . . . My God! You're Daniel Grant, the big tycoon! I've seen you on the vids!"

"That's me."

"You look awfu—I mean, I guess you could use some rest." She hobbled over to an empty gravcouch, and Grant, despite his weariness, was unable to take his attention off her delightfully swiveling hips. She turned. "I'd *heard* you were somewhere behind this mission. I didn't think I'd get to really *meet* you though!"

"Well, get used to it, Private," said Henrikson. "He's coming along with us for the voyage."

"No kidding! Well, isn't that . . . Isn't *that* news." She swiveled back over, unconsciously smoothing her hair, and gave him her hand and a markedly breathier delivery. "My name is Edie Mahone. Private First Class—but I'm still young, and I really think I have quite a bright future with the Colonial Marines."

Grant felt a little nonplussed and couldn't help automatically turning on the charm—and wondering at the same time what this particular woman was doing in the Marines . . . and on *this* mission in particular. As he studied her though, he got an impression of strength beneath the apparent ditziness. The oh-gosh business was just an act. Beneath it, Grant could tell, was strength, and it turned him on. It challenged him.

"You have an interest in xeno development then?" said Grant.

"The bugs? Oh, no." She shook her head, shuddered. "Hate 'em. But then, who doesn't? I can see your question coming. What's a nice girl doing in a place like this?" She shrugged. "I'm just a space natural, I guess, Mr. Grant. I wasn't fooling you . . . And on top of that, I'm a tactical weapons specialist."

"Weapons specialist?"

"Yes, sir. Top scores." A mischievous playfulness shaded her voice.

"I'm just glad you weren't carrying any grenades when you fell over me."

"Hmmm? Oh, yes . . . yes, of course. Mr. Grant, I really am sorry, and it's such a surprise . . . maybe this mission isn't going to be such a grim business after all."

"I certainly hope not. Now, Private Mahone—I hope you'll come to my cabin sometime for drinks and we'll have a nice long chat. In the meantime, my sanity could really use a little rest before it gets rattled by takeoff."

"Of course. Of course, Mr. Grant . . . sir. I'll just hop into a couch over here and leave you alone . . . And . . ." She did a double take. "Drinks? Did you say *drinks* with a tycoon! Of course, Mr. Grant. I'd *love* to! I'm a regular media hound and I watch you all the time. I even bought that unauthorized paperback about you—is it true that your wife divorced you when she found you in your marriage bed with four naked women?"

Grant chuckled mischievously. "And a parrot. Don't forget the parrot, Private Mahone."

He was pleased the legend lingered.

The starstruck private shook her head and rapturously wandered back to her couch. Was it an act? He didn't know. And he didn't care.

Drinks with an attractive private who would probably be disappointed if he didn't make a pass at her. After that tragic debacle last night, he was hardly in the mood for romance right now. But weeks into a space cruise with a bunch of scientists and hardened soldiers? The dominant Grant hormones would doubtless trot themselves out into quest-and-conquer mode. A willing female partner with the requisite assets was something that cheered him immensely.

Now, though, to sleep for just a brief sweet moment.

Grant let his head flop down into the cushion, gratified at the silence that the cabin had cloaked itself in. *Respectful* silence.

This wasn't so bad, shipping out on a boat heading light-years away from Earth with a bunch of scientists and marines. It was *his* mission, after all . . . And he seemed to be getting the appropriate obeisance from his people.

This was good. This was very good. A kind of calm descended upon Daniel Grant. His knotted muscles unwound, and a sense of control of his environment began to knit itself around him. Yes, yes, perhaps it *would* work out for the best that he was coming along to supervise, to oversee . . . no, to *control*. The boys in the office knew well enough how he ran things by now. They could do exactly what he would do, whatever the situation. He didn't have to be around. Instead, he should be doing exactly what he was doing. Heading for parts unknown, spreading his influence, his dominion.

Daniel Grant . . . a great man, destined for the stars.

The cadences of his self-congratulations lulla-byed him into that blessed relaxed land just short of slumber, where not even his mother was waiting to natter at him.

Ah . . . !

Sweet, gentle peace . . .

WOOOOOOONK!

WOONNNNNNNK!

The Klaxon rang like hell's own trumpet.

"That's the fire alarm!" cried Jastrow.

"Shit! Something's wrong with the shuttle. We gotta get out of here, Mr. Grant!"

"Please," murmured Grant. "Just let me lie here awhile. I'll die if need be. Just let me sleep."

"No can do, Mr. G!"

Grant felt himself being pulled up out of the couch, and physically carried down the ramp.

The cooler air outside was like a slap across the chops. He blinked, felt himself being jounced . . .

And then suddenly stop still.

"Let me down!" he demanded.

"Do what the man says, turkey! Now!"

Henrikson dropped him onto hard sheetcrete.

"Ow!" Groggily he scrambled up to his feet . . .

And found himself staring into the bores of 10mm blasters.

Connected to those blasters were Colonel Alex Kozlowski and a group of marines, travel sacks at their bags.

"Belay arms," said Kozlowski, striding up to them, arms on hips. If we were a group of bugs, you dopes would be bug food now! Emergencies demand emergency measures!" A toothpick stuck out from the side of her mouth. She worked it all the way to the other side of a scowl. "Isn't that right, soldiers!"

The marines, who somewhere in the midst of all this had managed to effect uncomfortable poses of attention, immediately responded.

"Yes, *sir*!"

Kozlowski worked the toothpick.

"Besides, I haven't assigned seats yet, have I?"

"No, *sir*!"

Kozlowski walked over to Grant, and stooped down beside him. "Welcome to your mission, Mr. Grant . . ." She spat the toothpick.

It stuck into the loose fabric of his pants.

"Welcome to *my* command."

Grant sighed and closed his eyes again.

This sheetcrete was actually rather comfortable . . .

9

Darkness.

Darkness and dreams.

Dream logic tangled in its own shreds and chips of reality and magic.

For six weeks, Daniel Grant dreamed or didn't dream, but in the overpowering darkness, the dreams were all he knew.

Moebius strips of dreams. Jump cuts. Swirls of victory and laughter and glory.

The depths of the past, into secret and overpowering fears.

Mostly, though, it seemed a short sleep, for the dreams were only brief releases of hypersleep to allow brain function and REM.

In the glass-case cubicle, embedded like a fly in amber, when the mechanism and gas mix slowly began to gently pry him from his slumber, Daniel

Grant only vaguely sensed the springing of the lock mechanism of his case. He clung to his dreams, clung to the darkness, a sleeper drunk on sleep.

"Mr. Grant?"

A gentle female voice. Whose? It was sweet and kind and understanding. The kind of voice his ex-wife used to use, in their early love, when he gave himself only to her.

She seemed very real now, very much a part of reality in this darkness.

"Daniel?"

Martha. He'd been dating a lot back then, back in the halcyon days of Neo-Pharm, when he'd first bought it and was working on the beginnings of his empire. She was a model his ad company had hired for commercials. He'd swooped down and never come back up . . . not for a long time, anyway. Still, to this day, he was not sure why there had been others, years down the road. Old bad habits? Part of the life-style he'd loved? Pure stoking of an overblown ego?

He wasn't sure, and he wasn't troubled about it.

Except for moments like these, upon waking, when he doubted himself, when he felt vulnerable.

"It's time to wake up, Mr. Grant."

Wake up? Where was he?

"We've got a lot to do."

That voice. It certainly wasn't Martha's. He realized that now.

"So hop to it."

It was a hard voice now, a voice used to being obeyed.

Grant realized that he was cold. He felt quite naked. Shivering, he raised himself.

He pried open his eyes.

Peripherally, he saw the overhanging cables and cold metal of the hypersleep chamber.

In front of him, crouching, was a good eight feet worth of talons, bony notched spars and open, angry jaws.

An *alien*!

He screamed.

He cringed.

Then he scrabbled back, instinctively throwing up his arms in a helpless gesture to protect him from this, the deadliest creature in the known universe.

Even as he squirmed, trying to grapple over the side of his hypersleep cubicle, what shreds of his rational mind that still operated realized something.

The thing wasn't moving.

It was just hovering there, a few feet away.

And come to think of it, couldn't he barely see a *bulkhead* through the murky black of its articulated body?

A shudder, a *zwip!* of light passed through it.

It wasn't real . . . It was a . . .

From the left a woman in khaki fatigues stepped, holding a modular control unit.

Colonel Kozlowski.

The beast before him was just a hologram.

"Thought you might need to get your juices flowing." She tapped a control, and moved the hologram away. "Welcome to the U.S.S. *Razzia*, Phase II."

"God *damn* you, Colonel!"

She raised a dark eyebrow. "You want to be a

part of the gang, don't you, Grant? Just consider this a very mild hazing. You're a member of the fraternity now!"

He wasn't groggy at all. The adrenaline had managed to kick weeks worth of sleepdirt out of his head. Still, his heart was racing and he was damned angry.

And, what with only a pair of briefs between himself and nakedness, damned near naked!

He hopped out of his cubicle, one of ten spiraled around a central control and supply center. All the duraplas casings were lifted now, like translucent insect wings.

They had obviously let him snooze awhile longer than normal. All the other cubicles were empty.

"Why am I the last to wake?" he said, getting up and out of the thing, steadying himself on the side.

"You seemed real tired when we left, Grant. We all thought you could use a little extra sleep."

"How far are we from our destination?"

"The gravitonic engines are cut off. We've got to use regular impulse engines to cruise among planets. We'll be in orbit around the Hiveworld in four days." She smiled. "Are you ready for some action, Mr. Grant?"

"It would appear I've already gotten some, Colonel."

"What. From Black Fang here?" She smiled. "Just a training hologram. No reason to be embarrassed. Some younger recruits have soiled their skivvies because of Black Fang. Looks like you pretty much did okay."

Grant snorted. "You have quite a warped sense of humor, Kozlowski. I guess we're going to have to talk about that, and some other things in a few hours. Right now, I'd like to get some pants on."

"Too bad. You look so cute that way." She laughed and started walking away. "Come, boy! Come! Fun's over. We've got some work to do."

The holoprojection ghosted along beside her as she walked away toward wherever.

Grant shuddered. He took a deep breath, got his bearings, and headed off in the direction of the locker room where he'd left his clothing.

In the few days aboard the U.S.S. *Razzia* before he was tucked away in hypersleep, Daniel Grant had had very little time to familiarize himself with the full extent of this very large ship. He'd spent some time overseeing the operations of his scientists and he'd spent time getting some natural sleep. That was about it.

However, he did make sure he remembered where he put his clothes.

He wasn't crazy about the immense and metallic coldness of the ship. The liner he'd taken from his home planet had at least catered to *some* human amenities. It gave some feeling of warmth and sociability. Here, aboard the *Razzia*, it was just a pure case of military utilitarianism. There was about as much decor inside the ship as on the outside.

All in all, Grant was just as happy to snore the time away.

What the hell was going on back on Earth now? he wondered. He'd warned his officers to stay inside, to hire security, and to reinforce measures. He'd even had them tender a small payment to Fisk's "company." Nonetheless, he couldn't help but wonder. Still, whatever was going on, there was absolutely nothing he could do out here, light-years distant in some godforsaken quadrant of the half-known galaxy.

The locker room was down a narrow corridor.

Showers, toilets, benches.

It looked, smelled, tasted, felt like something out of his high school sports hero's days. Funky, but somehow homey. Oddly comforting.

A tall blond man was in the corner, buckling the belt of his pants. Oddly enough, he was wearing dark glasses. They made him look more like the MacArthur school of officer than a corporal.

"Henrikson? You just get out of cold sleep, too, buddy?"

The corporal turned and looked at him. "Early this morning. Just finished exercising, sir."

"Just kicked my butt out of bed now. Wonder why they kept me down so long?"

"Maybe they just wanted things spick-and-span for you, sir."

"You have a first name?"

"As I told you before, sir. It's Lars."

"Oh, right. That's it. Lars. Tell you what. You can call me Dan."

The corporal nodded. "Thanks . . . Dan."

Grant found his locker. Racked his brain. His memory coughed up the combination. He twirled the dial back and forth. The lock snapped open. Inside were the civvie scientist grays they'd provided him with, since he hadn't brought along any of his own clothes, and the duds he'd come in with were pretty shredded.

He put his pants on.

"You know," said the corporal, "times like these make me wish I could pop a tab or two of that Xeno-Zip you make. Unfortunately, tests have determined that chances are pretty good I'd go berserk even on the regular stuff. Damned skittish metabolism."

"Oh, well," said Grant paternally. "I'm sure you're a damn fine soldier without it." He grew thoughtful. "I'll tell you, Lars. You must be pretty sick of that colonel of yours."

"Colonel Kozlowski. Our commanding officer."

"She had a bug holo waiting for me when I woke up."

"No kidding. She must like you then."

"*Like* me? Scared hell out of me. Said it was some sort of hazing."

"Tough. She's pretty tough all right, the colonel is."

Grant was surprised. "C'mon. We're friends. You don't have to pull that loyalty crap with me. Tell me the truth . . . you've hated her for months, right?"

In a we-men-gotta-stick-together tone.

Henrikson's face was peculiarly immobile. Behind those shades, his eyes were unreadable.

"Mr. Grant. I guess you could say I feel like I've taken you under my wing. You don't know much about the military . . . and here you are on a military craft. There are things you have to understand about the military . . . and I guess it's not that much different from business life. Maybe even simpler."

Grant smiled. "Right! I knew we could be chums." He continued Velcroing his suit. Damned thing! It sure as hell chafed!

"I'm a corporal. I haven't been in the Colonial Marine Corps that long. But I have previous military experience."

"Exterminating bugs?"

"That's not all the military does in this universe, Mr. Grant . . . Sorry. Dan. Sir." He sighed. "Whatever. At any rate, my point is that it's dog-eat-dog, here. Domination, but in a codified, respectful fashion. I've only served under the colonel since she culled me from the ranks to be on this mission. She's earned my respect."

"Oh. But she *seems* to have some kind of chip on her shoulder. Think she's just trying to make up for not having one between her legs?"

"Like I said, Dan. You've got things to learn. There are codes and games. Just like everything in life. You learn the ropes . . ." He shrugged. "Maybe these little attitude snits . . . Well, I guess you've pulled a few in your time at Grant Industries."

Daniel Grant considered. "I suppose I have. In my own charming way. Good point."

"The colonel is totally in command. And she treats every one as an equal. And if she chooses to dump a little extra shit on your ears . . ." A brusque shrug. "Well, then like I said, Dan. She must like you."

Grant thought about that a moment.

"Fair enough, Henrikson. That doesn't mean I have to like *her*, does it?"

Henrikson put a hand on his new friend's shoulder.

"Any woman ever treat you like this before?"

Grant considered. "Yes. My wife!"

"And what did you do about it?"

"I divorced the bitch!"

Henrikson smiled. "Well, you'll have to marry the colonel to do that! I reckon the captain of the ship's got the legal right to do that."

"Marry . . . Henrikson, I wonder who's got the more warped sense of humor. You or me!"

"From what you tell me, sounds like the colonel does. I'll watch for that little holo trick. She hasn't done that number on me—yet."

"She must not like you, Henrikson."

"No, I guess not." The corporal gave a farewell nod and started leaving the locker room.

"You're a lucky man, Lars."

"We'll see, Dan. We'll see."

The big man was gone.

Grant sighed. He Velcroed his ship shoes, and made a pit stop at the head.

Next stop: his scientists, and his little secret project.

That should make him feel back in the saddle again!

10

"How we doing, Pilot?" asked Colonel Kozlowski.

The man was bent over away from her, obscuring the motions of his hands. Around him ranged a convex field of lights. LCD screens played spectacular spectrum games. Lume-points glittered, waiting for computer input. From this angle, she could see his bald spot, like the top of a hairy egg.

"Fine, Colonel," he said in a monotone. "Almost finished."

His elbow swiveled. His head nodded.

One last telemetry check?

The culmination of a final primary diagnostic of the *Razzia*'s sys/ops and structural integrity after its long cruise through sub-Einsteinian planes of warped mathematics?

One more little flourish of his hand and he

turned to her. "What's up, Colonel?" He'd turned
so that now Kozlowski could see that his hand was
nowhere near any of the controls. He held a pencil
and a book of crossword puzzles. The blocks in the
puzzle were all filled now.

"An interesting form of duty report, Captain,"
said Kozlowski coldly.

The man's lined, pale face remained impassive.
He shut the book, slipped the pencil behind a
large, hairy ear, and folded his arms together. "You
forget, Colonel. You got a nice long snooze. I got to
wake up for a few weeks, to check on things. Part
of my job. Got to keep something going to prevent
the ennui from driving me nuts. Little diversion of
mine." He tapped the book. "Got a whole library of
them. After twenty-six years in the Marines, I got
lots filled, too. Next year I retire. Bought a nice little chicken ranch on the Ulna colony. And then, I
don't want to see the inside of another freakin' in-
terstellar vessel . . . or for that matter the inside of
another crossword puzzle book again."

"Just the inside of chickens."

The pilot-captain's name was Hastings. Phillip
Hastings.

Hastings shrugged. "The ancient Greeks used to
study bird entrails to predict the future. Wonder
what a split-open one would tell us now."

"A few tomorrows of many spilled bug guts, hopefully. I take it by your inaction that everything is
functional, we're on course, minor things like
that."

"We got navigators and copilots and engineers to
take care of that garbage, Colonel. I just oversee
and coordinate." Hastings looked like a good sol-

dier gone to seed. Beer belly. Slack skin that had that waxen look that toned muscular bodies get when they don't get exercised for a few years. He had thinning brown hair and a network of burst capillaries in his nose. From the look of him, he wasn't just going to raise chickens upon retirement. He was going to do some serious drinking.

Nonetheless, she—and doubtless Daniel Grant as well—had been assured that he was the best in the business. That he was a burnout did not seem to be important.

"What can I do for you, Colonel?"

"I'm briefing the troops. I thought you might like to join us."

"I'm not going down to that hellhole. Why should I?"

"I thought you might find it educational. These bugs have popped up all over the universe—and they spread via ships, as you know. Thought you might like to know some tactics against them."

The captain sucked a lip. "Thanks, Colonel. You going to tape the meeting?"

"Yes."

"I'll watch it some other time."

"Miles and miles of crossword puzzles to do before you sleep?"

Hastings scratched his nose. "Something like that."

"I *am* in command, Captain. I can order you to be at that meeting."

"Then you already would have, wouldn't you? You gave me an option and I'm exercising that option." He leaned forward and tapped LCD displays. "Besides, we're in a planetary system now. A strange system can have all kinds of phenomena waiting. Gravity wells, black holes . . . as well as the usual meteor showers, comets, asteroids . . . I like to ride close shotgun at times like this." He tapped his book. "Besides, I've got some more puzzles to do."

She was ticked off at the guy, but he'd rummaged up a good excuse, so she really couldn't pull rank.

She just wished the admiral had given her someone with a better attitude, that was all.

"Just make sure we don't crash into any moons, Captain."

Captain Hastings turned to his left where a miniature holotank filled with blips and sparks and readings hung. "No moons in our immediate future."

He opened his puzzle book and went back to work.

Kozlowski turned and stomped away.

She stopped at her cabin first. She went inside and splashed some water into her face. Had she done the right thing? Should she have made Hastings go to the meeting?

He was right about not really having to, but his lack of interest, his insolence, annoyed her. She had the command here. He should be doing not only what she told him—but what she suggested as well.

Kozlowski wiped her face with a towel, looked into a mirror.

She had a lost look to her eyes.

Light-years from home.

She'd fought for her planet a very long time. She'd learned the basics of space travel so that she could carry the battle against these creatures to their home. Now, though, like some mythological being, she felt cut off from a source of her power.

Nonsense, of course. Foolishness. All just knots and complexes of neural patterns, easy enough to blast apart. She was a fighting machine and she was just taking a ferry to another part of the battle.

Still, why did she feel so homesick?

She'd popped out of hypersleep a full two days before the others, so she could do some work with the tactical computers as well as knock some of the stasis sleep out of her brain. Wrapped up in maps and facts, figures and projections, inventorying weapons and supplies, and rebriefing herself on the armor, she'd been in her own little world.

Now, though, with a day full of the troops waking up, the whole thing was starting to get to her.

Thirty troops were going to jump down right into the thick of thousands, maybe even *millions* of creatures that could give even biblical demons a scare, with only some half-proven experimental weapons to do the job.

Okay, girlie, she told herself. Just knock that look right off your repertoire. Either that, or get it out of your system, here and now.

There was no reason for this kind of doubt. The Hiveworld had been raided before. True, there had been casualties. However, there had been survivors. She'd studied their reports. Wilks. Billie whatshername. Nasty stuff, but compelling.

Kozlowski had no illusions.

You deal card hands from the bug decks, you

came up holding some casualties. Now, though, here on her first big extra-Earth mission, she'd watched the troops get up today, stretch and go through their metaphorical thawing, and when she saw the vulnerability in their eyes, that moment of terror, that oh-shit-here-we-are expression, she felt what they felt.

Even with that asshole Grant.

Ever since what had happened with Peter Michaels, maybe she was just getting soft . . .

Of course there was a reason she'd pulled the holostunt with Grant. He'd been making noises before sleepytime that he wanted to jump down with them for the mission, to see it firsthand. She was just trying to discourage him, that was all.

Maybe, just maybe the meeting would rattle him. When she thought deeply enough about all the implications, it sure as hell rattled her.

She closed her eyes, did some inner self-composure exercises. What came up wasn't calm and a deep peace, though. What came up was Daniel Grant. She didn't feel good about him being here. Not good at all. For complex reasons she didn't care to deal with just right now.

Even though she'd promised herself she wasn't going to do it, she went to her bag and pulled out a medicine bottle full of the reason Daniel Grant bothered her.

She cut a tablet of Fire in half. She'd tried to give it up, no go. Maybe after this fracas was over.

She washed the half-tablet down with a glass of water.

Then she finished getting ready for the briefing.

11

The bug wavered, capered, lunged.

Drool cascaded down its mouth into the shadows.

Its exoskeleton seemed to glow with evil, spikes sticking out of its back erecting.

The thing looked like a dinosaur attempting to shapeshift into the Devil.

"Yum yum," squawked a reptilian voice. "Fee fie fo fum. I smell the blood of a bunch of bums!"

Uneasy laughter rippled among the assemblage.

"Any of you sweethearts want a date with my ovipositors?" it snarled. "Looks like we'd have a wonderful party. You all look like absolutely splendid *hosts*."

Groans.

Colonel Kozlowski twirled the dial of the holoprojector, and the bug program faded. She let her voice assume its normal timbre as she looked out at the group of amused, anxious marines.

"Okay, listen up, people. I promise you right now, this is going to be no party. But we didn't come all these light-years to party, did we? We came to help make this galaxy safe for peaceful, sentient life. As long as these things infest any of our planets or ships or space colonies *anywhere* in an uncontrolled and above all *misunderstood* fashion, the future of humanity is threatened."

The briefing room felt like the interior of a metal egg, subtly lit in the curved corners. All of the soldiers assigned for planetfall sat in rows of comfortable, slanted chairs, as though in some military theater. They sat at a kind of alert attention. Professionals. Damned good people all of them, and Kozlowski should know. She had helped to select every single one of them.

In the front of the room, alongside her podium, was a table where the big shots in the mission sat, ready to support her in her explanations. Grant. A few of his scientists. Some crew members.

"These killers, these reprehensible aliens, have just got their claws and their blood and their teeth and their incredible powers of survival as weapons . . ." She paused for impact. "Our *ignorance* is their primary weapon, and I hope to diffuse a little more of that with you today."

The soldiers all looked entranced. Hanging on her words. These people had been briefed on xenos before, but now they greedily lapped up the information she was presenting. She was familiar with the phenomenon. When you were a soldier, you could act as macho and as confident as you wanted to—but if you didn't listen and absorb every ounce of information handed to you, you could find yourself dead. Smart soldiers learned to listen. These grunts were smart and capable. Quirky, maybe, but she'd gone through the choices with the command herself, and not one of these people didn't belong here.

Too bad about people like the captain, Grant, and his castle of Frankenstein scientists. But then, if she had control over everything, *pfft!* The aliens would be instant slag, and Peter Michaels would be back.

Anyway, she had some interesting information here.

Her theatrics at the beginning had probably not been necessary, but she liked to put a little pizzazz into the proceedings.

She began with the parameters of the mission.

"Quite simply, people, as much as I'd like to say all this is perfect and noble in our mission, it's not. We're going to a planet which is the origin of the xenos in this sector of the galaxy. We'll be using a specially fitted lander. People, we've got the latest in technology at our disposal. Basically, we're going in to do a robbery. Now, ultimately I have no doubt this will be in humanity's best interest so take whatever nobility you can from your participation here. However, what we're up to here is the biggest heist of queen mother jelly in history."

Jastrow waved an excited hand. "Why?"

"Officially, I can't tell you. You're just supposed to do what you're ordered to do. Unofficially, though, I don't give a shit." She grinned. "Xeno-Zip."

An excited buzz sounded in the meeting room.

"*That*'s why Daniel Grant is here," someone whispered.

"Heck, I use that stuff," another said. "It's *great*."

"That's right, people," said Kozlowski. "We're on a glorified drug run. Take my word for it, though. I'm personally assured that it will make someone a great deal of money—"

Laughter.

"And maybe even help the human cause as well. In any case, be assured. We're taking the Alien-Earth War to the source, and we'll most certainly kill lots of xenos in the process. Call it hard-core vengeance if you like. Call it just another job. In any event, we're here together so I can provide you with some information and equipment designed to preserve your sorry lives."

Quickly she rattled off some of the basics about the xenos, their behavior, their attack patterns, individually and in groups. She summarized what was known about the Hiveworld, and what the main hive itself looked like, from the information provided by the previous expedition. It was all like a mantra, and she ticked off the info, point by point.

"Now then. As for the interior of the hive . . ." She thumbed the projector to a prepared setting, kicking in the holotank in the corner.

Like some magician she conjured up a vision from the depths of Hades.

Here was the familiar bowellike tomb, ropey with intestoid projections and ridged with tubing, bumps, and alien growths, organic in the very worst and most frightening sense. All hellishly lit in orange and yellow. In the central portion of this chilly sight squatted a huge bulblike protuberance, like a half-planted flower bulb. However, instead of bright and colorful plumage, from its pustulelike side it sprouted tubings that connected to other, slightly smaller bulbs.

And from its top, like Mephistopheles happily squatted atop a pile of his own excrement, rose a gently swaying royal giantess.

An alien queen mother.

"All right." She snapped on a cursor-blip pointer and guided it over to the central sack. "What we have here is a quite realistic computer animation suggesting what we might find in the alien central chamber, once we locate it.

"This is where we'll find that royal jelly that Mr. Daniel Grant has sent us after," she said.

Grant, seated at the table in a position similar enough to the chairman-of-the-board's attitude to make him comfortable, leaned back, hands behind the back of his neck. "That's right. And if you can trap a queen mother, that would be okay by me."

"Trap?" said Private Jastrow, a little dubiously.

"It's been done before," assured Private Ellis.

"Sounds awfully dangerous!" piped Private Mahone, looking quite doubtful about the whole enterprise.

"Private—this whole trip is dangerous. You knew that when you volunteered. *Anything* involving these things is dangerous ..." Kozlowski stepped up the magnification threefold, focusing in upon the queen. "Alice in Wonderland time, people. Listen up. We're going in the hive, and pulling this stuff out. Along the way, we will not be delicate. In any event, be assured . . . we've by no means come here to preserve the species. Kill all the creatures you want," she said brightly.

Easy laughter.

"So then, let's cook up a little preliminary strategy on how you pry open a bug hive, shall we?"

With the aid of more prepared graphics, she delineated the technology, science, and tactics that would allow a group of marines to storm a nest of the nastiest monsters in the universe.

"So . . . basically—guns, guts, and lots of *luck*!" she said. She paused for a moment as her people tried to assimilate her words.

She let them twist in the wind for a moment as a parade of aliens wilted before the onslaught of cartoon marines. The blasts from the heavy millimeter carbines tore through the heads and carapaces, splashing splinters of alien exoskeleton hither and thither along with gobs of alien blood that fell upon the marines and the scene like cancerous amoebas.

Kozlowski froze the animation.

"What's wrong with this picture?"

Jastrow raised a tentative hand. "Wishful thinking?"

"Yes. Fantasy, perhaps. Only showing the aliens eating marines wouldn't exactly be the best way to raise your morale, would it?"

"Not particularly, no," mumbled Ellis.

"Wait a minute," said Henrikson. "All that alien blood on the troops. It doesn't seem to phase them. That stuff makes toxic waste look like cotton candy."

Kozlowski snapped her fingers. "My *man*! Exactly!"

"What about the acid blood?" said Edie Mahone. "Can you tell us something about that?"

"Some good news for you all there. We do have something special for you. Something that's going to buck your morale right up." She smiled. "But first, let me remind you it's still very important that at close distance you try and avoid the torso. The splatter potential is quite bad. It's best to go for the knees." The cursor in the air flew to one of the strong and knobby alien lower joints. "As many of you have already discovered, a shot to the knee will not only hamper the alien's mobility . . . but such a wound also minimizes bleeding and spatter potential. A discreet coup de grace to the head at that point is made possible. But then, of course, if you haven't actually been in battle with the things, you've at least had simulation chamber experience . . . save perhaps for Mr. Grant."

"I'm hardly going to exactly participate in the mayhem, now am I, Colonel?" said Grant.

"As you've never handled a gun before, I hope not . . ." said Kozlowski dismissively. "Now then . . . I've kept you all waiting long enough . . ." She pulled out a com unit. "Thank you, Doctor, for waiting in the wings. You may come out now, and by all means bring your assistant with you."

She turned to the audience, most of whom were on the edge of their seats with suspense.

Kozlowski turned quite serious.

. . . *Michaels, his head molten and sizzling, skin sliding from naked skull* . . .

She suppressed the memory.

"I know the blood issue is of great concern to all of you, so I'm happy to present an innovation that should all but do away with your fears."

Yeah. Right.

Pep talk. Maybe that's what she'd given too much of to poor Peter. Maybe if he'd been properly scared shitless and quaking in his sweatsocks, he wouldn't have had to act like the Big Man and gone to that trap.

She swallowed down a dry throat, resumed.

"For more on that, I turn you over to Dr. Zato."

Dr. Zato, one of Grant's squids.

The man waltzed into the room like a stand-up comedian just called on to do his act. He was a toady little guy, who blinked as though the light was too much. Receding hairline. High IQ dandruff.

"Ladies and gentlemen," he said in a high, munchkin voice, "I give you your next best friend—"

The assistant walked into the room, slowly, clearly a little weighted down by what he wore, but not uncomfortably so.

Armor.

"Here it is, folks. The Z-110 Acid-Neutralizing Combat Wardrobe."

The assistant wore a streamlined, snazzy-looking jumble of plates, silver and blue in hue. A combination of insect and tortoiseshell. On the back was a compact storage unit. A narrow-visored helmet fitted snugly over his head. An antenna angled out of the back.

Kozlowski had seen it before, but the sight of it still impressed her.

And if it could do what Doc Z. claimed—well, all the better!

"Efforts to produce an armor resistant to the intense acidity of the alien blood have proved impractical."

Ellis waved his hand, got called upon. "Yeah. I always wondered about that. We've got the chemical composition of the alien's exoskeleton down cold. That isn't eaten up by alien blood, clearly. And it's light enough. How come its elements aren't used for armor?"

"Well, that would be all very good, Private, if you'd care to be encased in a toxic suit."

"You can't make an alloy . . . or have that stuff as the uppermost layer?" insisted Ellis.

"Incompatible. What we have here in the aliens is a different kind of chemistry. Part carbon-based, part silicon-based—and maybe something else."

"But we're starting to learn to use their DNA."

"Fooling around with genes and chromosomes doesn't necessarily mean we've got everything solved, Private. These things are still mysteries wrapped in enigmas. Believe me, your suggestions have been tried." He shook his head patronizingly. "Just doesn't work."

"So there *was* some kind of armor that wasn't affected by the alien blood?" said Mahone.

"That's right. But it was too heavy. Now if we were working in low-gee environments, maybe. Such is not the case on the Hiveworld. These suits were already in the works when this mission was established. We tailored the batch we brought along just for this occasion—with all your specific measurements in mind."

"No chance to return these, huh?" said Jastrow.

"That won't be necessary, I assure you. What

we've got here *is* a new process, but we've been testing it for years, and we've got it down exactly."

He went over to the suit and poked the side of the
arm.

The surface gave.

"What we have here is a light, effective armor,
covered with a permeable membrane controlled by a
mechanism in the back of the suit. It's kind of like
having the whole suit engulfed by a friendly jellyfish
that will grow back immediately if hit. Its function is
quite useful.

"Before, the suits that worked were too heavy.
Therefore what we have here is a self-contained os-
motic demi-atmospheric suit that does not resist, but
extirpates."

He poked the suit again.

"The moment alien blood touches this wardrobe,
the threat is eliminated altogether."

He took a vial marked ACID from his pants pocket,
twirled it open, and poured drops onto the shoulder
of the suit.

The top layer frizzled, bubbling.

Kozlowski had to make herself watch.

The bubbling was only for a moment, though.

Fluid welled, swallowing the acid.

The membrane closed up the hole within moments, and it was as though the acid had never
been.

"Yeah, but how *tough* is that stuff?"

"It's a form of plastic, and it can be cut . . . but it's
even better than skin . . . it naturally re-forms into
its previous mode within seconds, and chemically
rebonds itself. A healing process, if you will."

"What about inside. I mean, we haven't exactly

been trained in those sort of suits," said another man.

"That's one of the beauties of the things. In all details, the interior, the articulation, and the booster servos of the suits are identical to what you all have been trained to use. The other aspects are self-regulating. Maintenance will be needed, of course, but only after an encounter with the enemy. I should emphasize that this armor isn't perfect. It will wear out, though it should stand up during battle. Nonetheless *try* and avoid any alien blood you can. Don't go wading in it." He nodded to his assistant. "Go ahead. Let them have a close look."

The man strode around the room.

The soldiers poked and prodded the model.

"Goddamn. I'm going to feel like rubber-boy!" said Ellis.

"This is going to give a whole new twist of the saying 'Bouncing back!' " suggested Jastrow.

"Okay," said Kozlowski, after giving them a couple of minutes to handle the merchandise. "You'll all have the opportunity to get used to these suits in special exercises we have planned every day for the remainder of the journey. But for now, listen up! 'Cause this is how we're going to use these things."

And she told them.

12

One drink down.

Two more to go.

"Another glass of bubbly, my dear?" said Daniel Grant, pulling the bottle out of the thermo-adjuster and tilting it even as he asked the question.

"It is awfully delicious—but . . ." said Edie Mahone, holding out her hand.

Glug glug glug.

The quite large glass filled with bright, dazzlingly effervescent fluid.

"Of course you will. You're off duty, you need to relax, and we've got three whole days before your mission," said Daniel Grant. "*Our* mission!"

He refilled his own glass with the double-strength champagne. Damned good thing he was feeling generous with his team on the *Razzia*. He'd fitted them out with his own concept of hardship

140

supplies. Hell, if they had to go to the other side of nowhere to suck some bug juice from some god forsaken planet, at least they should do so in style. Now, he was reaping the rewards of his own munificence.

"Well, if you insist. I know your time is valuable and I hate to take it up by asking you really silly questions. But I *have* been following your career, and I *do* have more questions."

Somehow the alcohol seemed to have unlocked this woman's pheromones. She smelled good, damned good, and Daniel Grant breathed her scent in greedily. Of course she wore no perfume—a ridiculous and foolish luxury for a person on a highly unglamorous journey in a tin can through space with a bunch of males. That didn't make any difference. Hell, he was *tired* of perfume. What he had here before him was the dangling, rounded hair and breasts and lovely limbs of a full-blooded woman.

His last date had hardly been fulfilling. And the gritty details attendant to moving the *Razzia* and himself toward hyperdrive and hypersleep had pretty much put a hold on his appetites. But as soon as the sleep-rheum drained from his head, he immediately became aware of how *horny* he was. The incident on the shuttle made him naturally think of Private Edie Mahone. After Colonel Kozlowski's briefing, he'd suggested that after evening mess she might like to stop by for that promised drink. He always enjoyed talking to fans about his career, and he was quite *upset* about the gross inaccuracies of that trashy book about him, and wanted to set some things straight—

. . . uhm, so to speak.

Two to go.

He'd sized her up. She was a three-drink girl. In two drinks she'd be pliable. Three she'd sit closer, lean those dark eyes toward him, let that sweet, fresh, scrubbed scent of her dart in for a kiss.

Then *snap!* Like a patient angler fish, he'd swallow her up for a delicious hour or so, and then spit her back out. They'd both be happy, sated, and better able to deal with the grim realities before them.

She brought the topped-off glass up to those full, moist lips and drank half the glass in a couple swallows. He was impressed and gleeful at this. "My, but this is wonderful stuff."

"My own special vintage!" said Grant. "You're one of the few people who've actually tasted it!"

"Goodness! Then I shouldn't be so shy, should I? I don't want to be impolite when I'm so privileged!" With that, and a down-the-hatch determination to her face, she took the large glass and swallowed the rest of it.

That had been a very large portion. This, perhaps, would be very short work!

"Yes, right." In a moment she'd probably have to step off to his private toilet and he'd slip the last bit of liquor into her glass. He had to play it cool though now. "You were asking me about my youth?"

Edie Mahone had an odd expression on her face. She seemed not to be listening to him, just in a kind of trance.

"Edie? Edie . . . are you all right?"

"Mr. Grant . . ."

"Daniel . . ." he said. "I told you, you can call me Daniel."

She got quiet. She closed her eyes.

Hmm, thought Daniel Grant.

Maybe *two* glasses of the old id-tickler was all that was necessary!

He scooted closer.

"You know, Edie . . . We're basically just two people . . . a man and a woman with needs . . . out in the middle of nowhere . . . We should *comfort* one another, the way that normal human males and females do . . ."

Edie Mahone snorted. She sniffed, and the straight line described by her lips crumpled into misery. Tears dripped from the corners of her eyes.

"Oh, Daniel . . ." she mewled, and then dissolved into a quivering mess onto him, arms wrapped protectively over her abdomen. "I don't know what I'm going to do . . ."

"Uhmm . . . Edie . . . what's wrong?"

"I made a terrible mistake. I never should have come along on this mission. It just seemed like the right thing to do at the time. I just wanted to be light-years away. Light-years from *him*."

"Him?"

"Chuck!"

Chuck. Oh, yes. A boyfriend. The usual story.

Grant began to stroke her back comfortingly. He could feel her muscles relax. Oh, yes, this was going to be soooooo easy!

"Tell me about him?"

"What's to tell?" she said in a monotone voice. "Love with the wrong guy. He was in my troop. Started sleeping with our lieutenant. No way to compete. Only thing to do is to ship out. Chuck wasn't going to. So I'd tested high in all necessary categories, I've got the skill and the experience. And now the reason. But now that I wake up here . . . Now that I see those pictures, I remember what it was like, the one actual nest experience I had." Grant could feel her shudder. "It's worse than cold and forbidding out here. And those *things*. They're worse than devils."

"There, there, dear. I know how you feel." She was wearing a green fatigue shirt with buttons down the front. He slowly unbuttoned the top one.

"I know you do. I can feel it. You're really a sympathetic man, a good man . . . beneath that hard, caustic surface. I could tell that . . . even in the book."

Another button.

"You're a very special woman, Edie . . . You deserve comforting." Another button. He could see a fleshy swell of bare bosom, held in check by a tan bra. Out here in the harsh and cold of space, it struck him as one of the most erotic sights he'd witnessed.

He slipped his hand inside her shirt. Soft, warm, pliable.

Ah!

She said nothing. She hardly seemed to notice, wrapped up in her own misery.

Maybe she didn't really want this. Maybe she'd just let him have his way, like a trusting lamb, helpless before the slaughter. Maybe he really shouldn't take advantage of this vulnerable soul this way . . .

Bullshit, he thought, remembering his personal philosophy. Plunder while the plunder's available.

"You know, Edie, I can't think of anything more soothing than if we gave each other hot oil massages. You'll feel much better. Now let me just help you off with this scratchy old uniform and then—"

There was a pounding on the door.

Private Edie Mahone jumped about a foot in the air, eyes going wide. "Who's that?" she said, pulling away from his embrace.

"No one! I'll get rid of them!"

She stuffed herself back into bra and fatigues, sobering up in record time.

"Grant!" called a too-familiar voice. "I know you're in there. Answer the damned door. There's something wrong with your comm unit."

"Colonel Kozlowski!" said Mahone, jumping up and away from Grant's grasp for her. Quickly she ran into his toilet to straighten herself out. She turned back and gave Grant a harsh you're-just-like-the-book-says-you-are look. Then, in a rush of indignation and alarm, she was gone.

Pound. Pound. "Grant. We need to talk."

Daniel Grant had to take a deep breath and straighten his pants as much as possible. *Calm yourself. The bitch doesn't need any kind of salute from you.*

Then he got up and hit the door hydraulics. It slid open, and characteristically Colonel Kozlowski just stormed on in. "You know, with only three days to go, you can't expect to just hole yourself up."

"I was having a conference. Getting to know our troops," said Grant, rearing up to every inch of six feet two.

She glared at him, not buying his attempt at dominance for a moment. "Troops?"

"Private Edie Mahone. She's in the bathroom. She was having a few doubts about the mission."

Kozlowski raised her eyebrow. "Oh, yeah—?"

Edie Mahone came out of the head, looking perfectly composed and professional. "Thank you, Mr. Grant. You've been a real gentleman, but I have to go now . . ."

"Mahone. Why aren't you studying . . . ?"

"Free time, sir. I can use it according to my discretion. Permission to leave, sir?"

"Permission granted," said Kozlowski in a disgusted tone. She didn't even watch as the private departed, a study of healing wounded dignity.

Grant felt mightily vexed.

Sexual frustration piled upon a direct intrusion upon his privacy by a woman wearing confrontation over her head like a storm cloud.

Back on Earth, had this situation arisen, so might have the infamous Daniel Grant temper. A rant, a rave, a metaphorical chomping off of the head. Employee or associate, pressman or president, it would make no difference. Grant would have made mincemeat of them.

He could feel it burbling up, steaming through his capillaries. One little vent was all it would take, and the explosion would blast.

However something gave him pause.

Something odd aglint in this feistmeister of a woman's eye. She *did* present a fetching figure in those skintight duds she wore. And if you got past the cropped, patchy hair, the defiant lack of softening makeup, and those scars she wore like medals . . .

If you turned down the lights a bit and smudged

a little with mind and imagination, this Kozlowski bitch was really *quite* the looker.

He looked at her. He looked at the unopened bottle of champagne in its cooler slot. He looked back at her, suddenly oily with cordiality.

"Well, Colonel. As long as you're here—"

The gall!

She looked at him as though he'd just opened his zipper and wagged his privates at her.

The unmitigated *gall*!

"No, Mr. Grant. I will *not* have a glass of champagne with you!"

Daniel Grant stepped back as though she'd blasted a breath of fire at him. "You don't drink."

"I drink. That's not what I came here for, though."

"You don't like champagne. I promise you, you'll not taste better. Besides, Colonel . . . We're three days away from Death leering at us. Carpe diem. Seize the day!"

She wasn't sure why she was so annoyed at his offer. He was right. She'd pretty much finished most of her tasks for the day anyway, and the Colonial Marines were unfortunately not a military navy force known for packing away kegs of rum onboard for the officers.

She'd been working hard for three days. Her mouth was dry. And here was some high-quality, rich man's champagne being offered to her. She hadn't had a drink in weeks, and she could feel her tastebuds and her nerves, falling to their knees and begging her to accept the offer.

She told them to go screw themselves.

"I'm here, Grant, to officially request that you allow me to tour the levels assigned to your scientists on this mission. In the interests of the success of our journey, I feel the need to know everything going on in this ship."

Grant nodded. "Ah. I see. This, despite what your superiors told you. To wit: that is *not* your territory of concern."

"Yes. I have given it a great deal of thought. Any ignorance on my part could spell a danger to my troops and this vessel."

"I thought the captain was in charge of the actual vessel. He doesn't seem to care much what's going on on Decks E and F."

"The captain? He's a burnout. He does just the minimum to get by, counting things out by crossword. I honestly wonder why he was given this particular duty."

"He seems quite competent to me . . ."

Nonetheless, Grant did not say no.

Instead, he pushed a button that depressurized the seal on the champagne. He tagged another switch. Armatures extended and made short work of the cork.

Pop!

Kozlowski jumped despite herself. A brief spurt of white stuff ran down the upright thing. She licked her lips, a sudden tingling running down her spine.

Coolly, Grant went to a cabinet, pulled out two glasses. He poured these glasses full of the drink, and then carefully slipped the bottle back into its frigid place.

"I'll tell you what, Colonel Alex. Have a drink with me, I'll give you the Grand Tour."

He tapped the side of the glass closest to her. *Ting!* The liquid effervesced delightfully.

She made her decision. It was an easy one. She took the glass and drank a swallow, letting it drift through her teeth a moment. It was strong, but it was the lightest, tastiest champagne she'd ever experienced. Fruit vapor, dancing pirouettes on her tongue.

She glowered. A thought occurred to her. "You bastard. You were going to show me anyway, weren't you?"

He picked his own glass up, sipped it. "You'll never know now, will you?"

"Damn you." She couldn't help but sip the glass again. If anything, it tasted better on the second go.

"But here—I happen to have some pâté. Crackers, too. French and English, respectively." His hand motioned toward a tray of condiments. "So why don't you have a seat."

She finished the glass of champagne in one guzzle.

Heaven.

Her toes seemed to curl.

"Okay! If you pour us both another!"

"Absolutely!" He poured. "So nice to have company."

She sat and she sipped. She sampled the crackers and pâté. After what seemed like a lifetime of reconstituted Marine chow, it tasted like ambrosia. More champagne. Ah. Ambrosia and nectar.

"So then," she said, "I have two questions.

"Number one. What the hell is going on down on

those decks? I saw some of the strangest apparatus being boosted off for the *Razzia*."

"You're just going to have to wait until tomorrow for the answer to that," Grant said. "Then, though, I promise that all will be explained."

"Fair enough. Question two—" She drained her glass of champagne. It exploded inside her like a depth charge of flowers. "Have you got another bottle of this stuff around? This is the best alcohol I've ever had!"

Grant grinned widely. "I think that can be arranged!"

Daniel Grant listed. His eyes were half-closed, and his face was mashed against a cushion of the couch.

A half-filled glass of champagne wobbled in his hand.

". . . I should have never let her go," he mumbled.

Clear-eyed and feeling very good indeed, glass balanced on a raised knee, Alex Kozlowski regarded the scene. Totally in charge. Grant had extra champagne, all right. He'd had it trotted on up to his cabin, no problem. A strategy meeting, she'd explained to the surprised ensign sent to deliver it. A tumbled line of dead soldiers lay on the floor.

"Your wife?"

"Yeah. She was . . . she was the only person I ever really loved." He sighed.

An interesting evening.

Halfway through the second bottle of champagne, he'd put a hand on her left breast.

She'd cold-cocked him.

He'd flown across the room and landed on the couch fortunately, then lay semi-conscious for a few minutes, while Kozlowski thoughtfully nibbled at crackers and sipped the champagne, enjoying the silence and the boost to her ego. It had been a while since a man had been arrogant enough to make a pass at her, much less trespass her body. She enjoyed it.

She got some ice, wrapped it up in a cloth, and gave it to him. He thanked her and asked for another glass of champagne. The pain seemed to have leeched the randiness out of him, and the champagne helped with his sore jaw. He apologized and they drank more. Kozlowski finished off the pâté and crackers. Grant just sipped.

She wasn't going to be able to drink any more before the mission. Drinking now was stretching things. But she figured she might as well enjoy it—and enjoy this first-class liquor—while she could. Might as well have some sound effects while she did so, she'd told herself—so she pried Daniel Grant's life story out of him. Easy, since he was really getting snookered.

Pretty queasy stuff.

Cold mother. Distant father. Money the end-all be-all in the family. No love and affection. A football team approach to sex and affection as conquest. Massive insecurities covered over by efforts and dominance, arrogance and control.

All in all, fairly predictable. Textbook even, she'd imagine. She'd not read much psychology. Hell, most books and computer information had been destroyed.

She'd more or less drunken him under the table.

Either that, or her fist had knocked something loose in his brain. Unlikely. Grant looked like he had a pretty hard head.

She'd lifted the rock up and found a mass of worms and nightcrawlers.

The great man wasn't much different, deep down, from her. A few less nightmares, a little more civilized on the surface. But deep down—the usual writhing stew of human troubles.

"So," slurred Grant. "Your full name is Alexandra Lee Kozlowski."

"You did your homework. Yes. My parents named me after two famous generals."

"Grant and Lee. No wonder the antipathy. Hope we can smooth things out."

She shrugged. "We both want the mission to succeed."

"Yes," he murmured. "This trip succeeds, my company succeeds. I'm in the black, debts are paid off, I'm competing effectively against MedTech again, the mob gets paid off, and I get free of their contract—"

"Which you presume you're safe from out here."

He'd spilled the beans on that one under her probing questions, proving her suspicions correct. He'd come along on the mission because it was a convenient way to get off Earth, away from certain deadly factions. Now she knew why. Simple enough and understandable.

Only she honestly wondered if Grant knew that he'd jumped out of the frying pan into the fire. And there were a lot of nasty bugs in that fire, you betcha.

Grant didn't seem to hear her last comment. He

was just rambling on. "I get things *on track*," he was saying. "God, the world is my oyster, I just got to get through the shell. When I get straight with everyone . . . I'll ask her back. I swear I will. *That's* what I'm pushing for . . . Can't live the life I've been living so long . . . So empty . . . So useless . . ."

"Fast track. Candle at both ends. Strive strive strive so you can build yourself a fancy coffin. Dominance and dominoes—both falling-down games."

"Gotta stay on top. Gotta flash the smile. Gotta work, gotta survive," Grant mumbled.

"Gotta drink the best champagne," said Kozlowski. "Eat the best pâté." She downed the last bit of stuff in her glass, clapped it back on the table, and stood up. "I guess that's as good a goal as any. Thanks, Grant. I had a good time. Tell you what. We get back to Earth, we have a little party. You supply the champagne and eats, and we'll have a good time."

He looked up, bleary eyes startled. "Don't go!"

"Right. I'm gonna tippy-toe out of your place in the wee hours . . . or worse, at the beginning of first shift. Won't that amuse the troops?"

"None of . . . their business . . ."

"True, but it's also a good excuse to slip the noose here, Grant."

"I just . . . I just don't want to be alone."

"Yeah. I've heard that one before." She found herself angry for no explicable reason. "Take a snooze, guy. Let your dreams keep you company."

She half expected him to suddenly jump up and

run in front of her, begging her to stop. She made
a fist. Yeah. Just let the lecher try.

But he didn't. She stopped at the door and listened.

Peaceful, content snores.

She opened the door and stormed out.

Now she knew why she was ticked off, and it absolutely annoyed the hell out of her.

She was attracted to the jerk, dammit.

13

Daniel Grant didn't look so good.

He was sipping at what passed for coffee when Kozlowski found him on the observation deck, looking out at the specks of stars and planets in the vast blackness of space as though searching for dawn.

"Hey there," she said. "Captain told me I'd find you here."

"I'm trying to soak my head in the Big Dipper," said Grant, gazing out into the vastness.

"I'm here for my tour."

"So you are. So you are, Colonel Kozlowski."

She considered telling him to call her by her first name. He looked so . . . lost and vulnerable, a wisp of steam winding up from his coffee and misting a piece of the view. She decided against it. She didn't want to give him the wrong idea.

Silence slid between them, which surprised her for a moment. Silence didn't seem in Grant's lexicon of communication devices.

She coughed encouragingly.

Nothing.

Finally, she said, "I did earn my tour, Grant."

"So you did, Colonel. However, I wish you'd said you had a hollow leg."

She shrugged. "You were drinking before I got there. Head start. Besides, I really don't care for your sexual preying before a mission."

"All's fair in love and war."

"Foxhole love. I've had some of that, nice if you like watching your partner in the deed die the next day."

Grant nodded. Managed a smile. "You're far too dramatic, Colonel." He shrugged. "Severe hangovers have a way of putting things in perspective. I guess I'm a bit of the predator. I apologize."

"How's your jaw?"

He rubbed it gingerly. "I can still speak and I can still think. However, I believe you've actually improved my looks."

"You've lost me on that one, Grant."

"I think my face was a little irregular before. You appear to have whacked it back into proper symmetry. Doubtless hundreds of nubile young ladies will come to thank you."

"You know, Grant, if I didn't detect a little self-mockery in your tone, I think I'd deck you again."

A flash of alarm in his face. That immediately retreated into an accepting nod. "I'm an energetic son of a bitch, aren't I?"

"I guess there's a reason you got where you got. But now we're just short of our destination, a parsec and some change from home. And I need to see some more of exactly why we're here."

"Very well. Let me scrape some of my brain off my throat and reassimilate." He sipped some coffee.

She had a notion. "Here you go. I think I've got something that will help." She fished a small container from a pocket.

"Oh. How do *you* know?"

"Believe it or not, I've had a hangover or two lately." She did not get specific. She just snapped open the top and displayed the pills, neatly cut into halves and thirds and quarters.

"Pills? What are they?"

"Fire, Grant. Your own poison. Works damned well in this kind of situation. Check it out."

He shook his head. "Thanks, but no thanks. I never touch my own stuff. But please . . . don't let me stop you."

She'd been thinking of taking a quarter but now, instead, she snapped the container shut and stuck it back in her pocket, feeling annoyed, feeling like a junkie getting the brush-off by the pusher himself.

"Just show me those decks, Grant."

"This way, Colonel."

Corporal Lars Henrikson waited for them at the turbolift.

Kozlowski was taken aback. "Henrikson? What are *you* doing here?"

Henrikson remained stoic. "Mr. Grant called. He asked me to meet him here. I'm here."

Grant put a hand on the big guy's shoulder. Patted. "My kind of man, Colonel. Henrikson here's going to get a look at what we've got inside, too. Why? I'm glad you asked that question. Henrikson's probably wondering, too." He punched the button for the 'lift. The door slid open, and they all stepped inside. Whir of lights, compression, off for another level. "I'm not an elitist. I want to show what we've got here, to give you an understanding of what's going on. That knowledge on your part may come in handy later on. Helps us a lot. It also gives you a better idea of what we're going to need down on Hiveworld."

Kozlowski was a bit irked. First, because from the sounds of it, Grant had always intended to show her what was going on here. Second, because of Henrikson. He was a first-class soldier. During training, he'd come up as number one at all levels. His abilities were unquestionable. Plenty of references, and one of the troops she'd had no problem at all deciding should go on this mission. However, now it seemed as though Grant had taken him under his corporate wing—a corporal!—and was squiring him about, giving him the treatment that she as the commander alone deserved. True, Grant claimed that of all the regular troops Henrikson had the most actual combat time with the xenos. But still . . .

Basically, she felt a tad jealous, as though this selection of Henrikson was a *male* thing, some off-handed way of slapping the fact that she was a female.

"One little condition," said Grant as they walked along the catwalk on Deck E, approaching doors that looked like the entrance to a bank vault. "What I'm about to show you two is strictly hush-hush. I don't want anyone to know about this, especially not the other men—or women. That's why I'm just showing it to you two. I feel as though you can handle it."

Without further explanation, Grant cycled open the door and led them through. The lights were more muted here; it had almost a submarine quality. Aquas and red and shadows. As her eyes adjusted, Kozlowski immediately noticed the equipment.

Banks of it, spread along the ways. Tubing and bulking computers and flanges. Cables and glass and blinking lights. A number of men were clustered at the far end in front of a window that looked like something out of an aquarium. Grant's scientists, doing their geeky scientist thing, mystery wrapped in machinery and mundanity.

It smelled in here. Acidic. Oil, electricity, coffee . . . and something more.

Something that made Kozlowski's hackles rise.

She recognized it. Faint, but there.

Bugs.

No, she told herself. That can't be right. What would bugs be doing down here?

"Isn't this supposed to be a storage chamber?" she said lamely, trying to get Grant to talk, trying to get the creepy feeling out of the pit of her stomach.

"Oh, yes," said Grant, leading them down some

stairs. "And in a way, it still is. But the cargo! That's what's a little unusual."

The steps clanged and echoed.

"So, Grant," said Henrikson. "Why all the secrecy? Why just us?"

Nice of him to echo her own thoughts.

They were walking forward, and through the murky light in the glassed tank she was able to pick out a few details.

Cables, dangling equipment.

Something bulky and organic in the very middle.

And by it . . .

An egg sack.

And the discarded shell of a face hugger.

She walked up to the window in a haze, astonished, looking in upon the gruesome scene enclosed in metal and glass.

"Well, Corporal, I know most marines have come to really hate the aliens," said Grant. "I'm afraid that what we've got down here would really hinder the morale necessary for the operation."

A thickset man with a boyish face and a cowlick in his mass of blondish hair scuttled up to Grant, lab coat swaying about his ankles. In whispers they conferred together in the corner. The man produced a clipboarded chart that Grant nodded at and then pushed away. He took the scientist gently by the arm and pulled him over to meet his guests.

"This is Dr. Murray Friel. He's in charge of this project down here—the science part, anyway."

"Yes—I've met the commander, but not the corporal," said the doctor.

Kozlowski remembered now. There had been introductions and handshakes on Earth, and then the batch of docs, including Friel here, had been swallowed up on these decks. Brief glimpses in other parts of the ship—that was all. She'd met a lot of men like Friel. Plump red-cheeked guys, smart, but with no real experience. They all seemed to have the same arrogance as Friel here had. He was in his own little world—and owned every corner of it.

But it wasn't Dr. Friel that preoccupied her now. She was looking at something else.

It looked like a misshapen excuse for a body, but with limbs and head cut off and lengths of esophagus and intestine connecting it with organic machines nearby.

Liquids pulsed through these, feeding it.

"What *is* that thing?" said Kozlowski, recovering her aplomb, overcoming her initial horror.

"Friel . . . care to do the honors?" suggested Grant.

"Certainly. It certainly isn't very attractive . . . but then, neither would your interior bits, awkwardly displayed. You must excuse me, but I feel rather proprietary toward it. You see, in a way, it's a part of me." He stepped forward, a pudgy palm placed up against the glass. He gazed at it with an odd kind of pride. "You see, it's a donor clone, DNA clamped so that it would grow simply the torso, no brain, limited nervous system. A machine regulates it. These things are usually produced for the purpose of organ and tissue donation." His fingers drummed on the glass thoughtfully and then he turned back to look at her. "I'll admit, it isn't the most attractive creature, but it's proved useful." He

tapped his arm. "I'm proud to say its cells of orig-
ination were retrieved from my wrist."

The odd, smirky fellow who had been introduced
before to her as Dr. Amos Begalli sidled up. "We had
a little coin toss. We all wanted to be the one . . .
Dr. Friel won. He's like a proud father now, waiting
for a son to be born."

Friel shrugged. "It's an interesting experience, I
must say."

Kozlowski shook her head. She was finally allowing herself to assimilate the evidence presented
here to her. She turned to Grant. "I've seen this
before," she said through clenched teeth. "You're
breeding one of those damn things!"

"Take it easy, kiddo!" said Grant. "First, everything is quite secure here. The torso is in special
suspended animation. It can't blow until the right
switches are hit. There are reinforced windows.
Special alloy cages. Alarms and an automatic laser
lattice should something unforeseen happen."

"But that thing in there . . . it's living . . ."

"Only on the crudest terms," said Dr. Friel. "It
doesn't feel any pain. It doesn't think. It's just basically a mass of tissue that serves a purpose."

"But if a xeno gets loose on this ship . . ."

"Colonel, Colonel—the dangers are well known
and plenty of precautionary measures have been
built into the fail-safe system, I promise you!" said
Grant. "Believe me, at Neo-Pharm we've been
doing this kind of thing for years . . . And that
woman Ripley did it years ago successfully. Our
technology is far superior now. We know how to
deal with it."

"But why are you bringing along something like this when we're going to a planet full of them?"

"An experiment," said Dr. Friel. "Naturally, we'd like to come back with necessary alien DNA and queen mother royal jelly to create our own colony for purposes I've been told you are acquainted with. Also perhaps even captured eggs. But we want to work with the product of our own DNA manipulation. To create our own kind of queen, utilizing the necessary royal jelly from what you good soldiers are going to retrieve for us. We'd like to work with some different material than we've had on Earth."

Dr. Begalli beamed. "Yes! You see we've got *everything* thoroughly regulated here . . . Metabolic control. We've got it set up so that baby won't pop until we've got the jelly we need available for her queening."

"Lovely," said Kozlowski. "Just lovely."

"In addition, of course, on these decks we've got the necessary tanks and holding pens for the jelly and captured eggs, refrigerated alien DNA . . . Oh, all manner of good stuff, Colonel. But you can see why your troops might be a little upset."

Friel shook his head. "It's understandable why people are so afraid of these things. However, with the proper applied measures of science, Neo-Pharm is proving that what has up till now appeared to be a threat to humanity—can in fact be a great help. We've just begun our work in the area of drugs and medicine . . . Heaven alone knows how our understanding of the alien DNA will help us in the future." He sighed happily. "And to think . . . I'm to be like a *father* to a whole aspect of what may be the most significant advance in human evolution. Its chemical interaction with xenobiology! Who knows what wonderful new vistas await us!"

"Try horrible pain. Try death. Try species *extinction*!" said Kozlowski.

Dr. Friel flinched with the intensity of Kozlowski's response. "I don't think, Colonel, you appreciate the beauties and intricacies of the alien genetic gifts."

"I don't think, Doctor, you appreciate the *threat* these things are—" She paused, calmed herself down, took a gulp of air.

Grant seemed taken aback. "Colonel . . . Alex. You were there at the initial meeting. I saw you there . . . you heard everything. You're aware of our ultimate goal. You know what you're here for."

She swung on him, outthrust finger just short of his nose. "Make no mistake, Grant. I may be here to head up this mission to facilitate your personal and professional goals. That's secondary to my duty to the armed forces I serve—and my own purpose. Which is, quite simply, to do everything I can to make sure these bugs are either rendered into a threat equivalent to cosmic cockroaches—or thoroughly exterminated." She lowered the finger. "Any bugs crushed underfoot along the way are all the better."

With that, she turned and stalked the hell away from this charnel house in the belly of a starship.

14

Everyone knew that service chow sucked.

You didn't join the Colonial Marines for gourmet food, that was for certain.

Still, as Kozlowski accepted the food dumped unceremoniously on her plate at the cafeteria line, her stomach cringed at the lumps of colorless, reconstituted whatsits her meal comprised. She well knew that all the food groups were represented, that this was vitamin and nutrient rich stuff. There just wasn't much taste or appeal to it, that was all.

Still, the gig was two days away.

Gotta carb up!

She stepped over to push a button that would put a dollop of what the machine claimed was mashed potatoes on her plate. She positioned the plate under the nozzle, still not quite there . . .

She'd been a bit preoccupied ever since she'd seen that cloned torso down on Grant's deck. The merging of alien and human to her had always been the height of obscenity. Eradicating that threat had been what her life had been about now for over twenty years. Her use of Fire she'd rationalized as an exercise of dominance over the aliens . . . Now, though, she wasn't so sure. Unfortunately, she suspected she was hooked on the stuff. She'd been okay this morning, no bad champagne headache, just a chemical pall of gloom riding her. A quarter pill wouldn't banish it. A half pill didn't give her the buzz she realized she wanted to get through the day. She'd taken what amounted to an entire pill, something that she'd only done before in battle exercises and war itself.

And the stuff had unwound in her, like the talons of a bug, zapping her neurons . . .

She shuddered, tried to forget about it. When this mission was over, she was going to throw her pills in the garbage. Clean up her act. Live clean and healthy. But she knew that she needed the Xeno-Zip to deal with what was coming up in her life—and it pissed her off. Especially with her conflicted feelings about Daniel Grant. Especially after what she'd seen down there.

She tried to tune out the chatter in her head, to focus on getting some of this food down, despite her lack of appetite. She took her tray and sat down, alone, at the side of an unoccupied table.

In another corner of the room, Jastrow was noodling on his saxophone. The man didn't play well, but he didn't play badly either. At least, if it wasn't exactly melodious, it wasn't that grating either.

However, his buddy, who was sitting beside him as usual, didn't seem to appreciate it.

"Could you give it a rest, Jastrow?"

"What's wrong, Ellis? I thought you liked music."

"I like music fine. But not blaring in my ear while I'm eating."

Kozlowski listened to them bicker. Better than concentrating on this crap that she was stuffing into her face. Jastrow stopped playing and they talked. They talked about Henrikson, who had just come in, walked through the cafeteria, taken his food, and was walking out again.

"Hey. Check it out," said Jastrow. "Henrikson's doing it again. He's taking his food to the room. Oh, man, the bet's still on here . . . I say he's a synthetic!"

"Gimme a break," said Ellis. "They make models that eat, you know."

"It's not just that. He won't shower with us. I've never seen him shave . . . And from the way he talks in briefings, I'd guess he's never seen combat."

"Yeah. That is odd."

"I say he's a company plant. And I don't like it. Bad things happen to Marine ships with synthetics on board!"

The next thing Kozlowski knew, Henrikson was by the table.

"Jastrow. Why don't you just say what you've got on your mind—to my face."

He lifted the private off the chair. The sax banged onto the floor.

Kozlowski shot up to put a stop to this.

"Shit, man! Let me go!"

"Sure." The big corporal threw the private across the room.

"Henrikson!" screamed Kozlowski.

Henrikson froze. He turned around and looked at his commander, his face impassive. "Sorry."

Ellis was leaning over, attending to his buddy, who seemed okay, just dazed.

"We're all under pressure here, Henrikson," snarled Kozlowski. "Take it out on the bugs." She swiveled on the privates. "And that means you two. We're all working together on this. No divisiveness."

"You know, Corporal," a voice said behind her. "I admire a man who doesn't take any crap. I honestly do." Grant's voice. He came up to them, and his easy-going arrogance seemed to cut through the tension. "But the truth is I need every last one of these troops for this operation." He looked over to the fallen Jastrow, who was just getting up. "You don't have to kiss and make up, but please don't mash his skull, okay? Thanks."

Henrikson nodded. Kozlowski dismissed him. He took his food and went off again toward his quarters.

Kozlowski turned to the others. "All right. Back to the chow. I don't want any energy-deficient troops when we get down to work." As an example, she went back to her own plate, which had gone cold. Nonetheless, she began to stuff it in her face.

Grant came over to her.

"Colonel," he said in a low voice. "Can we talk a moment, please. Alone?"

"Pull up some vittles, Dan. If I've got to work my way through this stuff, so do you."

He didn't even try to argue. He went off, got a minimum order of gruelish reconstituted stew, and spooned it down, trying to look cheerful as they made chitchat. The sucker looked much better now. Probably had himself a cocktail and a nap and a good hot bath. He even smelled good. Oddly, Kozlowski enjoyed the small talk. She was still annoyed at her attraction to the asshole, but she didn't have to let him know about it—and she could enjoy the warped sex appeal he presented on her own terms. He probably sprayed on pheromones, the conscienceless bastard.

Finally, when she was satisfied the last morsel was gone from his plate, she agreed to go with him to somewhere they couldn't be overheard—but a meeting room, not his room.

"Look," he said. "I didn't know you'd react the way you did down there. Corporal Henrikson took it well. He's even volunteering to double-check security. I just want to make sure I'm still getting the best out of you on our mission, Colonel."

"There was never any doubt of that, chum. You asked for the best, you got the best—but I want to tell you, I'm not real crazy about your methods."

"What I'm doing is for the benefit of mankind!"

She laughed in his face. "You don't have to try and pull that one on me. You're doing this for the money."

"Ultimately, it will save lives."

"What are you talking about? You're risking good Marine lives for this damned jelly and what-all . . . For profit, pure and simple. You're a ruthless bastard. At least my superiors honestly believe they're doing what's right."

"I'm risking my own life here, too, remember."

"Only because you're too scared to face up to a souped-up loan shark back home."

He cringed. "Ah. I told you that, eh?"

"You bet. I'd pretty much guessed something along those lines anyway."

"Nonetheless. We figure a source for this—a safe controlled source—we can finance a full erasure of the aliens on the planet Earth. Studying them, we'll be able to know how to deal with them when we encounter them on other worlds."

"All sounds good. Doesn't change anything about what I think about *you* though."

"You'll honor my concerns about the others, though . . . Not letting them know."

"You think I want to undermine their morale by letting them know that a xeno's going to be prowling in some cage below them while they're helpless in hypersleep? They're my people, and I'll take care of them . . . You watch out for your own crew. Understand?"

"I'm glad we're clear on this, Colonel. I really don't quite understand your hostility, though . . . I think it's best for both our sakes if we got along much better."

"Don't push it, Grant. And most of all—don't push me."

She got up, and she got away from him.

If she hung around the handsome goon much longer she didn't know what she'd do—kiss him or kill him.

She wasn't sure which she'd enjoy more.

· · ·

In the dim lights of the Cargo Bay Nine, shadows moved.

Padding past open doors, feet paced over to controls. Fingers pushed, pulled, tapped. Status quo alarms were turned off. Serums were released and rheostats adjusted.

Inside the ghost-lit tank, the hanging torso jerked.

Satisfied that the necessary measures had been taken, the figure hurried back out of the room, door shushing closed behind it.

In the tank, the hanging torso jerked again.

In the hanging torso, the alien embryo, already formed and at full term, but previously kept dormant by electronic and biochemical means, shivered into full life over a matter of mere minutes.

It shook. It gasped. Sparked by the energies that had been shot through it, and the instincts that had been ignited, it flailed in its seating.

Membranes tore, muscles were yanked from their mooring.

Still it was not yet free.

Instinct activated.

With a preternatural power, it pushed up against the diaphragm, up through the tangle of lungs and heart and arteries.

Up against the rib cage.

Then, with its hard equipment prepared for just this moment, and every bit of its energy, it plunged through the bones, through the skin into the freedom of gaseous atmosphere.

The torso exploded.

Blood spattered. Bronchial tissue splattered up

like the eruption of a volcano. Bits of broken bone spanged against metal and glass.

Like a worm with a head of all teeth, the alien chest-burster reared up above the carcass of its birth, weaving in a sensory dance. Sensing no danger, it began to scuttle for the darkness of a corner.

The hands that had nudged the obscene delivery forward had not removed the precautions against just such an event.

Delicate motion detectors reacted to the scuttling, heat-seeking alien. Spectrographic readings determined its nature, double-checked, and then implemented the next step. Should the thing be born in unsupervised circumstances, there was no other alternatives.

Servomotors hummed as coaxial cables controlled three separate particle beam weapons, aiming toward the source and form causing the spectrographic abnormalities.

Had it not had to pause for a moment to attempt to get through the glass of the tank, the alien might have survived longer, rendering the mission an entirely different affair.

However, it did pause.

And the weapons did fire.

The beams converged into a fulcrum of energy.

The alien blew apart, adding its gore to that of the torso it had already scattered. The force lifted its little head up and off and through the hole it had smacked in the glass, followed by charred bits of its tail.

The teeth gnashed. The tail twitched.

Then both stilled, surrendering their last signs of survival to the alarm that blared to life.

15

When she reached the cargo bay of Deck D, and she successfully convinced the flustered scientist by the door that she had Daniel Grant's permission for access (a little determined pushing helped greatly), she found the cause of the alarm waiting for her, bathed in emergency light.

Hovered over the dead infant alien, wearing their acid suits, were the science team.

Daniel Grant paced beyond the reach of any acid, punching the air and cursing. "Goddammit. Goddammit! What the hell went wrong! I'm looking at a million-dollar loss here, minimum!"

He did not notice Kozlowski come up behind him until she put a calming, restraining hand on his arm. He jumped away from her, looking startled, then sighed and folded his arms. "I don't understand. I just don't understand."

Dr. Friel knelt the closest to the wreckage. Tears were streaming from his eyes. He looked as though he would have liked to have gathered the bits and pieces of the alien baby and cradled them in his arms. Acid-neutralizing liquid had automatically been splashed, but there were still pocks and holes in the floor.

Dr. Begalli stepped up beside Grant and Kozlowski.

"Looks like someone diddled with the equipment. Took off the safeguards. The baby bug popped early. The good news is no alien running amok in the sewage pipes. Bad news: damage, no alien baby on hand to queenify . . . and a little heartbreak, it would seem."

"Christ," said Grant. His face was white. "A saboteur."

"Who would *do* such a thing?" sobbed Dr. Friel. "So young . . . so very young . . . And she didn't even get to see *me*!"

"Uh—I trust you checked your doctors' psychological profiles," said Kozlowski. "Friel looks a bit on the edge here."

"He'll be fine, he'll be fine," muttered Grant. "Just a little too wrapped up in his work."

"No wife, no kids . . ." said Begalli. "Looks like Friel wanted to be a daddy. Bad."

The stricken scientist spun on the assemblage. He swung an arc with an accusing finger. "Which one of you monsters was it?" Tears runneled down his cheeks. "Which one of you killed my baby?" The finger stopped on Kozlowski. "Was it you, Colonel? You despised it the moment you saw what was going on here. I could tell!"

"No, it wasn't me, you fool," she spat back. "Would someone get a shot of something for this hysteric? Something strong? And maybe a strait-jacket." She motioned to the wreckage. "And douse this stuff in some more acid neutralizer fast, in case the blood wants to eat through the deck any-more."

"I trust you'll help me establish better security here for the return trip," said Grant.

"Of course," she said. She spun around and started away.

Grant caught up with her. "Colonel . . . Alex . . . Could I ask for a moment of your time? Alone."

She was going to spit back a curt no, but his eyes implored her. They looked frightened and haunted. The part of Daniel Grant that she'd seen when he was drunk was there, and she was startled by its humanity.

"Meeting room. Five minutes. I'll brew the tea," she said.

"Thank you, Colonel."

The meeting room was secured, peripheral sound dampers down, communications off.

The two sat across from one another, sipping a soothing herb tea.

"So," said Kozlowski, breaking the grim silence. "Who do you think it is? An emissary of the orga-nized crime boys you owe money to. Or one of your drug company rivals, like MedTech."

"I don't get it," said Grant, shaking his head. "I can't believe I overlooked this possibility. Everyone knows that if this mission fails, I'm history."

"If you ask me, it's better this way," said

Kozlowski. "Something tells me you would have gotten more than you bargained for with Dr. Friel in control of a queen alien."

Grant sighed. "You're probably right, but that isn't the point. This sabotage will continue, and a lot more than money could be lost next time."

Kozlowski shrugged. "It's hard for me to be frightened of a corporate spy or even of the mob when I've been fighting drooling monsters for years."

"Yes, but how often have you run into infiltration? Don't you see? You and your soldiers have always been united against an obvious threat. Take it from someone who knows—nothing is deadlier than the enemy within."

"You have any suggestions?"

"That's why I asked you here. Have you any clue as to who the saboteur could be?"

"You didn't set up your systems to safeguard against one or to detect the activity of one. I suggest you do so now. I haven't the vaguest. I can only tell you . . . it isn't me."

"No. You think I'd be talking to you if I thought it was you? No, Colonel. We'll take precautions. But we'll have to take precautions and remain vigilant. If you note unusual activity in any of your people, please report it to me."

"I could say the same about your people."

"Oh, you can be sure I'm going to check them *all* out." He sipped his tea. "Nonetheless, this is going to be one hell of a mission . . ."

"It's already that, Grant. But then, I've been to hell before, so I'll put in a good word with Beelzebub."

"Thanks, Colonel."

"Strikes me that you're getting awfully self-involved here. We're all in this mission together, and we're committed to its success. Remember that, Grant. The mission comes first. Everything else, later, including your narcissistic moans."

"That's all well and good, Colonel. Just pop a couple of pills and all *your* troubles go away."

"Bastard."

She got up to go, then had a second thought. She reached into her pocket and pulled out a medicine bottle. "Just a warning, Grant." She tossed it to him. "That's my supply of the shit that you make. I'm swearing off, so I'm going to be in a pretty bitchy mood."

Grant looked down at the bottle. "Okay, Colonel." He stuck it in his own pocket. "Maybe I'll take it along myself. A dose of my own medicine might be in order."

"I wouldn't suggest it," she said, turning away so she wouldn't grab it back. She regretted the gesture already, but she'd see the bastard in true hell before she took his poison anymore.

She did, however, take the tea.

The U.S.S. *Razzia* locked into orbit around the planet dubbed Hiveworld.

Hiveworld, of course, was not its official name. That would be G-435, for obscure classification purposes. It was the fourth of ten planets orbiting Achilles Two, a GO star. It was a class M planet, with a great deal of seismic activity that rendered it generally flat and comparatively barren.

Huge banks of clouds obscured the surface, but analysis sensors had already scouted out the geographic area that was known to be the location of the alien hive visited previously.

Zero hour approached.

The mothership, naturally, would not descend.

A class 9 lander would perform that duty, bearing with it the complement of marines who embarked upon the mission. The marines all knew their jobs, but there was a palpable pall of tension and dread in the lander's interior as the soldiers, already garbed in their special acid-neutralizing suits, began to file in and strap into their grav-chairs.

They all carried their carbines and the array of other special weapons in which they specialized.

Private Jastrow carried something a little extra.

His saxophone.

"So what are you going to do, Jastrow?" said Mahone, attempting a smile. "Scare the crickets off with free-form? A little late Coltrane?"

"Shut up, Mahone," said Jastrow. "You never know when I'm going to need to unwind."

"Yow! Just having a little joke! Gimme a break!"

"Cool it, Edie," said Ellis. "We're all a little on edge huh? These suits don't douse acid words."

Edie Mahone nodded. "Sorry, guys. I'll get off your case. How about some knock-knock jokes?"

Ellis grinned. "As long as they're dirty."

Nervous titters.

Dr. Amos Begalli walked in, and slouched onto a chair, looking a little preoccupied.

Ellis nudged his friend. "Hey, Jazz. I didn't know that old Big Nozzle was taking the plunge."

Jastrow shrugged. "I don't know. Something big went on down in Mysteryville Deck. Nobody got killed or hurt. I've been keeping track and I've seen them all. But from what I saw on the down list, that Dr. Friel guy was supposed to take the plunge. Looked a bit forlorn yesterday. Freaked out, I guess. Couldn't deal with it."

"Probably smart."

"That's okay. That Begalli seems to know his stuff."

"Yeah, but I get the creeps from him."

"You get the creeps when I play Sun Ra tunes."

Jastrow lifted his horn up to blow a few notes, but Ellis stopped him. "Look. These guys are all hyped up to kill things, Jazz. Don't make them practice on you."

"Okay, okay. So where's Grant and the colonel?" He looked at his chronometer, featuring dials and sensors capable of all manner of odd things.

"Humpin', you think?"

"Come on . . . I think dear Koz dug her gonads outta herself with a rusty spoon."

"I don't know, man. I feel some heavy vibes between them."

"Yeah. Hostility. Just be glad she's directing it at someone else and not us."

Jastrow shook his head. "You know, I've trained for this. I've killed bugs. I know everything by heart. They say I'm about as ready as a marine can be mentally and physically. Spiritually though?" He shook his head. "I ain't ready."

"Who is, buddy?" Ellis said. He shuddered. "Who is?" He looked around and saw his shudder echoed in the eyes of his fellow troops.

Colonel Alex Kozlowski entered the ship.
She'd already stowed her personal weapons and

supplies in the appropriate cubicle earlier that day, just before she ran through the checklist of the Mark Nine Planetary Surface Lander, dubbed U.S.S. *Anteater* by some wag. Now she carried a large steaming cup of coffee and a grim smile.

"Ready to waste some bugs, folks?"

A roar of approval greeted her words.

"Good. But remember, that's incidental to our mission. Our priorities are inside that nest . . . our appointment with the queen mother!" She sipped at the strong black coffee. The caffeine helped her cope with the downer she was experiencing from withdrawal from Fire. She'd put some regulation pills into her suit, things her system was used to. She didn't want to jeopardize the troops or the mission by lack of performance. She did not, however, want to fall back on Fire. Although the decision put her on edge, the boost in spirit and self-determination more than made up for it.

"Anybody see Daniel Grant around?" she asked.

"Last I saw him, he was talking to Hastings about something," said Corporal Henrikson.

"He'd better get his tail down here, or it's going to get left on the *Razzia* . . . and no big loss." She ambled over to Fitzwilliam and Tanarez, the lieutenants who'd been pegged as pilots for this boat. They were huddled over their banks of controls, doing final diagnostics of their system arrays. "How's it doing, guys?"

Fitzwilliam grinned at her. "I'm telling you, Colonel. We've got one mean machine here. Backup systems galore . . . Lovely and elegant."

"Yeah," said Tanarez, not looking up from a

screen he was reading. "War with the xenos has given us a boost in technology. We've got some pretty stuff in here. Gives me a huge boost of confidence, I'll tell you that."

"Too bad this thing can't just do the dirty work," said Fitzwilliam.

"What . . . robot-controlled? And miss all the fun?"

Laughter from the troops. A good sign. Ever since she'd shown them the acid-neutralizing suits, they'd seemed to perk up quite a bit. Without the big threat of the alien blood eating through you, this was a much less dangerous mission, and the troops seemed to realize that.

As though he'd taken it as a cue, the last passenger hurried on, lugging a sack closed by a zipper. He quickly stowed it where the other stuff had been placed.

"All right, people," Daniel Grant said. "You can close the access port."

The door closed behind him after a touch of a pilot's finger.

"Thank you. I just want to say quickly that this is the most exciting day of my life," he said, in a voice that had been clearly exercised much at after banquet speeches. "Down there," he said, pointing out a port toward the pearl and cerulean clouds swirling above a continental mass. "Down on this strange world are the secrets that will strengthen our country . . . Perhaps even point us all toward a better future. Down there are the brethren of the creatures that not only are a threat to humanity— but who devastated our beloved homeworld." He

paused for dramatic impact. "It's in our hands now.
In our power. Let's do our mission and do it well."

A roar of approval arose from the ranks.

Grant, smiling like a politician, took his grav-
chair and belted himself in.

Kozlowski gave him the thumbs-up signal.

Well, Grant you goat, she thought, get ready for
the panty raid of your life.

16

Docking struts released, the half-million-ton lander first parted from the mothership *Razzia* on retros. When it was at a safe distance, its powerful impulse thrusters in, pushing it down and away, deeper into the hold of the Hiveworld's gravity.

The U.S.S. *Anteater* descended.

This was still the part of space travel that Kozlowski had never gotten used to: planetfall.

She remembered when she was a little girl, before the aliens came, she had taken a ride on a roller coaster at an amusement park. She'd thought for sure, despite the strong and reassuring presence of her father, when the coaster took a long angled dip that she was going to fall out. Now, as the lander tilted down and began its powered descent, as her heart filled her throat, that was the way she felt here.

Only if she fell, she knew it would be forever.

She desperately wanted a tab of Fire. Maybe she was going to need it, she thought. Maybe Kozlowski now, without her drug, would be a crippled foot to the mission.

Later, she told herself. She'd make that decision later.

Initially, parted from the faux gravity of the *Razzia*, there had been the heady feeling of null gravity. But then, as the ship descended, she felt the butterflies flutter into her stomach and then chute up the back door to climb her spine.

Then the gees started kicking in.

The retros roared, slowing them down. Ablation reddened the hull slightly before a force shield kicked in. Landers went down much too quickly for Kozlowski's taste. She much preferred the mollycoddling you got on a passenger shuttle. A slow, smooth descent. Friggin' Marine landers, though, acted like sperm charging out of the gate for an appointment with a pretty egg.

They were still well above the clouds, but the atmosphere started buffeting the lander, shaking it like a toy. Kozlowski gritted her teeth. She looked over. The other troops looked intent. Some just had their eyes closed. Daniel Grant looked a bit green at the gills. Kozlowski suspected that she didn't look all that great herself, but there was no place to powder her nose now.

The suits had temp controls, but they were open now and the air-conditioning wasn't on. The cabin's air control wasn't working well, and it was a bit hot and humid. Kozlowski could smell her own sweat. It was a comforting smell. What she didn't like much was the sweat from the others.

"Turbulence!" called Fitzwilliam, up in the pilot blister, with the best view. She'd chosen Lenny Fitzwilliam herself. He was a top expert at this kind of planetfall, a ranging muscular guy with a Texas accent who could have been the reincarnation of one of those crazy pilots who broke the barrier between Earth and space back in the twentieth century. His wife had just died, and this was his way of getting back some life in himself, in what he knew best.

"No shit, Sherlock!" said Tank Tanarez. He flipped on the PA. "No smoking. No trips to the can. Fasten seat belts. All that stuff. It's going to be a rocky one."

"*Going* to be?" said Grant weakly.

Tanarez never exaggerated. He was a short, stocky guy with a buzz cut and a two-dimensional way of looking at the universe, which made him a gem in this kind of piloting situation. With his fierce concentration branded in those dark eyes of his below that sloping brow, he cut straight through problems to the solutions. He could drink everyone under the table but herself. Kozlowski knew. He'd tried. He had a mordant sense of humor that was just what Kozlowski needed to hear now.

"I'm reading some pretty fierce mid-atmospheric activity. This place ain't exactly paradise."

The lander began to rock and jerk violently.

This continued for some minutes. Kozlowski suspected that there were going to be some gouges in the armrests after this from the digging in of fingers. Including hers. Nobody puked though. That was something.

The twirling lengths of gray cottony clouds seemed to reach up like an ocean of mist and absorb them. The rattling and rocking continued, and then calmed down.

"Okeydokey, folks," said Fitzwilliam. "We're through the worst of it. We should be done in about thirty-five minutes. So sit back and enjoy the flight." Fitz was clearly from the Chuck Yeager school of pilots. Fly by the seat of your pants, but even if your wings had sheered off and your ejector was jammed, at no time abandon your laid-back Texas accent.

Kozlowski took a luxurious breath of bad air. It tasted good through slightly less constricted lungs.

"Can't see a goddamned thing," said Argento, the dark-haired mustached sergeant who sat behind her. Argento's brooding eyes and bushy eyebrows and bushier mustache made Tanarez look like the Blue Boy. He was like a Neanderthal with all that hair and stolid attitude. But there wasn't a man in the Corps who knew his way around artillery, light or heavy, better. Kozlowski had worked with Argento the year before, and when the possibility of his coming along arose, she grabbed it. He had a rich, deep voice that inspired confidence in him from the git go. He was a man's man and a fine poker player, too.

"Do you really want to?" said Jastrow, suddenly talkative. "If ignorance is bliss, let's enjoy it for another half hour, huh? Me, I'm just going to rest my eyes."

That seemed like a good idea to Kozlowski. Unfortunately, she was too high-strung to give herself even that much of a treat. She had to see it all. Somewhere, in this hellish cloud cover, might be something she needed. In the first break, when she got the lay of the land—that might make a change in her strategy that might save lives, might give this mission the edge it needed for a thorough success.

So, for long minutes she watched as the lander pierced the cloud cover.

Occasional comments arose from the troops, but generally there was silence.

Finally, the cloud cover started to break up.

Kozlowski peered out through the port.

As far as she could tell, they were still a couple miles up, but she could make out some of the landscape below. She'd seen pictures of it before of course in her studies of this godforsaken planet.

Like Mars, the report had said. A few mountains, lots of volcanoes, but for the most part flat and pocked. More atmosphere than Mars. Breathable even. Not nice, though. Not nice at all.

The pictures had clued her in to the starkness, the hellish wasteland quality this place had. There was something stricken about it, something *unholy*. Kozlowski wasn't a religious person, but that was the first word that came to her mind.

Unholy.

Damned, was the second.

Shakespeare could have used it for his "blasted heath" in the play *Macbeth*.

"Still can't see much down there through the cloud cover," Fitzwilliam was saying.

"Anything coming through the telemetry topography scan?" said Tanarez.

"Hey. What do you know? Calculations totally correct. The sucker's down there!"

A thrill of elation filled Kozlowski.

The moment the *Razzia* had entered parking orbit, its heavy-duty sensors, on full power, had gotten to work. The coordinates of the original alien hive were known. And sure enough, it didn't take long to locate the ugly hive, poking up from the flat land like a huge unlanced boil.

"What the hell is this?"

"What?"

"Just take a look, will you!"

Begalli's eyes grew bright with excitement. "I *suspected* as much!"

About a hundred miles away from the original hive, there was another hive. A hive shaped differently from the original, according to the sensors.

Sure enough, up close, the sensors were showing it was indeed an alien hive. So far so good. Now they just had to determine if it was the flavor alien they wanted.

The misty clouds swirled away from the ship, and they got a better view.

Somehow, even from way up here, Kozlowski could tell that things weren't quite right.

"Jeez," she heard Tanarez say. "This unit checks out. So this reading must be correct."

"Yeah? So what's it say?" Fitzwilliam shot back.

"Well, judging from the surface activity." She could hear the slight gulp in Tanarez's voice, breaking up that Yeager effect. "There's some kind of *war* going on down there!"

"Let me look!"

Grant's eyes were suddenly open and eager. He strained forward on his belt, his hands frantically scrabbling at the catches.

"Grant!" she barked at him. "We haven't landed. Keep your goddamned butt parked. We don't want your brains all over the ceiling."

Grant halted his efforts to release himself. Nonetheless, his desire to see what was going on down there had not diminished. "What's going on? Begalli! Talk to me! How does this work into your high-flown theories?"

Begalli was wearing a shit-eating grin. "Couldn't be sweeter, boss."

"We're looking at aliens swarming like ants around a hive and that's supposed to be sweet?" said Grant.

Kozlowski wasn't too worried. They had the technology to deal with this. Just a detail. The brass were going to like this—they were going to be able to check out how well the new stuff worked.

"You bet. You ever hear of the xenos fighting among themselves wholesale, Colonel?"

"Nope. Not the batch that came to Earth."

"Exactly. Because they were all the same breed, the same race. They smelled the same to each other. They worked together. The fact that there's conflict down there tends to prove that what we suspected would happen, has."

"Like *what*?" demanded Jastrow, eyes round and a little protruding with fear.

Kozlowski didn't blame him. Looked like a goddamned African ant war down there. Hundreds and thousands of the bastards, swarming, swarming . . .

"Okay, okay. Classified material. Sorry. Shouldn't have brought it up in front of the troops," said Grant.

That pissed Kozlowski off, but she didn't say anything. Wouldn't do the soldiers any good anyway. Would just take their minds off the job at hand. Nonetheless, she knew what Begalli was talking about, and dammit, it did make sense. She just hoped it wouldn't complicate things, mucking over the mission beyond redemption.

The theory was, of course, that aliens without a controlling queen would branch off into different packs. Breeding might (and apparently did) give rise to bugs with recessive traits. If these bugs were allowed to continue to breed, the result would be a new race . . . and hurry over to start up a new hive, complete with a new queen.

This was a new hive here.

Call them the Democrats.

But apparently, the old fart bugs had gotten things together and spawned a new queen mother . . . and millions of workers. And although the new Democrat hive was a long way away, eventually they'd located it. Their queen mother had sent off her armies to destroy the interlopers into the genetic xeno broth.

Call them the Republicans.

She looked out at the troops. There were naked questions beside the fear and misgiving in their eyes.

"What are you assholes looking at! Plan C takes this kind of situation into account." She smiled grimly. "Just look at it this way . . . We're going to be able to kill more bugs."

"Pardon us, Commander . . ." said Fitzwilliam. "Plan C starts the same way they all do . . . Land as close to the hive as possible. There are thousands of aliens down there now."

Colonel Kozlowski grinned. "And hopefully there will be thousands there when we land—only *burnt* aliens."

Grant shook his head. "Well, I guess those bugs aren't the only specialists in genocide."

They continued their descent.

17

When they were a mile above the hive, the mist had cleared enough to use optical magnifiers to good effect.

Sure enough, there was a war going on down there. As vicious a war as Alex Kozlowski could imagine. Thousands of struggling bugs going at each other.

Fangs and talons.

The ruddy landscape was running with alien parts, alien blood, spasming monsters.

How long had this been going on?

Kozlowski's best guess, offhand, was that this was just the latest of many attacks. She saw alien skeletons littering the landscape. One more battle.

That wasn't all the crew of the *Anteater* saw, though.

"Run this over with me again, Begalli," said Grant.

"Very quickly, sir, the creatures have had a freak genetic offshoot. Normally a queen mother would stamp this out immediately. With no queen mother, though, another colony has been allowed to take root and thrive. As for the possible difference caused by the recessive gene theory . . . we'll just have to examine them closer, won't we."

The most important thing the magnified view on the screen pointed out was that Begalli's theories were entirely correct.

One set of bugs had a vague reddish cast. The rest—the defenders, it could be seen, because they were the ones streaming from the portals of the huge hive below—were the usual dark color that Kozlowski was accustomed to.

Begalli whooped. "What did I tell you. And ten to one, they've got unpredictable internal differences. I can't wait to find out. There's also got to be other kinds of life on this planet that have learned to survive the xenos. If possible, I'd like to check on them."

"Celebrations later, fella. For what I'm not sure. They all look nasty as ever. And as for other forms of life—yeah, I guess the critters have got to eat something. But that's not why we're here, is it?" Kozlowski unhooked her belt and hurried up to a place beside the pilots. "Okay, fellows. I've got this wonderful idea. You usually use force impellers as well as a few retros to land, correct?"

"That's right."

"Anything to stop us from using the thrusters to land? That should cook a lot of them pretty good."

"Sure. Lots of fuel consumption though," said Fitzwilliam.

"We just need enough to get back."

"We've got plenty to spare for that," said Tanarez. "I could do a configuration of the primaries and tertiaries that would do the trick."

"Good. Then do it. Burn the bastards, and make sure they're well done."

"Okay. That looks like the main entrance to the hive. Not as close as we'd like, but it's the only option," said Fitzwilliam.

"That'll be just fine," Kozlowski said after studying the computer schematics that the pilot had called up on the screen to illustrate the lay of the land.

"You'd better sit back down, Colonel, and buckle that seat belt. Rockets are a little bit rougher than force impellers . . ." suggested Fitzwilliam.

"So I've noticed."

The craft was rumbling and rocking like a son of a bitch. Kozlowski stumble-walked back to her chair, strapped herself in again, and watched the action, eyes gleaming.

The *Anteater* slowed down.

There was a mighty wrenching as the rockets cut in. Fitzwilliam was right. It felt like they were riding a jackhammer down. She had to clench her teeth to keep them from rattling.

She looked up to the magnification screen. The bugs had stopped fighting. Some were waving their heads, as though attempting to look up, to make out the source of the terrible rumbling in the sky with their primitive photosensors.

"I hope the bastards don't have the sense to run," she said under her breath.

"Unfortunately, the instinct for survival is paramount in the creatures," said Begalli, above the roar. "They're disoriented, but as soon as they sense the presence of the ship, they'll start to scatter. Fortunately, there are enough of them clustered that they can't scatter fast."

"Can we go down quicker?" said Kozlowski, excited.

"Not and get the effect you want!" screamed Fitzwilliam.

"Besides, we want 'em good and crisp! We don't want any of that blood eating away at the hull or support struts," said Tanarez.

True. Very true. C'mon, Koz. Use your head . . . not your hate and bloodlust.

She looked up again at the screen.

The shadow of the craft showed now, spread like a blot on the land and the mass of aliens.

Who began to scurry.

The shadow narrowed, darkened.

"Shit!" cried Tanarez. "That outcropping over there!"

"Yeah. I see it," said the other pilot. "I'll take her another twenty-five meters away. Tight fit, but I can land this baby on a dime."

The confidence in Fitzwilliam's voice encouraged her.

She could feel the shift of the ship. It slewed sideways, and started down again.

Catching a bunch of the bugs by surprise.

The tongues of intense puce and orange and

ocher shot down to the ground, licking across the
arid ground.

Lapping at the creatures.

Unable to take her eyes off the scene, she
watched as the rocket flames covered and consumed hundreds of the beasts. Hundreds more not
directly in the fires nonetheless burst into incandescence at the horrible heat.

Fried.

"Incredible," she whispered.

She watched as long as she was able as the
aliens were immolated. A black swath of alien
ash . . . lovely. The *Anteater*, in just a minute, had
wiped out enough to fill a couple of nests back
home.

Unfortunately, it looked like there were plenty
left to take their place.

"Hold a moment. Scorch the ground a little
more before we land," said Fitzwilliam. "We've got
about all we can. I just want to make sure these below are properly cooked."

"Sure."

The craft jerked, and hung for just a few seconds.

Smoke was curling up now past the viewports,
obscuring the scene. Kozlowski closed her eyes.
Afterimages of the skeletal demons torching up
flickered across her vision.

Then the ship descended again, this time landing on its struts with a wobbling jolt. It swayed,
then stilled.

A red light shifted on.

"All right, grunts!" snapped Kozlowski. "We've

got ourselves an emergency combat landing on our hands. It's *showtime!*"

Now everything was in the hands of an Irishman named Seamus O'Connor—and the marvelous new technology at his fingertips. O'Connor was a guy she didn't know that well. He was a technician who'd helped develop the procedure he was about to use, a sandy-haired gentleman with a soft voice and a twinkle to his eyes in social situations, but a rock-solid attitude of concentration during briefings and exercise. He looked like the kind of person who got a job done, and then went off to the pub to play pipes and whistles and have a few pints.

She looked out at the heaving mass of aliens, outlines in the soot. And if that didn't work, they might as well just take off again out of here!

"All right, O'Connor," Fitzwilliam's voice crackled through the 'lobephone. "I've cut the engines. The smoke is pretty much dissipated. "Do your duty before any of the things put on their boots and stomp back in."

"Roger, Skipper."

Corporal Seamus O'Connor scratched his beard. He adjusted his grav-chair for a better view of the control panel. He'd been training for this moment for months in virtual reality sims. Unfortunately, somehow it wasn't quite the same here. He'd never had xenos crawling all over the place before. He'd never had a field of dismembered and burnt bugs to negotiate before.

What O'Connor operated were the PEHs—the Perimeter Extension Harpoons. The marines had learned pretty damned quick that in dealing with hostile life forms—i.e., bugs—force fields were quite useful. They'd been in use to a certain extent in the routine humdrum of company galactic life, but as soon as the nasty things with a penchant for destruction were discovered, necessity became the mother of invention yet again. Power was increased, but in landings like this one it was rapidly discovered that the Fields could only be beamed out a short circumference around the ship. In situations involving the need for expanded territory, their reach had to be expanded.

Some kind of fence had to be constructed, utilizing force-field generating devices. However, in a theoretical hostile situation, neither men nor robots could be expected to trundle out and erect these posts.

Hence the harpoons.

They'd been tested before in the field, of course. Out in deserts and plains, among rocks and what have you. You just played Moby Dick, and shot them out to likely-looking spots. When they thunked in properly, you pressed a button for remote control and—ZAP. You had yourself a wide but snug little force-field cap within which to work.

O'Connor's job now was to get those harpoons out.

He touched a button and the ports opened.

He did a quick analysis, adjusted the aim, said a prayer . . .

And fired.

Four harpoons—each seven meters tall and two thick—burst from their ports, sailed out into the alien atmosphere, trailing their power cables like baited hooks tossed from fishing rods.

They sailed majestically and gorgeously.

C'mon you beauties, thought O'Connor.

Hit your marks.

The sharp points, capable of boring into rock, struck the surface of the alien planet and—marvel of marvels—stuck.

"Bull's-eye!" O'Connor cried.

The radio crackled. "No time to rest on your laurels. Looks like those bugs haven't been discouraged much. They're coming back in!"

"No problem!"

O'Connor leaned over and pulled the switch.

The posts sparked. A shimmer of power traveled down the lines, and then spread like electric coloring in water, connecting the posts, the cables, and swirling along the ground.

"Outwall activation has been initiated," O'Connor reported, a note of triumph in his voice.

Dozens of aliens caught in the power grid were simply sheered in half. Others heading back in toward the lander simply bounced off the field, limbs and heads bent or smoking.

O'Connor grinned to himself, and put the field on automatic. He'd done his job.

Now the troops were going to have to do theirs.

This was why they had worn their suits:

So they could go into action at a moment's notice.

"We've got some cleaning up to do, people," said Kozlowski, motioning for the troops to hurry along into the hangar deck. "This is what we came to do."

The rest of the crew already had their helmets on, so she couldn't see what their faces registered.

"It's why we're drawing a salary."

She put her own helmet on, tongued on communications.

"Gentlemen," she said. "I do believe we're ready."

"Roger, Colonel. Hatchway opening initiated."

The carbines, plasma rifles, and other automatic weapons of the assembled rattled upward, positioning themselves for firing.

No depressurization was necessary. However the PSIs were not the same, so there was a distinct escape of air as the hatchway opened. A chiaroscuro of dark colors and smoke wavered between them and distant jagged rotten-tooth mountains. Before her oxygen-rich mix started to whisper through her suit's ducts, she fancied she smelled the land beyond.

Burnt carbon.

Burnt silicon.

Alien acid.

Never-ending death beneath an eldritch, evil sun.

She had a regulation upper-pill in her hand, ready to take it. Looking out, though, she realized she didn't really need it. She threw it away.

A surge of victory ran through her.

"C'mon, people," she snapped through her microphone, staccato calling of a parade into a battle on shores not made for humans. "Let's earn some money."

18

The operation was basically a clean-up proposition.

The landing had cindered hundreds of the bugs. The force-field perimeter had locked out the remainder. Only about twenty-five of the aliens had made it past the harpoons before the field crackled on.

These were the current targets.

These were the bugs that had to be crushed.

Vague colorings or internal differences didn't seem to matter. From the way these things acted, all were every centimeter the crazed berserkers their cousins were.

The lip of the ramp had not been touched down, and one of them leapt on it, scuttling up toward them, slavering and tearing away at the air.

"Simultaneous!" she cried and lifted her own rifle and fired.

The blast of weapons was so strong converging on the bug that the force lifted the thing up a good meter and slammed it back another ten. Damned good thing, too. It disintegrated into a splatter of parts and blood in midair.

"Keep that shit off the hull!" Kozlowski cried. "Okay now, move it!"

As practiced before, the troops moved out, plasma weapons first. A robo-wagon trundled out after them, bearing extra weapons, supplies, and automatic support keyed from the *Anteater*. As soon as the first four marines cleared the bottom of the ramp, they started blasting. A wave of fire, like a manic flamethrower on amphetamines, roared out, whacking into a group of five bugs scampering into the melee.

They all fell apart in the hellish fire.

Kozlowski and the others were out in a flash, bringing up the rear and selecting targets. Kozlowski felt as though she'd just downed a couple tabs of Xeno-Zip. Adrenaline? Yes, and bliss, too. It had been a long time since she'd fought real xenos, and there was nothing like the satisfaction of the prospect of one's slugs putting out the lights on a bug to get a gal's heart to thumpin'.

"Fire at will!" she said.

She jumped off the ramp and swiveled over to cover the underside of the lander. A space of about seven meters existed between the base of the lander and the ground. All in shadow. Unlikely that any had scuttled under here, but you never knew.

She nudged the correct com switch. "Turn on the bottom lights, Control!"

"Roger."

The lights started to blink on, but even before they were up, through the heightened "ears" of the suit, she heard the telltale hissing.

"Damn!"

One was coming toward her.

They had descended to Mission Control, to stand and watch beside Corporal Seamus O'Connor as the monitors flashed the frenetic details of the conflict.

Daniel Grant felt giddy victory turn his skin to goose pumps.

What a spectacle!

Whatever doubts he'd ever felt about the competency of this batch of marines disappeared within seconds as the group fanned out in perfect formation, their weapons efficiently blasting away. Out in the open, the alien strategy seemed simple: charge and destroy. The Marine strategy seemed equally simple: blast the things to bits.

The marines acted like precision-sensored robots. Their aims were deadly. Like a phalanx of destruction, they performed this grisly, pyrotechnic ballet. Grant suddenly wished for some appropriate music. Sturm und drang!

O'Connor was clearly equally impressed. "Wow." He turned to Dr. Begalli. "Those suits you produced are working great. Used to be, you couldn't fight these things in such close quarters."

Indeed, Grant noted.

As the radium bullets, the plasma blasts, and the

tossed explosives struck the aliens, rupturing the chitinous material of their exoskeletons, they tended to burst apart like ripe tomatoes atop M-80s. Their "blood"—a viscous green ichor—hurled every which way, slapping across the white armor and helmets the marines wore.

The skin of the suit ruptured, fluid leaked out, instantly neutralizing the horrible full-bore effects of the acid. Then the skin "healed." And voilà—no harm done to the marine. Nonetheless, the troops seemed to be trying for the knees and the heads, as Colonel Kozlowski had instructed them, waiting till the aliens were prone before they blasted the torso apart.

Whatever they were doing, whatever the plan had been, it seemed to be working just fine. True, the alien blood was leaving pocks and craters in the ground, but the soldiers were trained to deal with them.

Particularly impressive in his efforts was Corporal Henrikson. Like some military juggernaut he moved over the battlescape with fierce speed and agility, his plasma rifle snuffing out aliens and putting them to fiery deaths in what seemed like speeded-up film.

"Man," said Grant. "Look at Henrikson go!"

"Quite something," said Begalli. "He's a regular one-man army."

"I've heard rumors. Some of the troops think he's a synthetic," said O'Connor.

"What the hell does it matter?" said Grant. "He's doing his job and damned well!"

Dr. Begalli shook his head. "True. True. With soldiers like that, we're going to get into the nest."

Grant looked up just in time to see an odd look pass over Begalli's face. A squinting feral look, like a rat considering the implications of a maze—and looking forward as much to shitting in the passageways as to getting to the cheese at the other end.

But then, Begalli had always struck him as one odd customer, and so he just set the observance aside and turned back to this marvelous bloody sport up there on the screen.

All he needed now was a beer and some peanuts!

It was a big one.

The alien under the lander scrabbled for Kozlowski like some frenetic dinosaur closing in for the kill on what it considered a soft-bellied mammal.

"Just try, asshole," said Kozlowski, whipping her gun up.

The lights came on full bore, stopping the thing not one stride, but illuminating it thoroughly.

She fired.

The burst of bullets from her semiautomatic rifle fanned out perfectly. Textbook. The explosive slugs caught the thing in the kneecaps, exploding them. The beast went down, snarling and hissing, scrabbling for her without missing a beat.

She drew a bead on its bananalike head and squeezed off another burst. The thrill of competency seized her as the head burst apart. The blast kicked back a dollop of blood onto her suit.

Her reaction was knee-jerk terror. Experience had taught her that a burst of xeno blood on armor meant trouble.

Then her brain kicked in, salving her trained reaction with reality: this was a special suit.

Time to see if it worked. The guinea pig: herself.

The junk immediately sizzled and bubbled through the plastic lining. Like oozing pus, the neutralizing agent flowed out, and swallowed the acid.

Sizzle.

Bubble.

The plastic shell moved back over the hole and the suit was whole again.

Unfortunately, there wasn't a lot of time to feel good about it. Already three more aliens were running her way underneath the lander. She picked off the right one. Knees. Head. Torso. The weapons these days were so *good*. The shells just cut through that damned exoskeleton like it was the thinnest of tin. So *satisfying* just seeing them *burst* like that.

Overripe gourds in a shooting gallery!

Another soldier was beside her.

The nametag read MAHONE.

No discussion. Just quick efficient drawing of a bead, and then her gun coughed off, dealing amazing damage to the beast to their left.

They swiveled as one, and their fire converged on the central alien, only five yards away now.

The strength of their blasting shattered the thing, and its blood blew back as well, among the tumble and tatters of its wasted body.

"He looked like my last boyfriend!" said Mahone over the radio, her voice sounding immensely satisfied.

"No," said Kozlowski. "Seems to me the others look more like boyfriends."

"Yeah. I think you're right. Let's waste 'em!"

Mahone's grin showed through her faceplate.

However, before they could go and look for any more, a voice crackled over Kozlowski's radio. "Colonel. We got one on the ship!"

"Damn," said Kozlowski. "Not good!" She turned to Mahone. "Stay here and cover me. I have to check this out."

"Roger."

She turned and started running for the other side of the ramp to gain a vantage point on the situation.

Intellectually she'd been aware that the gravity here was only .9 of Earth Standard. However, she was shocked at how quickly she was able to move. True, these suits were a little lighter than she was used to . . .

She didn't complain at all. She just had to adjust herself accordingly.

"Okay, hotshots," she said to a soldier she immediately recognized as Jastrow. "What's going on?"

Things looked pretty well contained. The rest of the bunch were killing either the last standing alien, or raking their weapons across the remains of ones already shot down, making sure they were dead.

Jastrow pointed. Sweat dripped down his temples and forehead despite his suit's air-conditioning. Kozlowski followed the direction of his forefinger.

The xeno had somehow leapt up to one of the gemlike pilot blisters. Its talons were scratching

along the structural spokes and its tail whipped
hard against the material, attempting to break
through.

Even as she stood, considering, Private Ellis
puffed up, raising his rifle.

"Hold on, soldier," said Kozlowski, holding out a
halting hand. "Shoot the thing with that, we'll have
bug blood all over the hull."

Bang! Bang! The tail whipped the blister. Probably giving the pilots fits.

"Jastrow! Haul the wagon over here," she commanded.

Speedily, the private obeyed, grabbing hold of the
robo-wagon. Kozlowski punched open a latch, lifted
the lid, looked.

Selected what she needed.

The thing was like a squarish grenade launcher,
with various tangly things extruding. She picked it
up, put it up against her shoulder, aimed at the of-
fending alien, and fired.

The projectile that shot out progressed half the
distance in a blur, but then at the top of its trajec-
tory bloomed out into a net drawn by three guided
bolos. Expertly directed, they whacked past the
bug, scooped it up in the net.

Electricity arced and zapped.

The bug was pried off its hold, and carried off
meters away to bounce hard upon the land. It
rolled, and lay there, just a faint hiss and crackle
emerging.

"Dead?" asked Jastrow.

"No way," Kozlowski said. "I doubt it. The electri-
cal charge in the mesh is probably just enough to
stun it."

"What should we do?"

Kozlowski considered.

Her first inclination was to just kill it. Quick. However, she well knew that Grant was watching the proceedings, and may want to imprison it with a force field in order that his scientist could examine it. She tongued her com unit, hating having to do it.

However, like a bolt out of the blue, before she could do a damned thing, a plasma blast fried the bug and the net.

She swung around to see the perpetrator of this, wondering whether to chew the soldier out or thank him.

Standing there, looking totally competent and unfazed, was Corporal Henrikson.

"It looked like it was about to break free, Colonel," the man said.

The colonel shrugged. "Yeah. Next time, though, check with me."

"Sure."

She looked around the field of devastation.

The bugs were squashed here, totally.

She took her helmet off and sniffed.

"Ah. What a stench," she said. "Nothing like it in the universe."

19

Soldiers, still helmeted and suited up, were carrying burnt and destroyed bodies of the enemy to collect them in a single pile. A vehicle was building a border of dirt around this pile, to prevent any possible spread of lingering acid.

Although he wore no suit, Daniel Grant *had* taken the precaution of donning acid-neutralizing boots. What with the lower gravity, though, he did not notice the extra weight or bulk.

On alien soil.

Grant had been born on a colony, but his own homeworld had not been that much different from Earth. His years on Earth had made him feel like a native. So it was an odd sensation indeed to actually be walking on ground so far from home, and so distinctly different in taste, touch, smell, and general atmosphere. Too, there could be no doubt that he was walking over a battlefield now.

Or that another war entirely was going on beyond the background buzz of the force-field perimeter.

Tune that out for now, man, he told himself. Take it a step at a time. Right now you're a lot safer here than you were back on Earth with that gangster Fisk breathing down your neck!

A couple of the troops were standing by the edge of the encampment, looking out past the clear shimmer of the force field to the events beyond.

Swarms of bugs were moving, dodging and sparring, occasionally dashing out and tearing one another to bits. Not exactly a melee, and the oddest battle that Daniel Grant had ever witnessed. Flashes of green and black. Fillips of splashed blood. Limbs flying and occasionally crackling into the field, bouncing back off in a spray of sparks, singed.

"Sun's up. Clouds are off," said Private Jastrow. "Feels good."

"What, you're enjoying a nice sunbath?" said Private Ellis, sarcastic. "God knows what kind of deadly radiation is coming down from that sun!"

"Like this whole planet is a health spa! Look, Ellis. You take your pleasure where you can get it! I'm taking mine here! Right now!" He held his arms outstretched. "Ah! Wonderful! I may come back with a tan."

"Just be happy if you come back."

"Actually, Ellis, I gotta tell you. I'm feeling relief. Great relief."

"Heaven's sake, *why*?"

"Everything is working great. That last bit wasn't so bad. Not too bad at all." Jastrow smiled. "Hell, this operation's going to be a cinch."

Ellis looked out at the mass of bugs, the hive, the stricken panorama. "Yeah . . . right."

Grant stepped up to them. "Hello, gentlemen. I just wanted to tell you how much I appreciate your work today."

They spun around, slightly alarmed. "Mr. Grant!" said Jastrow.

"Sorry to creep up on you like that. I didn't mean to, really. I just want to personally congratulate you. I was watching you guys. All of you. On the screens. You operated like a well-oiled, absolutely brilliant machine. It's good to be working with such fine people like you."

The two could not help but break out into broad smiles. "Thanks, Mr. Grant," said Jastrow.

"You know, you two may not be in the marines all your lives. Whenever you're out, Grant Industries is probably going to have positions for guys like you."

"That's *wonderful!*"

"So just keep up the good work!"

He moved away, to go have a look at what was going on at the side of the *Anteater*. That little speech should help boost the morale. Those two would probably spread it among the others, and he would be happy to repeat it. It wasn't bullshit, either. He really meant it. He'd be happy to hire all of these people.

First thing he'd do was set them on that maniac Fisk.

On the side of the lander, a huge portion of

metal had flipped down on hinges, exposing a bank of gleaming guns. A regular arsenal.

Grant felt a lilt to his step, a bounce to his walk as he approached.

In the command control area behind this array of weaponry, Sergeant Argento was doing a double check to systems.

"Looks like some mean machines here, Sarge," said Grant.

"That they are, Mr. Grant!" Argento said from beneath his drooping black mustache.

"What's the plan?"

"Pretty simple. We've got about seventy more yards to go before we can start thinking about getting into the hive entrance. Unfortunately, there's a lot of activity going on out there, what with alien species war going on."

"So I've noticed. Lovely to see them going at each other, instead of at us."

"Yes, sir. Well, we synchronize openings in the field to allow for explosive discharges. Then we bomb the territory between us and the top of the entrance, to clear off as many bugs as possible. Once the things are either dead or scattered, we blow out another PEH. Sink it in, turn it on—extend the force-field perimeter. Little trickier on this kind of rock but nothing harder than what we've just accomplished, really."

"And then we go for the gold."

"Exactly."

The silvery weaponry gleamed in the alien sun, sparkling with promise.

Grant gave the sergeant a thumbs-up sign.

"Here's to a campaign without a hitch."

"Yes, sir." Argento returned the gesture. "Without a hitch and then back home for the biggest party in one of your best casinos."

"You've been to one of my casinos, Argento?"

"Yes, sir. The Beach Blossom, last year. Lost my shirt, but I had the time of my life!" Argento was grinning, showing even, white teeth.

"You don't know how happy I am to hear that, my friend. Yes, an excellent concept. A party for you all . . . At my casino, the Beach Blossom at New Atlantic City!"

"Without a hitch!"

"That's right, soldier! That's pretty much what I promised your commanders before we started this trip—and now, thanks to the wonderful technology here, look where we are!"

He walked over and stood just meters away from a red and a black alien, slashing at each other.

It was like watching a movie.

He felt totally safe.

He put his hands on his hips and laughed.

Piece of cake!

They were playing horseshoes outside the lander.

Alex Kozlowski wasn't quite sure where they'd gotten the stuff. Probably fashioned it in the metal shop on board the *Razzia* for just such a possibility, and then stashed the stuff on the *Anteater*.

Clang!

Private Ellis's throw was a ringer, twirling around the post.

"Good shot!" said Jastrow.

Cheers arose from the audience.

Those two! What a pair! When they'd asked permission to set up the game, Kozlowski's first inclination was to say no. However, the pressures were so much that she not only assented, but went the next step.

Why not a picnic? The clouds had cleared and there was a sun shining through. They'd done the first part of the mission extremely well, and there was still a few hours till the rest of the operation could be properly set up.

So, instead of making her marines eat their meal inside the cold and antiseptic *Anteater*, she'd allowed the sandwiches and sodas to be set up on a folding table just outside the ramp. You had to be a little careful—if something went wrong with those force fields, you wanted to be able to make it back into the hold of the lander ASAP.

Jastrow finished his game, then moved to stand by the force field of the perimeter with his saxophone. He serenaded the aliens with John Coltrane-like free form squawking, with an occasionally more melodic passage thrown in for fun.

She was eating a tasteless sandwich layered with energy-rich Vit-C sauce for a boost, listening to Jastrow's jazz, and along with some heavily carbed macro-drink, when Daniel Grant sidled up, chomping confidently on his sandwich.

"Regular holiday."

"A bit bizarre, I agree," she said. "They need it though. There's worse ahead. Much worse."

"What? Things are going great."

"Grant. This is a war. Already we weren't quite expecting conflict on this level. Me, I would have preferred to wait until these things killed each other, then moved in."

Grant shook his head. "Not in the schedule. Things like fuel involved . . . money . . . time . . . Most especially time." His jaws worked thoughtfully around a mouthful of sandwich. "I don't have much time, back on Earth. Can't waste any hovering above this Hiveworld. Wonder what's going on back there, anyway."

"Maybe you better concentrate on this particular hellhole."

"Yeah right. But I came here because I need to talk to you a moment."

"You are talking to me."

"Alone, I mean. Not in earshot of the troops."

"Ah." She examined her wristwatch. She was out of her suit, taking the opportunity for a little bit of freedom. She didn't know how long she was going to be in next time she donned the thing. Probably *too* long. "How about inside the ship?" She wasn't that crazy about it out here now, anyway. Sun or no sun. Those bugs crawling and lumbering and fighting out there *bothered* her, dammit.

"That will be just fine."

She took another bite, another sip, nonchalantly gestured for him to follow.

Even as she walked into the locker room, she felt a little better. There was the smell of B.O. and gym shorts, sure, but at least it was human and familiar. The whiff of those bugs out there triggered all her inner alarms.

She spun on him, slapping her fingers clear of crumbs. "What's up, Grant?"

He sat down on a bench. "These troops . . . they're good."

"You're telling me something I don't know?"

"I'm sure they're going to pull this mission off, just fine."

"I sure as hell hope so. You dragged me in here to tell you *that*?"

Grant got up and began to pace.

"I don't know. That sabotage thing has got me worried."

"Consider yourself reassured. I think if they were going to strike, it would have been by now. Besides, think about this one, Grant. Right now, the numbers are down. They're in the same boat we are. We sink, they sink." She shrugged. "Besides, if there is a saboteur, I'd be happy to lay odds that it's one of your scientist bozos. Now there is a collection of premium losers."

"We do have a scientist along, remember. Begalli."

"Rat-face. Yeah. I'm watching him, don't worry. I'm watching everybody. But take it from me. I'm watching my own ass most of all."

"Me, too! It *is* a nice one."

She laughed out loud. "You're a hard case. Even while you're sober, and I smell like a horse after the Derby."

"You smell fine."

She nodded. "That's what Michaels used to say."

"Michaels?"

"Peter Michaels. Old lover. We used to fight together. Hell, we used to *waste* those bug hives, he and I. What a team." She shook her head. "God, we got into this incredible habit. After a gig, we'd come back. We'd be so hot, we didn't even bother to shower. We just stripped our suits and screwed. Sheesh. Couple of crazy horny kids."

She looked over at him. His face had turned a bright pink.

"Something wrong, Grant."

"Nothing. Nothing, Alex. Only . . ." He smiled. "I know women. Sorry about the old drunken stupor the other night, but you know, you're not bad-looking . . . And you're pretty damned tough and not exactly the most feminine creature I've ever encountered . . . I like you. Moreover . . . I think you like me. I can sense these kinds of things, kiddo. So I was wondering, once this is all over . . ."

"You touch me, you asshole, and I'll cut your genitals off and stick them up your nose."

He shrugged. "Just thought I'd try." He got up to go. "Well, off to my possible death."

She stepped over, spun him around, yanked his head down, and devoured his mouth with hers.

Just as the surprise wore off and Grant warmed up to the osculation, she pushed him away so hard he almost tumbled over the bench.

"God!" he said, catching his balance. "What was *that* all about?"

"Just don't let it go to your head, okay?" She smoothed her mussed hair and stormed from the room, enormously upset at herself.

She'd liked that a lot, dammit.

20

The troops were lined up and ready, their helmets back on and properly secured, their weapons cocked, primed, fully loaded and hungry for action.

A silence descended upon the troops, bordered by the buzz of the force fields and the snarling tumult of the fighting aliens between them and the entrance to the blacks' monolithic hive.

Kozlowski could feel their tension.

Or was it just her *own* tension, multiplied by twenty-five? This was going to be the make-or-break of the mission.

Thankfully, the ranks of the bugs had thinned somewhat. Whether many of them had simply been killed or crawled into holes somewhere she didn't know. She just hoped they hadn't gone into the hive.

She tongued her comm. "Troops ready."

The bounce-back from Control Central. "All set here." O'Connor's brogue. "Sergeant Argento?"

She looked back to where the sergeant sat, behind his banks of big weapons.

"Guns are sighted and ready," said Argento, fingers playing expertly across the controls. "I don't see a more optimum time."

Kozlowski looked up. She could have wished for a little more light. The clouds had closed back up, tight.

Oh, well, it didn't really matter that much. They had a good five hours till darkness. That would be more than enough time.

"Right," came O'Connor's voice. "Opening force-field apertures."

Kozlowski looked up toward the top of the force field. The field looked like a thin wavering skein of gray normally. It would open just—

There!

A wide hole sphinctered, and Argento wasted no time.

The big guns thundered.

The many millimetered shells sailed out perfectly, hammering onto the landscape. Whole clusters of bugs were destroyed, even more thrown back in the explosions.

More shells, differently directed, hammered out of the guns, exploded on the landscape.

When the smoke cleared, Kozlowski saw that a wide swath had been cleared. A trail of craters lay in the valley that led up to the opening of the hive.

"Harpoon away!" called O'Connor.

The appropriately aimed gun on the side of the lander thumped. Amid an explosion of gases, the harpoon launched. It sailed over their heads swiftly and majestically, trailing its cable like a kite caught in a gale. It threaded the hole in the force field easily and whooshed toward its target.

Even back here, many meters away, Kozlowski could hear the large harpoon thunk into place, burying itself in the ground right on target.

A hearty "Hurrah" sounded from the troops.

"We have a successful landing!" chirped O'Connor's voice. "Prepare for perimeter extension."

The troops grew quiet. Kozlowski braced herself, getting her rifle ready. Theoretically, when O'Connor pushed the right combination of switches and levers, the force field would move out like an arcing gate—only expanding as it did so.

Whacking all bugs en route.

However, in the activity, there was always the possibility that one of the aliens would slip through unharmed. That alien would have to be dealt with, immediately, hence the preparedness of the troops.

She could see the force field flicker erratically as it moved.

"Take it a little slower," she instructed.

"Can't," replied O'Connor.

With a whoosh, the force field was patterning out and then—*snap!*—was in place.

Leaving behind a scattered handful of aliens, in various states of disrepair and shock.

"Kill 'em," said Kozlowski.

The troops moved forward, bullets and plasma leaping out to smack into the survivors. It was all over in a matter of moments, bug pieces scattered to the winds of destruction.

And the force fields were buzzing away, the tunnel within easy striking distance.

"Yes!" Private Ellis's fist smote the air.

Cheers broke out among them all as they broke ranks and several broke out and headed deeper into the newly taken territory.

"Wait a minute, you assholes!" screeched Kozlowski. "I didn't order you . . ."

The force field wavered.

The troops all stopped in their tracks.

Kozlowski could *feel* something wrong before she saw anything.

But when she saw it, what was wrong was pretty obvious.

The newly planted harpoon was starting to list.

"What the hell—"

"Shit, what's going on—?"

"Oh, my God! We couldn't see it when it struck . . ."

"The thing landed on a couple of intact bugs."

That was the only explanation, and the veracity of it, and its implications swept through Kozlowski like electricity.

"Fall *back*!" she cried.

The alien acid must be eating through the base . . .

The upright harpoon shifted more, and the force field flickered again.

Then the thing toppled, its extended antenna breaking up.

The southern force field went down.

For a terrible moment she felt like an EVA astronaut with her suit ripped off.

"Get back to the original lines!" she screamed.

At first the surrounding bugs didn't seem to notice. But then, with the damnable speed of their breed, they perceived that the strange almost-invisible wall that had kept them from new prey had evaporated.

A few tentatively began to straggle toward the troops.

The soldiers who had gone the farthest out turned to run back. The aliens coming through seemed to sense their fear. They loped forward in the attack.

"Cover them!" screamed Kozlowski. She fired a volley as close to the troops as she dared, catching a couple of the bugs in their thoraxes, stopping them cold.

But others took their places.

"Okay!" she said after chinning her com. "They're past the original wall. Get that back up."

"Trying," said O'Connor. "Something's short-circuited!"

"*Do* it, dammit!"

"Argento!" said O'Connor. "Get that other harpoon off. That will do the trick."

By this time, Kozlowski had her hands too full to make commands, let alone comments.

The bugs were starting to come in.

Not the whole horde, thank God, or they'd be as good as dead.

She started blasting, just hoping her people had the sense to come in out of the storm.

"Shit!" said Daniel Grant. He pounded his hand hard against a bulkhead. "Shit shit *shit*!"

"Steady, Mr. Grant," said Dr. Begalli. "I'm sure they've got alternative plans."

O'Connor was leaning forward, stabbing at the controls. "Goddammit, Argento. Fire the thing! Manually!"

A voice crackled over the radio. "Can't. Can't find an opening. The things are swarming back into the crater."

"Then *make* an opening!" said O'Connor. "That's what you've got the starboard guns for. Blow 'em off!"

Grant watched disbelievingly.

Without a hitch.

Falling apart. Right before his eyes. If those troopers came out of this one without a casualty, it would be a miracle.

The point man—the one the farthest out—had to turn and blast with his weapons.

Grant watched with helpless horror as a bug scuttled up the backs of two of its fellows and leapt high into the air, landing directly on the man's back.

The soldier fought.

Grant had never seen such a fight.

Even though suddenly the aliens were all around him, like ants around a lump of sugar, they quaked and blew apart from the plasma blaster.

Then the havoc there stilled, and Grant could see the things scrabbling away, carrying bloody bits of suit, and pieces of the soldier, like trophies.

He had to turn away.

Without a hitch.

He'd never before seen his optimism turn to sewage, right before his eyes. His stomach turned, and he felt as though he was going to throw up. He contained himself, though. He reached down deep for strength, found it.

"Hell with the perimeter. Just have him blast those things! Cover the retreat!"

"I'm sure Argento is doing what he can."

"Look, can you get at least a *partial* up. Use what you got, man! Give them some time!"

He'd come light-years with these people, eaten with them, come to respect them in an odd but compelling way. And now they were being torn apart before his eyes.

O'Connor nodded. "I can try, sir. I can try."

Sergeant Argento cursed.

How the hell was he going to kill all these bugs alone? Should he start blasting, like O'Connor seemed to want—or should he clear out a crater and send off a harpoon?

He decided to do both. He blasted away with all the guns, making sure he didn't hit any of the troops. The shells streaked out, scattering whole swaths of bugs, and making craters.

Not exactly as far as they would like, not as close to the entrance of the hive as they needed—

But it would have to do.

He sent off another volley.

Excellent! It was giving the troops a fighting chance.

He swiveled the guns slightly to the right, concentrated on aiming—

And then heard the hissing.

Damn!

He reached down for his hand weapon and spun

around, but it was too late. The bug jumped down from the hull of the *Anteater* like a spider pouncing on its prey.

Its secondary set of jaws rammed through Argento's neck, speckling his guns with rich arterial blood.

They were moving back.

She'd watched Rodriguez go down. Go down bravely and well, taking a lot of bugs with him and maybe giving them a second or two extra to retreat. No time to grieve now, Kozlowski knew.

It was time to fight.

And she'd never fought quite like this before in her life.

Her rifle was discharging so quickly she could feel the heat come off the thing even through the gloves of her suit. With skill and precision she didn't know she had, she slammed away at the monsters, blowing them apart as fast as they came at her.

The thing was, she didn't have to think about what she was doing, it was all coming automatically. Because of these suits, the acid-splatter factor was not significant. She didn't have to aim at the knees, and then finish with their heads. She could just keep the rifle level and rip off fire at precisely the moment her instincts and skill dictated.

All the rest of the soldiers seemed to be doing equally well. The aliens were going down in huge numbers. The problem was that their numbers kept on getting replenished.

Sensing something on her peripheral vision, she wheeled around and found one of the bugs almost on top of her, its gooey saliva dripping as though in preparation for a feast.

She fed it a blast of plasma.

The thing's head lifted up off its neck in the gout of fire and flipped back like some obscene rocket aborting in its takeoff. She ripped off another round of fire to give herself some breathing room, and then took stock of the situation.

They'd all made it back to within the original perimeter . . . all but one.

Private Jastrow was just outside the area, his rifle blasting away.

"Jastrow!" she said. "Step back, dammit! Step back so we can put the field on!"

The man's radio apparently was not working. He did not respond. He just kept firing away at the things.

She was going to have to go out there and *drag* him back in, dammit. She started wading through the pile-up of dead bugs, firing away, then stopped dead as she looked back in the direction she was going.

The bugs covered Jastrow.

One was blasted away, but another took its place.

The radio screeched. "Ellis! Ellis, I need some backup! Ellis!" There was a muffled scream, signaling the end of a jazzman's military career.

"Argento! Start pounding the perimeter wall!" Kozlowski radioed.

No response.

What had happened to the guns, dammit! What was going on!

"Argento! Push them back with the guns!"

Another voice on the radio: "Argento's down, Colonel. There's a bug up there!"

Shit. Only one recourse now.

"O'Connor! Reactivate the southern wall! ASAP!"

Another bug charged her, dripping with human blood.

For some reason, Daniel Grant could not take his eyes off the gory demise of Private Jastrow.

He was stricken by grief, an unfamiliar emotion. He'd actually liked Jastrow, he suddenly realized. He hadn't realized before that he could *like* anybody. That concept just didn't seem appropriate to the kind of businessman he was.

He felt helpless. If only he could do something!

Then he heard Colonel Kozlowski's command come in.

At least she was still alive.

"Will do, Colonel," said O'Connor. "I've got the thing rerouted, and I think it's possible."

No more from the colonel. Grant watched as she swiveled and her plasma rifle shredded an approaching alien.

O'Connor leaned forward, hand outstretched toward the switch that would effect the renewal of the force field.

Dr. Begalli reached forward and stopped him. "Wait!" he said.

"Wait my ass! What's going on?" said Grant. "More and more of those things are starting to notice the breech. You've got to close it up. Lives are being lost down there!"

O'Connor reached for the switch again.

Begalli said, "No!"

Grant stood up and pulled Begalli back. "What are you trying to do, Doctor?"

But O'Connor paused as well. "He's right!"

"Right? What are you talking about?"

"Marines!" said O'Connor through his headset. "Get someone up on those guns!"

"What are you doing?" demanded Grant.

"Dr. Begalli's right, Mr. Grant. There are too many of those bastards down there. Only thing that's going to kick them out is that gun array. First off, there's going to have to be someplace to go to. Second place, using those guns with the force field up full is damned dangerous to the lander. *That's* what Dr. Begalli means."

Begalli looked furtive about the whole thing. "Uhm . . . Yes, of course. That's what I mean."

"Does the colonel know that?"

"Yes, sir," said O'Connor. "They *all* know that."

When she killed the alien that almost got her, Kozlowski didn't have time to enjoy its death throes.

"Get that bug off those guns! Get 'em going again, dammit, or we're *cooked*," she said, surveying the situation. "Private Mahone! You're the closest. *Do* it, dammit!"

"But, sir—"

Mahone was on one knee, spraying charging bugs, keeping them at bay.

"We'll keep them at bay. Do it—"

A pause . . . and then Private Mahone was up. She sidled on, and Kozlowski got a look at her face through the mottled faceplate. She looked uncertain and scared.

"Mahone. That xeno squatting up there by the guns. Looks an awful lot like that old boyfriend of yours, doesn't he?"

"Yes, sir. He kinda does."

Immediately the private began to hustle. She moved up the steps on the side of the lander. The alien hunkered over the remains of Argento. It hissed at her, wobbling like a spider guarding its prey.

"Don't let it bleed on the guns, Private."

Two steps forward.

The private dropped to the steps, avoiding a lunge from the alien. Brought her plasma rifle up at just the right angle.

Fired.

The force of the fiery discharge impacted on the thing's torso, pushing it over the edge even as the blast cindered it. The thing wilted to the ground and dropped, a flaming husk, not even giving a good heartfelt spasm.

"Good show, Mahone. Now, you think you can fire those guns?"

"Yes, sir." The private clambered up the stairs and over the body of Argento. "They're all starting to look like somebody's boyfriend!"

She jumped into the seat.

Immediately the guns started to swivel, pointing downward at the bugs already inside the force field, and those still crawling through.

They spoke.

The shells came hot and heavy . . . and well placed.

"Okay, guys. Let's get out of the rain, before we get blown up as well," said the colonel, motioning an ally-alley-in-come-free.

The troops seemed all too happy to obey, retreating and contributing their own fire.

The result was a rout. Between their concentrated wall of blasts and the powerful guns above them, those aliens not smart enough to retreat through the opening of the force field were obliterated.

Soon, all that moved among their ruins was smoke.

"Okay, O'Connor. Give it a try now."

The force field shimmered back into place.

"Okay, people," Kozlowski said. "Fan out and finish off any still alive!" She sighed. "Then we can count our dead."

21

The task was grisly, and it took a while, but the remains of the dead were placed in body bags, zipped tight, and then lined outside the ramp to the *Anteater*. All it would take was the okay from Kozlowski and they would be carted back into the freezer inside the lander.

When the bags lay in a row beside the lander, Colonel Kozlowski called for a moment of silence for the dead. When that was over, she spoke.

"I'd better say something now, because I might be the next one to go into one of these things. These were good people. There will be plenty of time to honor them properly and grieve later. They gave their all to the mission. Others may not recognize their contribution later. But we always will. Argento, Jastrow, Rodriguez, McCoy, Lantern, Chang. Their shells may be zipped up, but their spirits are still with us, and will be as long as we do our jobs with dedication and sincerity."

She bowed her head and observed her own moment of silence. In her mind, she heard a sweet snatch of some tune that Jastrow had played once. It sounded like hope, even now.

"Okay," she said, keeping herself stern and businesslike.

The bags were put on a wagon and taken up the ramp.

A raucous squawking made Kozlowski jump.

She turned around, hand going to the sidearm she was wearing.

Sitting on the edge of a folding chair that had been used for lunch was Private Ellis, lips around the end of Jastrow's saxophone. He moved the mouthpiece. "Sorry, Colonel."

"That's all right, Private. I'm just a bit on edge."

"Think I can ever learn to play this thing?"

"Why would you want to?"

"Jastrow. He always wanted me to try. I always told him I had no musical ability and besides, there was spit all over it." He sighed. "That part doesn't seem that important anymore."

"Sorry about your friend."

"Yeah. I figure we've gotten about a thousand or so bugs for every man killed here."

"It's not worth it, is it?"

"No. It's not."

She felt someone looking at her. Turned.

Daniel Grant was walking down the ramp.

She was about to get on her soapbox and rant at him, but then she noticed his face. It was white. In his eyes were the beginnings of tears.

She turned away and let him come up to her. Let him start the conversation, if he wanted to.

"I want you and your people to know how sorry I am," he said finally, after a long silence. "I guess when you see life turning into death so abruptly, it puts thing in perspective."

"Some business we're in here, eh, Grant?" she said.

"Some business." He nodded thoughtfully. "My problems . . . they can't compare with this." He sighed. "We can't quit now, though, can we?"

"No. My country sent me here to accomplish something. It's my duty to do that. You'll get what you came here to get, Grant."

"And maybe more than I bargained for."

"Definitely."

"Colonel. There's going to be a linkup with the *Razzia* in ten minutes. We're going to confer on the situation and decide a course of action. Naturally I want you to be there."

"Yes. I'll be right there."

She turned and continued to do what she could in the time remaining to her to give her the confidence and grit that she herself felt rapidly escaping from her.

It was a makeshift conference table at best, but it would have to do.

"I've just finished a full transmission to Captain Hastings of the events that have just occurred here," said Corporal O'Connor. He swiveled and turned a switch. "He's waiting to join the conference. Permission to let him in?"

Grant nodded.

"Permission granted," said Kozlowski. "We'll need all the input we can get."

Captain Hastings bid his regrets at the turn of events. His voice sounded even more subdued than usual.

"Now then," said Grant. "We've got a situation on our hands. I'd like to say, why don't we just give it another try with the perimeter extension harpoon. However, after what we've just been through, I don't think so."

"It's possible we're going to have to," said Kozlowski. "But that doesn't mean we can't explore other possibilities. Dr. Begalli . . . you seem to be the resident expert on the present situation with the aliens. What's your prognosis?"

"Clearly our projections were quite accurate," said the man, after scratching his large nose. "There is a genetic offshoot of the aliens, and the originals are attempting to eradicate them. Only we never anticipated this kind of scale . . . Or that it would hinder our actions to this degree."

"Not quite true," said Kozlowski. "We've got the technology. It's just not working as well as we would like."

Begalli's ferretlike eyes flicked back and forth over those assembled. "Despite our feelings of loss and frustration, I cannot forget just how correct my projections were about the recessive gene. Something that was quite unlikely. Naturally we're sorry for the loss . . . But after years and years, my science seems to be correct." He tapped his finger emphatically. "What we all want is in that hive. It's the answer to our dreams . . . Maybe, ultimately even to the whole alien conflict."

"Why would you say that?" said Henrikson.

"We came here to get the queen mother royal jelly and we've got to do that. Do you know how much we've been working with in these last two decades? About two hundred gallons' worth, that's all. Our tank here can go up to well over two thousand gallons, and I'm sure we can fill it. With that amount to work with, all kinds of possibilities will open up.

"We can learn something, I suppose, from this red and black alien business. Still it's all academic curiosity. There are no practical applications yet. With the jelly, those applications may be possible."

"Oh. Like what?"

"The key to the genetic control of the aliens! It could be in the queen down there and her royal jelly! Sorry, Mr. Grant, but there's a lot more at stake here than money for your company, and hyperspeed for the armed forces." He tapped the table emphatically. "Why do you think the red aliens are attempting genocide on the blacks?"

"Isn't it the same old story? They're different?"

Begalli shook his head. "You've got to have a certain amount of intelligence to be bigoted. The xenos aren't that smart. No. It's because on a very real level, the *existence* of difference threatens each other.

"Eradication is programmed into the species. I would daresay that in hives every once in a while red eggs are laid—and immediately destroyed by the queen or the queen's guards. When we removed the queen from the black hive and killed her guards, it probably allowed time for these freakish red eggs already laid to develop and grow . . . And then escape and build their own hive."

"Look, this is all very interesting," said Kozlowski. "But how is it going to get us past the *war* going on down there, and into the hive, where we can do our job? And get out with our butts intact, I might add!"

"Yes," said Grant ruminatively. "A definite priority."

"Let's look at it this way then," said Begalli. "What we have here is warfare on a grand scale. Each of these alien races would like to eradicate the other. Annihilate. This mission is deeply embedded in their chromosomal structure." He shrugged. "Now if we just tilt that warfare in the favor of the blacks, that would be to our definite advantage. We don't want mutant jelly. We want the black jelly, the stuff we know something about and can use."

Hastings's voice crackled over the radio. "I got lots of great weapons up here, folks. If you want, we can just nuke the red hive."

Begalli nodded. "Excellent! That might just work."

"How?" Grant asked.

Kozlowski nodded. "Well, it would kill off the red queen mother for one thing and with her any psychic control of her drones. Which would send the red army into disarray."

"More than that," said Begalli. "Without that control, instinctively the red army would retreat toward their hive. Equally instinctively the black army would pursue!"

Grant snapped his fingers. "Leaving the black hive wide open!"

"That would be the theory, yes . . . It's the best choice, in my opinion," said Begalli. "We'd still have to deal with the black guards, and they will be bigger and fiercer. But they would be limited in number. What we're facing out there is a problem of sheer oppressive volume."

Grant smacked the table. "Yes. We're going to have to do it, I think! Opinion, Colonel?"

"Sure. Why not. At the very least we're going to kill a lot of bugs!"

"Captain. How soon can you have those warheads ready?" said Grant.

"Couple of hours," came the voice.

"Excellent. We can accomplish this well before nightfall," said Kozlowski. "Get started, Captain. We can always postpone till morning if necessary."

"I don't think that will be necessary," said Hastings. "I'll get right to it."

Grant was nodding, his face intent. "One more thing, Colonel. I'd like to come with you when you go into that hive."

"What for?" said Kozlowski. "You're a civilian. You're not trained for this kind of work."

"I feel responsible here. I feel a moral obligation. You need extra people. I can aim a gun and shoot it. I—"

"Okay," she said.

"I want—" He blinked. "What?"

"I said you can go. There's a spare suit about your size down in the holding tank in the locker room. We'll go over the situation here in a few minutes, I'll brief you on a few things you'll have to know . . . And then you can suit up."

Grant's mouth flapped for a moment like a fish out of water.

"It'll be good to have you along, Grant!"

Henrikson and Begalli excused themselves to start preparations for the next assault.

"All right, people," announced Kozlowski. "Now that we've got a plan, let's chew over some details."

She felt charged again.

Those bugs were going to pay.

Big time.

Kozlowski was letting him go along!

A few minutes after the hour-long meeting, Daniel Grant was making his way down to the locker room, brain buzzing with the "briefing" that he'd just received. He felt beat up with facts and instructions, as though somehow Kozlowski had put him through a brief but intense boot camp under the whip of Drill Instructor Koz herself. Not fun!

Not that he wasn't *sincere* about wanting to go along.

He just hadn't really expected for her to agree to his volunteering.

Well, nothing for it now, old man. You're in for the full nine yards now. Play it out, do your job, and this will turn out fine! Just fine!

He entered the familiar smell of the locker, particularly ripe now from the recent press of ripe bodies that had just passed through.

Where was it that Kozlowski had said the spare suit was? Oh, yes, over in the cabinet yonder.

No lock, no latch.

Sabotage was the last thing on Grant's mind, he was so preoccupied with the lessons he'd learned about alien killing.

He opened the door and saw the suit, and reached for it.

What he did not see was the alien egg pod sitting in the shadows.

22

The thing stood like an obscene, fleshy orchid bulb.

Grant smelled it before he saw it.

That now-familiar, intense acidic blast of stench.

As he reached for the suit, his foot stubbed against the growth. It gave like a stink cabbage.

He looked down.

At first, he didn't want to believe his eyes.

Then he saw the tangle of talons, wiggling at the opening of the bulb, like the beginnings of a sand crab, emerging from its shell.

He froze.

He'd seen alien larvae before, of course. He'd seen them prey on test animals plenty of times. Only they had been behind thick glass at the time . . . Now this one was mere inches from his face.

It hissed at him, and began to come out faster, bending the petals of its deadly flower as it came.

"Screeeee!"

It launched.

Directly for his face.

Sheer desperation somehow prized the freeze lock off his muscles. Off to his right was a hanging suit. He reached out, grabbed it, and pulled it between himself and the face-hugger.

It bounced off it and flopped onto the floor.

Grant had just enough time to let off a yelp and take a step away from the thing before it animated again, leaping up toward him as though its legs were spring-loaded. As though his face were metal and the thing were a magnet, it headed straight for his eyes.

He reached out and caught it.

The talonlike claws tore at his skin. The pain shot up his arm, causing him to throw the thing down. It hit the floor, but it had clearly discovered its mission. It jumped around and was about to leap back up at him, when a blur flashed off to the left and a suited foot kicked it square in its crabby ass.

The thing hit the wall like a hockey puck smacking the sidelines, sluiced along the floor.

A rifle went up, tracked, sighted.

Energy sizzled out.

The blast smacked it like the finger of God, smushing a demon. Some of its acid came out, bubbling a small hole in the floor . . . But most was consumed in the incendiary blast.

He stepped back, his legs hit a stool, he sat down hard.

"Thanks," he said.

"Just my job," the person said, with bite.

He looked over to his savior.

It was Colonel Kozlowski.

"Looks like one of your pets wandered off the beaten track," she said, already going for a bucket. She put it in a shower stall, started filling it with water. "I'm losing count of the screwups in your 'harmless' project, Grant."

Grant shook his head. "I don't understand. I only authorized *one* creature for incubation." He drew in a breath, savoring it. "Take a look in the armory closet there!"

"In a moment."

She took the bucket and sluiced the water in the small crater. Hissing steam rose up, and that was that.

"The closet."

Grant nodded. "That's where the thing came from."

She looked and grunted. "Yep. You got yourself a pod here, Grant."

"I was the only one not armored, so it's obvious this thing was planted to get me when I came back here." He smacked a fist into a palm. "It's got to be Begalli. He must still be working for those scumbags at MedTech. I want you to put that bastard under arrest—hang him . . . keelhaul him . . . something."

"Yo! Rein yourself in, Grant. Then come here and take a look at this."

Grant walked over reluctantly. He looked in the closet. Kozlowski was pulling something off the side of the pod.

She pulled it into view.

"You know what this is, right?"

In her hand she held some kind of metal clamp, attached to a bottle-shaped thing.

"Of course," said Grant. "It's a timer clamp. It's used to hold the lips of an egg shut to ensure the creature can't escape during transportation."

"And it automatically falls off when the timer expires," she continued for him. "The planter is nowhere near the eggs when it activates. Looks like it's got a motion sensor on it, too. Anyone could have walked into this trap."

"So."

"So anyone could have planted this egg." She stood up. "Even me."

"This is just a regular chest-burster. I did not authorize this to be shipped out. Just that larvae queen." He shook his head. "I still don't feel good about that guy Begalli. He's been acting strangely."

Kozlowski sighed. "He seems clean to me. Anyway, he's the only alien expert in the landing party, and he's been giving us *good* information, by my lights."

"I don't know."

"Maybe you don't know this, but all radio signals are scrambled by the content of the shell in those hives. Once inside, we'll have no communication with the lander. We're going to need 'that bastard' in there more than any other crew member. Without him, this operation is dead in the water. You still want me to bust him?"

Grant thought about this.

He didn't like it, not at all. MedTech could very well be behind this whole sabotage business, and most certainly Begalli had been purchased from MedTech.

Had they purchased him back?

Was Foxnall back on Earth rubbing his hands with glee, waiting for the news of the demise of this mission, the death of Grant . . . Or would they just act when the mission got back? How could they possibly hope to pull off something like that?

At the same time, he well knew that Kozlowski was right.

Begalli knew his stuff, and they needed someone with knowledge of the inner workings of the alien queen's chambers, and what any change in the norm might mean.

"No. I guess you're right."

"Good. I'm glad we're agreed on that." She started out of the room. "I'm going to get the team ready for our push. Take a break, have a cup of tea—but if you're coming with us, I want to see you out there in an hour. *Capische*?"

"Yes. And Colonel Kozlowski . . . Alex." He tipped an imaginary hat. "Again, thanks."

She stopped and turned around. "Mr. Grant . . . Daniel . . ."

"Yes?"

"This isn't exactly the kind of mission you had in mind, is it? I know your type. The enduring optimist under fire. The sturdy campaigner who uses ignorance as a positive. Overconfidence, Grant. That's what I think it's called."

"Sounds like a defect, Kozlowski. Why are you letting it into that hive?"

"Because it's also called 'spirit,' Danny boy. It's infectious and it might just put us over the top here in a very ticklish situation." She winked at him. "Besides, it turns me on like hell, and your goddamned Fire has got absolutely nothing on good old-fashioned hormones to get me in the mood for action."

Grant found a grin coming to his face. "You going to save some of those hormones for me, Alex?"

"Sure, Danny. Next time I get PMS."

She turned and strutted away.

Grant shook his head.

What a woman. He wasn't sure if he could handle her.

But he sure would like to try.

23

The tactical nuclear weapon struck the red alien hive dead on.

Kozlowski watched the event inside the lander on the screen from the *Razzia*'s perspective. These tactical strikes had an extremely limited radius of effect, with minimal fallout and radiation, but nonetheless they had carefully ascertained the weather conditions beforehand. Everything had been perfect for the strike. The execution had been precise and professional.

"Good shooting!" she told Hastings.

Then she went outside where the troops were waiting for her.

They'd heard the news on their radios and were cheering.

"Just the start, people," she said as she strode into their midst. "The uphill road is ahead." She'd already noticed that the ranks of the battling aliens had thinned out somewhat. "What's going on out there?"

"Just seconds after detonation the reds just kind of stopped whatever they were doing and started spasming. Lots got killed, I think, and lots more are starting to take off," reported Mahone.

"Whatever psychic link they had with their queen mother must have been broken when the bitch got wasted," said Henrikson, nodding.

Kozlowski visualized that moment of intense destruction, the impact as that multimegaton nuke tore through the chambers of the reds, decimating all in it, shrieking caroming nuclear wind.

Had queenie gotten off one final scream of agony, one bitter nasty farewell to her evil crew?

Kozlowski hoped so. She hoped that bitch knew who'd been responsible. She was only sorry the thing didn't have a little picture of her to take down to bug hell with her.

Kozlowski turned to where Grant stood, looking uncomfortable and anxious in his suit. Doubtless, he was regretting his volunteering for the move into the hive. He'd be okay, though. He had the stuff.

"There it is!" said Henrikson, putting down the pair of binoculars and pointing. "You don't need glasses to see that baby."

Sure enough, off to the east, she could see the telltale mushroom cloud, rising up past the horizon of this flat, bleak landscape.

Black and poisonous.

"They're taking off in droves!" someone shouted. Kozlowski swiveled. Sure enough, the reds seemed totally disinterested in the conflict now. They were taking off in waves. Racing away back toward their blasted hive.

Why? Instinct? Whatever the reason, it wouldn't do them much good. Still, Kozlowski was pleased. They wouldn't be hanging around here.

The blacks hung back for a moment, perplexed.

Then, as though the thunderbolt of realization had hit them, they started after the enemy who had attempted to destroy them.

Totally ignoring the interlopers behind the shielded vessel from another planet.

"Yes!" said Kozlowski, stamping the ground with unalloyed glee.

Just as planned.

"It worked," she said. "The reds are retreating to the other hive. This one should be clear in a few minutes."

Grant was fidgeting. He clearly wanted this all to be over. "Then let's get moving! Who's going in?"

"Everyone but the technical crew," said Kozlowski. "And Ellis."

"Makes sense," said Grant. "He's taking Jastrow's death pretty hard."

"Yeah," said Mahone. "They grew up together, joined the Corps together, and fought for years in the same unit."

"He's a good marine," said Kozlowski. "He'll be okay in a few days. But I'd rather not have him in close combat right now. Besides, someone has to man the guns." She walked over to the bank of guns poking out the side of the lander. "How are you doing up there, Private?"

"All set, Colonel."

Luckily they'd trained all the troops to use these things.

"Right. I'm sure you'll do just fine." She turned back and walked toward Grant. "How about you? You sure you want to do this."

"No. But I'm *going* to."

"Good. It'll be good to have you along.

"All right then, helmets on." She fitted her own on above her suit, clicked in the radio, waited for the rest of the troops to check in. When they did, when it was all finished, she chinned her radio again. "Okay, O'Connor." The troops lifted their guns, released the safeties. "Drop the southern border."

They moved out.

There were still a few red aliens lingering about, and these charged in when they got a whiff of the intruders.

But this was the kind of operation that the marines had expected, that they had trained for. The blasts of their rifles easily dealt with the charging aliens. It was like a shooting gallery.

Meanwhile, Ellis and O'Connor were doing damned fine work with the PEHs. They spiked a few home to either side of the hive's opening and moments later the marines had a nice tunnel of force field to make their way through, cleaning up the couple of xenos left over and not having to worry about the ones who'd been excluded from the party.

Kozlowski turned to see how Grant was doing. She'd put him in the back, to guard the rear so he wouldn't shoot any of the troops.

He was doing a damned good job of blasting apart the fallen aliens, making sure they stayed down.

When they reached the opening of the hive, Kozlowski put a hand up, halting the party.

"What's the reading say, O'Connor?" she asked through the radio.

"Sensors show they're still on the run. No party's coming back."

"Good news." She turned to the group. "I don't know how long we've got in there before the three bears come home . . . but I do know we're going to go in there and get us some porridge."

Laughter. Cheers.

"However, let's be quick about it, okay? No sight-seeing, no rubbernecking. We picked up enough DNA from dead reds already, so we don't have to pack anything in ice. Moreover, we don't have to take 'em back alive. Now as we discussed before, what we're going to be up against in there are some pretty nasty bugs, bigger and smarter. Take this into account."

"Kozlowski!"

She turned and found herself helmet to red face with Grant. He'd undone his top and was holding it at his side, getting himself a breath of fresh air. "Well, Colonel!" His eyes were gleaming with excitement. He looked like a Boy Scout who'd just fired his first BB gun. "Were my combat skills satisfactory?"

Kozlowski granted him a patronizing scowl. "Pat yourself on the back later, Grant. And put that damn helmet back on!"

She got back on the radio.

"O'Connor. Send up the cargo drone."

That was what they were going to be using to carry the royal jelly back up with.

"When it gets up here, we'll drop the southern border and head out. We all ready?"

She surveyed the covered faces, knowing already they were about as ready as they were ever going to be.

"This is the last radio contact till we get back out," said Kozlowski. "Open her up, O'Connor. Over and out."

The skein of force frizzled off.

Perfect.

O'Connor was getting really good in his manipulations. The tunnel of the force field that led from the rounded entrance of the hive back to the bubble around the *Razzia* was still intact.

There weren't too many of the blacks left out there, but they couldn't get in.

Unless, of course, there were other entrances . . .

Likely, but the things didn't seem particularly interested. They seemed more interested in the cargo drone that had crawled up the slight incline. It was an automatically controlled vehicle with eight thick wheels. Omni-terrain. One of the marines took over the controls when it reached them.

They started down.

The tunnels were recognizably of alien origin. Kozlowski had seen plenty of hive tunnels, that was for certain. Nonetheless, these were a little larger than usual, with a different consistency of building material.

"I've never seen an alien nest so empty before," said one of the soldiers.

"I have," said Kozlowski grimly. "And it was a trap."

The nest on Hollywood and Vine.

It was flashing back on her.

The walls, like inside a tumorous colon . . .

The prickly fear, the sick-in-the-stomach . . .

Having people with her she respected, cared for . . . smack dab in the vat of trouble and fear . . . Along with someone special, for whom she feared the most.

She remembered her feelings for Michaels. It welled up inside of her, and she had to push it back down, along with her fear.

This time would be different, she told herself.

She shut out the memory and went into her automatic "competent" mode.

Nonetheless, she could feel the memories crowding in on her.

About forty meters down it became apparent that things were different in other ways as well.

There was a convergence of tunnels.

Three separate ways to go.

"Okay, Dr. Begalli. Get your butt and that machine up front."

Dr. Begalli shuttled forward. In his hand he held a device with a pair of green sensor extensions. A pheromone detector. Begalli tapped a few buttons and pointed the device in each of the directions in turn, scrutinizing the results carefully.

"Well, Doctor," said Kozlowski. "Which way to the buried treasure?"

The helmeted head bobbed eagerly. "Well, the

pheromone readings seem to jibe with what I expected." He pointed to the left. "Let's try that way."

They started down the corridor.

"This is why we need Begalli," she told Grant. "The tunnels of this hive are much more mazelike than any I've encountered on Earth. Without him, it might take a *long* time to find the queen mother."

Grant shook his head. "If you say so, Colonel. But I'm still keeping my eye on him."

"That's it, Grant. I've found the perfect job for you. Begalli watch. Sounds wonderfully exotic," she said.

"Sure. That's what I'll do." Grant's helmet turreted back and forth. "Where *is* the little creep, anyway?"

"You're not doing your job . . . But don't worry, there's a curve just up ahead. He just went around that. We've just lost sight—"

"Colonel," said Private Mahone. "The motion detectors show significant and sudden activity up ahead."

"Begalli!" Kozlowski yelled. "Get your ass *back* here!"

Just then, the suited Dr. Begalli returned around the bend where he'd disappeared.

Kozlowski could hear him screaming without benefit of the radio.

24

She didn't know the little guy could move that fast—let alone that fast with the hindering weight of a full battle suit on.

"Yaaaaaaaaaaa!" screamed Dr. Begalli as he ran for all he was worth around the corner. He ran past them, toward the cover of the cargo drone carrier.

"Begalli!" said Grant. "What the hell is it?"

Kozlowski didn't have to ask.

She could pretty much guess.

"Arms!" she yelled.

She needn't have bothered. The others were ready, angling their weapons down.

However, ready as they were, all the preparations were pretty much in vain.

The first of the queen's guard came around the corner and Kozlowski had to stop herself from gasping.

It was big and it was fast, and it was mean.

The blasts caught it full in the chest, and it kept on coming for what seemed like a full second before it was lifted up and slammed against the wall. It tried to scrabble back up and tackle them again, before a final plasma stream knocked its head apart.

"There's more," yelled the point man. "There's—"

The next one was even bigger, and even faster. Before they could swing their weapons away from the first and onto the new arrival, it was on the first soldier.

Horrible claws tore the man's chest apart.

"Jesus!" cried Private Mahone as she was sprayed with blood. She swung her gun around and let off a spurt of plasma, but missed. The beast was incredibly fast. It finished one more ripping shake of the point man and then leapt toward the rest.

Lesser soldiers might have lost it right then, so horrific was the sight. But they kept their cool, aimed their weapons, and let the thing have it.

Two more "guards" attacked.

Another soldier was torn apart before the guards were subdued, blasted to pieces.

In all her time fighting inside hives, Kozlowski had never seen such an intense battle conflagration. The queen's guards were incredibly quick and agile, almost imbued, it seemed, with superpowers. Fortunately, this crew was also the best she'd worked with, and they'd half expected something like this.

Within violent minutes, four aliens and two humans lay smoking and quite dead upon the ground.

"God," was all that Private Mahone could say, lying slumped against the wall, gasping for air and still grasping her weapon, ready if another bug should care to call.

"No, I don't think God's around here," said Henrikson. "This is more like the Other Place."

For her own part, Kozlowski was just numb.

"Okay, we'll pick the bodies up on the way back. Take a quick moment for a breather, because that's all the time we've got if any of us wants to get out of here."

Two more dead. She couldn't believe it, even when she looked down at their twisted and torn remains. This wasn't worth it. But she had her orders, and she had her duty, and she knew nothing more than that she had to complete this mission, or their lives and the lives lost earlier and the months spent on this project would have been for naught.

A suited figure peeked around the corner of the cargo drone. "Is . . . is everyone all right?"

Dr. Begalli. Apparently, his head had been well stuffed in the sand.

Daniel Grant, who had been leaning on the side wall, exhausted, pushed himself off and walked over to the man. "No. Two more dead. You couldn't have warned us this would happen?"

"We knew about the guards. What we didn't know was that they'd come charging up at us like that," said Kozlowski. She got her second wind, went over to have a look at the only xeno head that had survived the mauling. "Ever see anything quite like this, Doctor?"

Begalli gave the angry and suspicious Grant a

wide berth in coming around to look. "Oh, heaven, what a mess—No, Colonel, I had no idea . . . Loathsome beasts. I don't recall the report from the last visit here giving them full justice. We knew they were bigger, but not this nasty. This is fascinating." He looked up from the dead beast. He took a small piece of blasted "skin" in a bottle. "I'll have to do a genetic workup when I get back. The queen mother may equip her guards to continue to evolve." He shook his head, mystified. "Or could the things have *devolved* rather than evolved. What a fascinating mystery! So much is down here!"

"Let's get a roll on."

"Yeah, Begalli. And you go first," said Grant. "Let's see a little courage for a change."

Begalli nodded, picked up his pheromone meter, and they were off again toward the depths of the alien hive.

"The queen's chambers should be down there," said Begalli.

The electric torches stabbed down into the darkness—but beyond their reach, Kozlowski saw the beginnings of what appeared to be some kind of bioluminescence.

"Okay," she said. "This place has had a few surprises that we weren't prepared for. There still might be more. Dr. Begalli, Corporal Henrikson, Daniel Grant, and myself will head on down to the chamber. Dicer, Clapton, and Mahone, stay here and guard our backs. I don't expect the radios to work, so let's just say if we're not back in an hour, get back to the lander and get out of here."

Private Dicer was a skinny guy with big eyes that

seemed about to pop out of his head. He'd put on an excellent display of bug killing, but clearly the pressure was getting to him. Sweat pasted his long stringy hair down over his forehead. Private Clapton was a little more poised. He was a thickset easy-come, easy-go sort with a ready humor that he'd somehow lost now. Private Mahone looked as though she simply could not even believe she was here. But they were all good soldiers. They'd been good soldiers up above and they'd be good soldiers down here.

"Yes, sir," they chorused.

Kozlowski took the controls of the drone from a trooper and motioned the party onward.

It took another ten minutes to get down to a place where the lamps were necessary to see. Still, Kozlowski kept the side lights of her suit on, just in case things suddenly went dark.

The tunnel went around a bend.

Suddenly opened up.

It was the biggest chamber that Kozlowski had ever seen.

Eerily lit by the bioluminescence was the scene that the scientists had more or less predicted.

The four huge pods, radiating around a larger pod, above which the queen towered, a true giant, like a devil tilted atop her evil throne.

Only the sketchy holograms could never have hinted at the textures or the colors, the bizarre organic geometry here that threatened to drive a mind mad if concentrated on too closely.

The queen's pod glistened and oozed with what Kozlowski knew to be royal jelly.

The stuff that would make Grant an incredibly

rich man, that would give the armed forces what they wanted, that would spell a success to this bloody campaign.

"Incredible," said Grant.

However, his eyes did not glow with avarice.

"Amazing," said Kozlowski. "We've hit the motherlode of royal jelly here." She looked at Grant. "You're going to get your tank filled, I think."

She patted the metal, and it echoed hollowly.

"Little problem," said Grant. "What about queeny?"

The gigantic creature perched atop the center mound did not even seem to notice they were even there. Its attention seemed focused off into space, as though it were meditating.

"I'm sure it's psychically directing the rout of the reds," said Begalli. "Must be. It's so absorbed, it didn't even notice the death of its guards." He quickly scanned the room again. "Four pods. Four guards. Excellent correspondence. Looks like we've got this place all to ourselves. All we have to do is to deal with the queenie, and she's just a sitting duck!" He smiled broadly, skipping a little closer to the gleaming, gooey treasure hoard. "Looks delicious, doesn't it? Ah, what wonders that stuff must hold. I can't wait . . ." He cut himself off suddenly and looked furtive.

"Can't wait?" said Grant. "This is *my* expedition. What *exactly* can't you wait for?"

"Uhhmmm. Nothing. Nothing, sir . . ." He drifted closer to the pod. "Look at it all. I never thought I'd see this much up close. God, it's beautiful."

The queen mother was as still as a statue. As still as death.

Beautiful? Was fear beautiful? Dread? Terror? All the primitive juices battled now at Alex Kozlowski's barrier.

Michaels's beautiful head boiling apart with acid.

His scream.

Her guilt.

She wanted to turn and run from this place. It was worse than she had ever imagined it. The dead body of her lover seemed superimposed over everything.

She calmed herself. She'd known that she would never get the trauma of that dreadful Hollywood day off her mind, that she'd have to live it all over again in her head.

She just never realized she'd have to live it over again in reality.

And this time it could be *her* skin bubbling off, to expose the grinning skull beneath.

"Beautiful?" said Grant. "I'm not so sure anymore. People have *died* for this stuff. I feel . . . responsible."

"No time for self-remonstration," said Kozlowski. "Glad to hear you've got a conscience, but we really should finish this mission up. Begalli, get away from there. We can't take any chances. I want that thing up there dead, and I'm going to do it myself, right—"

Grant, though, was on a jag. Apparently the deaths of the other three soldiers, so close, had really shaken him up.

"I don't know," said Grant. "I just don't know."

"Mr. Grant! You started this whole thing rolling."

"Yeah, and I'm going to have to live with it for the rest of my life, too. I'm paying for my ignorance. But you, Begalli—" He brought his gun up. "You've been sabotaging this mission from day one, haven't you?"

"What?" said Begalli, turning back to him.

"Come off it! I've been watching you, Begalli, and I know damn well you're up to something," said Grant. "You're still working for MedTech, aren't you?"

"Okay, sure . . . I have been up to something." He took a breath. "I'm doing research, independent of Neo-Pharm. I'd planned to publish articles on my findings."

"Articles?"

"A new kind of alien. I'd go down in history. I'd be famous . . . forever!"

"Articles?" repeated Grant.

"I've got more than enough money, Grant. And I always hated MedTech—what I want is to be acknowledged for my scientific efforts. *That's* why I wanted to come down here. Maybe I'll even write a book . . . Yes, a bestseller!"

"You heard it, Grant," said Kozlowski. "The only thing he's guilty of is scientific greed. Now back off . . ."

"So how do you know he isn't lying . . . ?" Grant started to say, before a sudden hissing shriek froze his sentence.

Without warning, the queen mother jumped.

It sailed through the air, and it landed just short of Dr. Begalli. Stunned and disbelieving, Begalli tried to turn.

A long set of secondary jaws streaked out from
the alien's mouth, slicing and hammering into the
back of the scientist's head, boring through and
pushing his eyes out of their sockets like red Jell-O
being squeezed through cookie cutters.

Kozlowski was stunned. The thing wasn't supposed to be able to do that. Wasn't its ovipositor
fastened to the pod? But then wasn't that just
something else they didn't know about these
aliens?

Only a flicker of a second of thought, though. Already her rifle was going up, aiming, squeezing off
a round.

Henrikson fired at the exact same moment.

Their fire converged upon the exact same spot
on the queen. It hissed and wailed, a hole blown in
its thorax. Its blood rained down upon Begalli's
head and boiled his face away. The alien started toward them, forelimbs clutching and seeking.

Kozlowski lifted her rifle and aimed at its head.

It still came forward.

Henrikson's blasts joined hers, and the thing's
head burst asunder like a ripe melon.

They backpedaled to avoid the spurting acid, and
the great queen mother writhed and spasmed in its
death throes.

Kozlowski stepped forward, looking down at the
massive thing.

Fortunately it had come far enough that it hadn't
spoiled its own jelly.

"Right," she said. "Too bad about Begalli. Let's
get this tank loaded out of here, quick."

She jumped over to the vehicle and pulled out

ADER

ALIENS: GENOCIDE　　　　**263**

the vacuum tap. This bit was going to be the easy
part.

Only when the cargo drone's tank was topped
off, did Kozlowski pull the tap out of the membrane. There was lots more jelly, but they just
couldn't take it.

"I hope this will be enough," she said sardoni-
cally.

"Yes," said Grant. "Yes. It will have to do, I suppose."

"Something wrong, Grant?"

"I think you know what's troubling me." The
man sighed deeply. "Besides, I don't get it. Only a
few people knew about the alien incubation project. If Begalli didn't sabotage it, who did?"

Casually, Alex Kozlowski grabbed ahold of her rifle. She'd been thinking about that very same
thing.

And she didn't care for what was floating up on
her mental screen.

She was about to turn when Henrikson's voice
sounded behind them.

"Thank you, folks. That looks just fine," he said.
"Please drop your weapons. This close, one blast of
this rifle can deal with you both."

25

"**H**enrikson?" said Grant. He knelt and put his rifle down behind him. "You?"

"That's right, Grant. MedTech pays a lot better than the marines. Damned interesting ride, too. Been enjoying myself." He motioned with the tip of his rifle. "Come on, Colonel—sir. Get that pretty finger off the trigger and set your gun down."

She obeyed. "You're going to kill us and leave us here, aren't you?"

"Absolutely. And no one will be the wiser. And by the time we get back to Earth, a goodly part of this royal jelly will be siphoned off—and some of the DNA samples will be gone as well. Just in case . . . I daresay, once it's been announced you've been killed in action, your creaky empire will be up for grabs. And the Neo-Pharm scientists will pretty much disperse . . . The best ones bought up by MedTech."

"I checked your credentials, dammit. They were spotless!" said Kozlowski. She knew there was somebody giving them trouble, but she'd always felt that she could contain any problems. She thought she'd read this guy, that he was straight as an arrow. He'd given absolutely no previous sign of disloyalty.

"Hey! You've got an eminently corruptible bunch you're working for, Kozlowski." The man was grinning maliciously now, savoring his victory.

"What! Are you really a synth, Henrikson?" said Grant, clearly just as shocked as Kozlowski at this turn of events. And no wonder. Henrikson had been Grant's main man, his apple polisher. He'd brought him down to show him the alien incubation. There'd been a trustworthiness about the guy. A big brotherness.

Why hadn't they seen *through* him, dammit, she thought.

"C'mon. I'm no synth! If I were a synth, I could have taken those Xeno-Zips with absolutely no effect!" He nodded over to the royal jelly. "I avoid the crap."

"But . . . but I *trusted* you." said Grant. "I've got such a good nose for this kind of thing."

The grin got broader. "There's where MedTech has got your company beat all to hell, Grant. Every day I douse myself in a special pheromone, designed specifically for leader types to sniff. Makes you trust me, gives type A's like you confidence in big guys like me. That's why the other grunts didn't care for me . . . they weren't the kind that like this pheromone. You guys bought it!"

"But you've risked your life with all the rest of us . . . You've been a damned good soldier!" said Grant.

"Yes, I have, and I've had a good time, too, folks, let me tell you. I am a soldier. A soldier of fortune. I raid alien nests with buddies for money. I'm an independent and damned good at it. Only there's more money in this for me than I'd ever dreamed of—and I get to see the stars, too." He shrugged. "Don't look for anything deeper here. That's all there is."

"But the death of the alien baby . . . that pod . . . the sabotage . . . it just doesn't add up."

"Sure it does, Grant. I caused confusion. I hurt the program, and I pretty much framed poor old Begalli. Fact, when I get back with this liquid gold here, that's what I think I'm going to tell them. Yeah. 'It was Begalli, guys. He's dead now, though, along with poor old Grant and Kozlowski. Boo hoo. Mission complete. Now let's get the hell out of here.' You see. Piece of cake."

He started laughing.

Unless she acted, they'd be dead within seconds.

However, since they'd all taken off their helmets, there might be a shred of hope here.

Without a further thought, Kozlowski dived for her rifle. She scooped it up, put her finger under the trigger.

And was blasted by the quadruple barrels of Henrikson's weapon.

Grant watched in horror as the blast hit Kozlowski's left thigh. She spun around and fell hard onto the ground.

The next thing Grant knew, he was on top of Henrikson. The man had been swerving his rifle for the coup de grace—but Grant's fist sailed into the man's bare face with a solid impact before he could pull the trigger again.

Where that had come from, Grant didn't know. But it felt so good that he found himself doing it again.

The attack surprised Henrikson so much he clearly wasn't sure what to do. To defend himself at close quarters he'd have to drop the rifle. But Kozlowski wasn't dead yet, and to give up the weapon meant certain defeat. He lifted his other arm—but Grant countered.

And nailed him with another punch.

Thank God he'd worked out regularly! He hadn't done it for fights. He'd done it for his self-confidence and for the ladies. But his reflexes were good, and it had all paid off.

The blows had opened up Henrikson's face. He bled from the nose and from the mouth, and he went down like a fighting suit full of potatoes.

Grant kicked the rifle away from him, and then booted him in the head again. Hard.

"Unnnh!"

The lights in those bright blue eyes dimmed.

"You don't smell so good to me anymore, Henrikson!"

A groan from behind him. He picked up Henrikson's weapon, and then went over to Colonel Kozlowski.

"Ooooh," she said. "I think my hip is broken."

Indeed, there was a smoking hole in the overplating of the hip area of the suit, exposing underpart beneath.

"Yes," said Grant. "The underplating of this armor is designed to withstand severe concussions.

Still, you're probably right about that hip. You're going to need some help."

He helped her up. "Yeah. Thanks." She cringed. "I'll make it."

"Good."

"Looks like you did a number on Henrikson there. Surprised you didn't take his rifle and blast him."

"Don't think the thought didn't enter my mind. No, if we can get him back, I'll be able to use him to string MedTech up by its dangling prescriptions."

"Sounds good. We go now?"

"We go."

They revived Henrikson with a few slaps across the chops, and then they made sure that he knew which direction their rifles were pointing.

Grant propped Kozlowski up on the sideboard of the drone. She could walk, sort of, but he figured he'd better save that for later.

The suit was getting too heavy for him, so he took off the top.

"Helmets?" she said.

"Forget the helmets. We've got enough weight to slow us down as it is."

"At least stick them up here on the drone, dammit."

"Yes, sir."

He had Henrikson do that. The traitorous corporal performed the task grudgingly, without comment.

"The creatures should be miles from here," said Grant.

They started trudging back the way they'd come, with him keeping a bead on Henrikson while Kozlowski controlled the cargo drone.

They were just at the tunnel opening at the end of the chamber when they heard the rumbling.

"What the hell . . ." said Henrikson, looking behind. "It's coming from that other tunnel, on the opposite end of the chamber."

"Oh, shit," said Kozlowski.

Grant watched, disbelieving, as an alien ran into view in the dimly illuminated distance.

Followed by another.

Followed by three . . . four . . .

A clot of the monsters burst out of the tunnel.

"They must be coming back through another entrance!" said Kozlowski. "They must have sensed the death of their queen, dammit, and started to head back."

"And took a short cut! Well, let's get a *move* on here. I—"

He'd taken his attention off of Henrikson for one moment—one short moment!—and had been rewarded by the big man, big time.

Henrikson's body plowed into his, knocking Grant down, bashing the rifle from his hands. It clunked down beside him, and Grant grabbed it up again.

Henrikson jumped on top of him and they wrestled for the gun. They were on the other side of the cargo drone, away from any chance of Colonel Kozlowski interceding immediately.

"For chrissake, you asshole," said Grant. "They're almost on top of us."

"I'm gonna make it out of here, Grant," said the big man. "I'm going to be the only one who does."

As they struggled, the bottle of Xeno-Zip fell out of Grant's pocket, cracking open on the alien floor beside him, spilling its contents.

Henrikson was distracted.

Grant used it.

He wrenched the rifle away from the man's hands and whacked the butt across the man's chin.

Stunned, the man fell back.

Kozlowski was limping around at that point, holding a rifle. "Stand back, Grant. I'm going to kill him!" she said, nostrils flaring with anger.

Grant took a look at the groaning Henrikson and the fallen bottle of Xeno-Zip and then at the approaching aliens.

"No," he said. "I've got a better idea."

He scooped up a handful of the pills, and he stuffed them into Henrikson's mouth, holding his hands over the man's lips so he was forced to automatically swallow them.

"Get yourself on the front of that drone, and let's get the hell out of here," he said.

"What . . . ?"

"Let's just say that it's a far, far nobler thing that Corporal Henrikson is going to do today than he's ever done before."

Grant put the rifle down between the Corporal's arms and then he grabbed Kozlowski's arm and helped her over to the lander.

The man's eyes popped open.

Inside he felt as though an atom bomb had just gone off in his brain.

He rolled his head, and saw, just meters away, a horde of charging, hissing aliens.

In his arms was a rifle.

Fire raged through his bloodstream and nervous

system. He felt the familiar flight-or-fight response, only flight didn't seem necessary.

Henrikson, after all, was God!

And in his hands was a fistful of lightning bolts.

Grinning, he got up as the aliens approached.

"C'mon, you bastards!" he screamed. "Let's play!"

He'd kill them all.

Then he'd go back up and nail that bastard Grant and that bitch Kozlowski.

Yeah!

The gun in his hand started blazing.

Something was going on down there. Something huge. The motion detectors were going nuts in Private Mahone's hands. And her own internal warning system, her instincts, told her that it was danger, pure and simple.

"Cripes," said Private Dicer, his eyes bulging, a tic working at his mouth. "I can even feel it in my feet!"

Sweat had broken out on the brow of Private Clapton. "Shit, man. What are we going to do?"

"Colonel says if they're not back, we should cut and run. I say we obey orders."

Every cell in Mahone's body agreed. She wanted to run and hide. She was exhausted in every respect but for the terror that had filled her from the very first. This mission was worse than she'd ever imagined.

Something deep inside her though surged up. Something strong inside of her took ahold of her, and she realized that it was as much her as her fear.

"No."

"Say *what*?" said Clapton.

The rumbling was building.

"Shit, Private, those idiots down there are probably getting torn to pieces. We wait here, and that's just what's going to happen to us," said Dicer.

Dicer started moving away toward the exit, eyes rolling with terror. Clapton started following him.

"You assholes move one more step, I'm going to blast you," she said.

Dicer kept moving and she put a blast a yard short of him, and then aimed in a fashion that they well knew could take them both out with a simple tug of the trigger.

"Jeez, Mahone? Are you crazy? Our asses are in a sling here!" whined Clapton.

"Well then rock in 'em, guys. We're going to stay right here and give aid and succor." Her eyes blazed. "And you know what! I've half a mind to go in after the others."

"You're nuts!"

"I'm looking at my watch here. We've got a good ten minutes to wait this out. I'm just following orders." She grinned. "Just doing my job."

Sweating and fidgeting, the others stopped.

Private Mahone smiled to herself. She was getting something out of this crazy jellybean hunt. She was getting her soul back.

She just hoped she was going to have a future to use it in.

"What happened?" said Mahone. "What the hell's going on down there?"

The three soldiers were still waiting for them patiently where Kozlowski had placed them. Seeing them there was a great relief, a testament to her ability to judge people.

"No time to explain," said Grant. "We've just got

to get *out* of here. There's a batch of aliens coming up through the tunnel."

That was all it took.

The cargo van kept going, rolling along with a few more guards.

Behind them, she could still hear the echoes of Henrikson's blazing gun.

Then it stopped, and there was a shriek the likes of which she'd never heard before.

"If we're lucky, enough of the dead things piled up that they're going to have to clear them out first," said Grant. "C'mon, can't we get this beast to move faster?"

"It's flat out," she said.

Running speed. It would have to do.

It seemed to take forever, but finally they saw the lip of the tunnel's entrance.

They rolled out, and there, like a delightful promise, was the *Anteater* patiently waiting for them.

With her excitement, Kozlowski could almost ignore the pounding pain in her hip.

She chinned her radio on. "O'Connor! Drop all walls of the perimeter and tell Fitzwilliam to start the engines!" she gasped a breath. "Prepare for an emergency lift-off!"

"Yes, sir!"

"Ellis. Get those guns ready. We're going to have some visitors coming out of that hole too damned quickly. Try and stop them, if you can!"

"Yes, sir."

They hightailed it.

They were halfway there when the aliens started gushing out of the tunnel.

"Now, Ellis!"

"Roger."

The private started blasting. The shells devastated whole sections of the emerging aliens. One blasted the side of the hive, sending down clumps of stuff to crush a few.

But there were so many of the things that they just kept on coming, regardless.

And coming too damned fast.

"Hurry it up!" called Grant.

Fortunately they hit a decline, and gained some speed.

They were almost there.

The ramp had been lowered for them. All they had to do, thought Kozlowski, was make that ramp. Roll up. Get in, and nip off.

That was all.

Grant was running alongside her. "Alex . . . how's the thigh?"

"Better. Why?"

"I think we can run faster than this drone. We might have to abandon it."

Kozlowski shook her head. "No freaking way, Grant. We came all the way to get this stuff. We're taking it back with us. Do you hear? I for one want to see you take a bath in the shit!"

Grant grunted. "Only in the nude, and only if you'll join me."

"If we're both lucky, Grant. If we're both lucky."

Somehow, they made it to the ramp.

The drone rolled up like a champ.

"Fold up shop!" cried Kozlowski. "Ellis, get your butt in here."

The hydraulic struts of the ramp started squealing up, hauling up the platform.

Through another door Private Ellis raced in, still clutching his dead friend's saxophone.

"Closing up the guns."

"Damn. We've got nothing to shoot them with now," said Kozlowski, hopping off the cargo drone, letting the side serve as her crutch.

"Engines firing."

"The damned hatch has got to close first!" she cried.

Then, a flicker of nightmare:

Talons, scrambling for a hold on the ramp, coming up now like a castle drawbridge in the face of vandals.

The too-familiar banana-shaped head, the drooling fangs . . .

A hissing insinuated through the sound of the hydraulics.

Guns raised to shoot the alien scrabbling in.

"No!" cried Kozlowski. "The blood will eat through the door. We won't be able to lift—"

"Hell," said Ellis. "I can't play the stupid thing anyway."

With all his might he threw the saxophone.

Its metal base bashed directly into the alien's head. *Bonk!*

The creature was knocked off the door, and it closed, tightly and firmly, no alien blood acid eating through it.

The lander rumbled and throbbed, and Kozlowski could feel its rockets kicking off this foul planet's dust with fiery disgust.

Epilogue

She was lying in bed, with a beautiful view of the stars through a viewport window.

She was safe and sound, and a few simple, nonaddictive drugs were running through her system, killing the pain of the fractured thigh.

She was off the Fire. The mission was complete. The Corps was going to be happy, and maybe she'd even get a promotion. She felt the loss of her troops heavily, but then she'd lost people before. Old hat. The emptiness went away. Eventually.

She felt no imminent sense of danger. She had some books to read, and some vids to watch.

Why, then, Colonel Alexandra Kozlowski asked herself, did she feel so bored and antsy?

This should be a time to celebrate.

After they'd gotten the *Anteater* safely back on the

Razzia, and off-loaded the tank, they realized they had twenty-five hundred gallons of the stuff. Grant's scientists were totally blissed. It was enough to work with, and absolutely top quality, no sign of that red strain whatsoever. There was a good chance now they could even create their own queen mother.

They'd nuked the black hive as a parting shot.

There were probably xenos left on the planet. But it would take a long, long time to regroup. Kozlowski imagined one playing a soulful sax as its hive burned.

Yeah!

Turned out, according to Friel and others, this whole "red aliens" thing was a fluke. The queen mother and the queens were dead now, and all their eggs. They'd never come scratching on their door again.

The generic brand though . . .

They'd be around. They were the universe's cockroaches, with a vengeance.

And she'd helped step on her share.

A time for rest and relaxation and recuperation. A time for peace and meditation and—

Whatever.

So it was that when Daniel Grant came to see her later that day, she was overjoyed at his visit— though she'd be damned if she'd let him know how much.

"Hello, Colonel. How are you feeling?"

"Okay. Not an extreme fracture. The machine set it, and it should heal while I'm in hypersleep. A little physical therapy on Earth, and I'll be right as rain."

"Good. I'm pleased. Very pleased." His eyes

seemed to drift toward the stars and into abstraction.

"You come here to talk about something?"

"Nothing in particular. I just wanted to make sure you're all right."

"I'm fine. Nothing more?"

"Well, everyone seems to be on the emotional mend. Lot of people are just sleeping . . . I guess in reaction to all that stress."

"And you. What are you doing? Taking any baths in your royal jelly yet?"

"No. No . . . Waiting for you." He laughed. "The scientists are just tickled pink. They've already started to work on it, along with the samples of the red alien DNA. They say maybe they really have got something here."

"I hope so. We had to dole out a few lives for it."

"I'm going to make sure that those lives were not lost in vain, Alex." He looked down at the bed, smoothing the linen thoughtfully. "Actually, you know, maybe there *was* something I wanted to talk to you about."

"Shoot. I'm not going anywhere."

"I was impressed by your work here. When we get back, I'm probably going to need someone to head up a security team for Grant Industries. The job is yours, if you want it."

She laughed. "And leave the marines? No way. I've got a mission in life, Grant. And it's not to guard your butt."

He shook his head. "I don't understand, Alex. How much longer can you do things like this mission? How long do you think you can survive?"

"I don't know any other kind of life . . . except . . ."

"Except what?"

"Except for maybe when I was a little girl. Yeah. I had a real good life when I was a kid, Grant. Perfect. And then a bunch of monsters came down and destroyed that life and destroyed a lot of lives." She shook her head. "Think about it, Grant. Think about it while you're sitting up there in your ivory tower when you get back. This may seem like hell to you. It's pretty rough, sure . . . That mission was one of the roughest. But chew on this—most wars get fought between people arguing over some relatively silly matter . . . usually involving money or land or possessions. People kill people. It's stupid, senseless, and a waste. History is drowned in the shed blood of martyrs for meaningless causes." She shook her head. "I don't know if I'm even going to make any history books, Grant. But I do know that whatever I accomplish against . . . against this *plague* against decent life . . . this *evil* that has infected the galaxy . . . It's not meaningless." She took a deep breath. "Now how many people can be positive . . . absolutely feel-it-to-their-toes sure . . . That their lives mean something. That as full as foibles as they are, they're living and fighting for something *good*."

Grant seemed to consider that for a moment.

"I can't argue much about that, Alex." He slapped his knees and stood up. "But we can't all be Joan of Arc. Somebody's got to get the engines of commerce running. And somebody's got to be in charge of those engines."

"Well, maybe you've got a different view of things

now that you've looked at life through the jaws of one of the monsters coming at you?"

"Sure. Sure. Of course, now I've got to figure out how to look at life without worrying about mobsters or MedTech."

She laughed. "I'm sure the generals and admiral back home will be so pleased, you'll have no problem, Grant."

"I don't know . . . I just hope that what we've done on this journey *does* make a difference."

She smiled. "I've been watching you, Grant. I think it already has, jelly or no jelly."

"Thanks. I guess maybe you're right." He started to leave, then paused and turned.

"Alex?"

"Daniel?"

"If you won't work for me . . . Maybe you'd like to have a little bubbly, a little caviar, a little gourmet dinner with me sometime?"

"Hell no!"

He sighed, nodded, and turned to go.

"But if you want a beer and some pretzels sometime, Daniel—I keep my larder well stocked with those."

He seemed confused for a moment, looked at her.

She winked at him.

His face flushed and he laughed.

"Count on it, Colonel. Count on it."

He blew a kiss at her and turned.

"Oh. And, Danny boy," she called after him.

He turned. "Yes?"

She'd pulled out the cigar he'd given her, along

with a lighter. She puffed the thing alight. "Thanks for the smoke."

"Anytime, Colonel. Anytime."

He left.

She looked back out at the stars.

She hadn't seen stars as beautiful as these, she thought, as filled with wonder and awe—

Well, since she was just a kid.

Suddenly, unaccountably, she found herself craving pretzels and beer as she blew thick puffs of smoke at the bright points of light.

ABOUT THE AUTHOR

DAVID BISCHOFF is the author of 40 novels spanning almost every genre: science fiction, fantasy, horror, historical, YA and mystery. He is the author of the *New York Times* bestselling novel *Star Trek: The Next Generation—Grounded*. The scripts he's written for television include two episodes of *Star Trek: The Next Generation*. He lives in Eugene, Oregon.